THE STARLIGHT
CONTINGENCY

THE STARLIGHT CONTINGENCY

KYOKO M.

FALSTAFF
BOOKS
WWW.FALSTAFFBOOKS.COM

For Sharon Sibley, who believed in my work even when I didn't.

CHAPTER ONE

DUKE

The binoculars in my hands were stolen.

Stealing wasn't hard. The clerk had been swamped on a Saturday night when it was still warm and people populated the street like schools of fish. Besides, Scarlett was perfect for distraction if he hadn't been anyway. The process is simple, almost childishly simple. Scope out the shop two days ahead of time. Mind the cameras. Browse. Remain casual. Ask the clerk questions about the products, make it look like you're gonna make a purchase. Clerks think that shoplifters avoid eye contact and immediately head for the corners of the store. Those are the amateurs. The kids looking for cheap thrills. The poor single moms struggling to make ends meet. The pathological liars.

We weren't like them.

A leather jacket would be too obvious. Cargo pants too. My favorite was a pair of old, ratty jeans that hung low off my ass. The clerk was a straight guy, so he wouldn't be paying attention to my ass when I carefully slipped the binoculars inside the back pocket after skillfully removing the tag with my pocketknife. 3.2 seconds. I had it down to an art.

I'd met eyes with Scarlett, and she knew the deed was done. We weren't twins, but people thought we were because we had so many non-verbal cues. Thieving wasn't like in the movies. We didn't have elaborate schemes and escape plans. We didn't wear rubber masks with nuns or presidents on them. Though, we did wear all black at night robberies. That was actually pretty useful.

My mind reeled itself back in to the task at hand. We had been planning this haul for a month. No more petty crooks. Big leagues. But more money also meant more time in jail and so we had to be careful. Cautious. Smart. Direct.

"Traffic?"

"Nothing. It is three a.m., after all." Scarlett stuck out her hand for the binoculars. I handed them to her and lowered my hands to the belt. The darkness of the alley concealed us. I didn't need light. I felt the tools one by one with my fingertips to check that they were all there and breathed a sigh of relief. Things would be fine. Just fine.

"Alright, let's cross. Head low, casual."

"Yes, boss," she snorted, tucking the binoculars on her belt. I walked across the street first, scanning for cars or people. It was a cold October night, and no one was around. I liked it that way, even when we weren't working. The rear entrance to the privately owned jewelry store—embarrassingly cliché, I know—was directly across from a pet store, which provided us with cover. No cameras on this street, but there were some two stoplights down, which was why we were on foot tonight.

Scarlett came over a couple minutes after me. I pried the rear entrance open, having already turned off the alarms. That was why we'd chosen this place. Large chain jewelry stores had intricate security systems that couldn't be externally shut down even in the event the power went out. We'd cased the place last month, getting to know the owner and the staff, and we'd worked out that it was minimum security and, therefore, worth the risk.

Cold silence and shiny linoleum greeted me. I walked inside, holding the door for my sister. I motioned for her to put her ski mask on and then did so myself. I shut the door and locked it before doing a quick scan of the employee lounge. Everything was laid out just like Scarlett said. Perfect.

There were a lot of ways to crack a safe, but we had found the fastest method was using a handheld welding torch. The modern safe of a place like this one wasn't spectacular. It sat in the corner of the room. Like most retail stores, there wouldn't be a sizeable amount of cash inside because most customers paid by card or check and the employees made weekly drops to the bank, but some bills were better than none. But that wasn't all we were here for anyway.

Scarlett burned through the metal door of the safe and flicked the welding torch off, her gloved fingers tugging at the mostly melted lid to reveal the drawer inside. I unfolded a bag and dumped the drawers from the cash registers inside, calculating that we had maybe two-thousand dollars in cash. Not bad.

The next priority was the loose diamonds, which were kept in a separate container with labels for where they went in the displays. This was the real reason we'd come. The private owner had a handful that amounted to about fifty-to-sixty grand altogether. I'd had a friend in our apartment building who said he could find a fence for the diamonds. All they needed to do was make sure there weren't serial numbers etched inside them and we'd be home free.

We walked out of the back room to the front display and split up. She went to the far side of the shop near the window, staying low, and I worked on the alarms set up on each display case. Once they were open, I stuffed the important pieces in individual sacks: necklaces first, bracelets second, and rings last. Anything else wouldn't be worth the trouble because we only had another two minutes to get the hell out of dodge. Scarlett always called me a Five-Minute Man. I found that both disturbing and irritating, but it was still better than my usual nickname.

I lifted my eyes toward her to let her know I had finished my half, but then I saw it: sleek and shiny like a Great White cruising through the surf, aching for prey. My mouth felt as if it had been filled with sand, but I pushed the words out anyway.

"Lettie, drop!" I hissed as the cop car glided past the window. She hit the floor with a loud *thunk*, and I did as well, panting for air as panic gripped my chest. I froze, listening for the sound of the tires scraping against the road but heard nothing. Slowly, I tilted my head upward to see the cop car had stopped in front of the building. I caught a glimpse of two patrol officers climbing out and one of them touching his walkie talkie. As soon as both of them shut the doors to their car, I hollered at my sister.

"Go!"

Scarlett leapt to her feet and raced toward me. The officers spotted us and broke into a run. I slung the loot across my shoulder and led the way out of the shop, kicking the door open once I'd slid the lock back. Our feet punished the ground, but it wasn't enough. I could hear the unintelligible jabber of their radio as they called in the robbery and ran even faster, turning down alleys left and right until we reached our escape route. Three streets and then straight into the woods. Five minutes and we'd be out of here.

Car horns blared as we pounced into the street. Scarlett had to do a front-hand flip over the hood of one that didn't stop in time. Sirens cut through the air, meaning that the cops had a second unit nearby, further mucking up our plans. The ski mask stifled my heaving breaths. I wanted desperately to take it off as we crossed the second street, climbing over stone dividers across the freeway.

We reached the last and most dangerous road and had to stop as an eighteen-wheeler thundered past. My foot hit the concrete and then everything flashed white for a second. At first, I thought I'd been hit by a car and died, but then I heard the unmistakable roar of helicopter blades and squinted up into the sky to see a police copter.

"Are you fucking kidding me?!" my sister spat, reading my mind.

I jerked my head in the direction of the forest. "Keep going!"

We crossed the last street and dove into the woods, eluding the spotlight for a few precious moments by hiding beneath a rotting log. Dirt and loam clung to my ski mask, making it even harder to breathe, and mud clumped on the front of my pants. We flattened ourselves as much as possible as the copter continued searching for us in the dark, but I knew we couldn't stay there. I could see the pair of cops who had spotted us crossing the second street. They would find us in mere minutes.

"This wasn't part of the plan," Scarlett hissed, her brown eyes slicing into mine.

"I know," I snapped. "Will you just give me a second to think?"

"Sure. You take your second and the cops crawl up our asses. Where did they even get a chopper? How are we this unlucky?"

"No one gets away with everything." I craned my neck to peer at the forest behind us, trying to remember where it led. Then it hit me.

"The Rosewood mansion."

Scarlett stared at me. "You're kidding me, right?"

"They haven't spotted us yet. If we make a break for it, we should be able to get on the grounds before they see where we went."

"Duke, we don't know what's in there. We don't know how their security system works. For all we know, they have attack dogs with lasers on their heads!"

"We move on the count of three."

She swore at me, pointing a long finger in my face. "Duke, this is a stupid idea."

"One..."

"We're gonna get caught!"

"Two..."

"If you say three, I'll punch you in the nuts."

"Three!"

I jumped to my feet and bolted. Scarlett let out an unearthly growl and came tearing after me. Branches smacked my chest, leaves scattered beneath my feet, and the cold air made my eyes tear up, but I kept going until the sound of sticks crunching and my ragged breath were all I could hear. A soundtrack of desperation and the need for freedom. A snide little voice in the back of my head told me it was pointless, that we'd get caught and locked up, but I didn't listen. Maybe God had one trick left up His sleeve and He'd slide it to me under the table.

The Rosewood mansion was surrounded by a four-foot brick wall with black fencing atop it. Lanterns adorned the front gate, giving me a point to focus on as we ran. Not that we were going to use it. One does not simply walk into Mordor, nor does one simply waltz into one of the most expensive homes in the state of Virginia.

My lungs ached and my hands shook as I hoisted my sister up over the fence in the back yard, straining to hear where the helicopter had gone. I saw dashes of light in the forest and followed the skyline until I spotted the flying mammoth thirsty for our capture. Briefly, I wondered if there were families at home eating buckets of popcorn and watching us like we were the circus, their entertainment for the night. They were programmed to hate us, the bad guys, the criminals, the scumbags. Bastards.

Thankfully, no attacks dogs with lasers on their heads greeted us as we hurried uphill toward the mansion. We might have tripped a silent alarm triggered by cameras, but I hadn't seen any wiring in the fences to indicate otherwise. It was possible that the mansion itself was wired instead of the premises.

The spotlight hit the grass four feet away from us, and I shoved my sister forward, pointing to the wooden porch connected to the third floor. We scurried over to it and flattened ourselves against the wall, praying that they hadn't seen us yet. The light veered back and forth on the ground like a drunk driver, drifting closer, making my heartbeat drown out the sound of the helicopter blades beating in the air. It passed over the porch, and the slats let in some of the blinding light, shocking my dilated pupils to tiny stars. Then, mercifully, it vanished.

Scarlett's shoulder bumped mine as she slumped down, her chest heaving as she tried to catch her breath enough to make a smartass comment.

"Well, wasn't *that* fun?"

"Exceptionally," I replied, yanking the horrid ski mask off my face and mopping up the sweat dripping down my skin. Once clean, I pulled it back on and crooked a finger at her.

"The cops will be searching the premises in no time. Let's get inside and get supplies so we can move on."

Nodding, she pressed her face to the plate-glass window of the first floor. I watched as she scanned what she could see of their kitchen.

"What kind of system?"

"A damn good one," she admitted, flipping her black hair over one shoulder. The ponytail had come loose during our escape. She'd have to tuck it under the mask, which she hated to do.

"From what I can see, there's a security pad on all the doors. Cutting the power might give us enough time for a hit-it-and-quit it, but not much else. The alarm system might be on a separate power source."

"We'll have to risk it. We've got to get out of here before the cops come. Let's just hope none of the Rosewoods are night owls."

I took out my flashlight and crept around the long brick wall, searching for the power line. It was about three feet behind the porch, nestled just out of range of the garden and the tree line. I reached into the last pocket on the left side of my belt, lamenting that I'd have to use a miniature charge. These things weren't cheap, and I'd only gotten three of them over the course of the past year. Emergencies only. But I'd be damned if this wasn't an emergency.

"Spot me," I said, sticking the flashlight back into my pocket and climbing up the pole. This was private property, so the pole had thin metal sticking out to serve as steps for maintenance purposes. I ascended as quickly as possible, occasionally checking for the helicopter's current position, and then withdrew the flashlight and charge.

I stuck the small explosive on the transformer between the lines leading toward the mansion. It would shut the power off, then the backup generator would kick in and reset the security system, but we'd already be inside. I set the charge and climbed down, motioning for Scarlett to follow me beneath the porch for safety. We both plugged our ears just before a muted pop crackled through the back yard, punctuated by sparks and a bright flash. Power out.

Scarlett went to the sliding glass door and flashed a nervous look in my direction. I nodded once. She picked the lock and gingerly slid the door back as I held my breath. Silence. Thank God.

She crept inside and I followed, closing the door and pulling the curtains shut. We both stood still, breathing lightly in unison, ears straining to hear any commotion in the house. I estimated that there were probably six rooms on this floor, maybe more in the basement. The main goal was to get a set of wheels, meaning that we were heading for the garage on the other side of the compound. The cops would be looking for people on foot, not in a vehicle, until they found out that we'd broken into the mansion, and by then, it would be too late.

I found a knife rack on the counter and took two of them. Scarlett took three of the smaller ones. Neither of us intended to kill or maim anyone, but they were good for intimidation.

I held the long knife in my left hand as I started past the den and down the hallway, mindful of every creak of the hardwood floor. There were four closed doors on either side. I stared at them, keeping my steps as light as possible. They looked like gigantic mouths waiting to swallow us whole.

We were past three of them when I heard an unmistakable click of a light switch. I whirled to see the light at the end of the hall was on and heard a doorknob turn. Two choices: run or hide.

Cursing, I opened the door to my right and waved Scarlett in. We darted inside and closed it, praying no one heard us. I pressed my ear to the door, listening. No footsteps. I couldn't tell if that was good or bad.

"Duke," Scarlett whispered, but I shushed her. She grabbed my arm and squeezed, saying my name again.

I glared at her. "I can't hear. What are you—?"

She was looking at the bed. I shut my mouth, my throat going dry as I realized there was an elderly black woman sitting there, staring at us.

She was short and plump with long white dreadlocks tucked in a messy bun at her nape. She wore a plain, light blue nightgown, her feet bare, the bed unmade from where she'd been lying in it. There was a cane leaning against the nightstand and a pair of slippers nearby.

Immediately, I lowered the knife to my side and held out my other hand toward her. "Ma'am, I need you to stay calm. We're not going to hurt you. We just need a car and we'll be out of here, I swear."

"They're waiting to take us," the old woman said.

I glanced at Scarlett. She shrugged. I kept my voice low as I addressed the woman. "What?"

"Waiting and waiting. Long time. Cold, where they are. Dark too. It's all they know."

Her voice was soft and trembling, but the Jamaican accent made it sound cryptic. The darkness made it hard to tell, but she looked to be nearly eighty years old. No wonder her mind had gone. She didn't seem upset by our presence. It almost felt like she had been expecting us.

Scarlett spoke up this time. "Ma'am, where is the garage on this property? Is it connected to the house?"

The old woman put her bare feet on the floor and walked toward my sister. Scarlett tensed, not sure of her intentions, but the old woman lifted her frail hands and touched her hair—ran her fingers down the black satin and the steaks of red at my sister's forehead.

"Chosen, you two. Never thought I'd see the day."

Scarlett glanced at me. "What the hell is she talking about?"

I opened my mouth to reply, but then a screeching sound tore through the silence like a knife through a veil. I clapped my hands over my ears, nearly keeling over at the volume of the alarm. It was unlike anything I'd ever heard—louder than ambulance sirens, louder than police sirens, damn near louder than God Himself.

"What is that?" Scarlett shouted, panicking.

I shook my head. "I don't know! Just hide! Now!"

I ran to the closet and pulled the double doors back, stuffing myself inside next to the fur coats and silk pajamas. Through the slats, I could see Scarlett flattening herself on the carpet and crawling beneath the bed. The old woman didn't move from her spot as if she were deaf, staring at the door as if expecting something.

Seconds later, a bald black man in his fifties opened the door and spotted her, wrapping his large hands around her forearms.

"C'mon, Mama, we've got to get ready."

He pulled her into the hallway and disappeared. What the hell was going on? Why were they leaving? Had the police notified them of our presence?

I could hear some sort of commotion from the hallway—panicked voices, footsteps, the clamor of dishes hitting the floor—the urge to run increased tenfold. I closed my eyes and counted to ten, trying to slow my heartbeat, but my pulse wouldn't cooperate. It beat hard and fast in my throat, along my tongue like the salty flavor of sweat, clinging. I couldn't think with this damn alarm slamming against my eardrums, plowing the sanity from my skull.

The carpet beneath my muddy boots started to vibrate. At first, I thought it was because of the alarms, but when I knelt and pressed my gloved hand to the ground, I knew it wasn't them. It rumbled like thunder had been trapped underneath the house. What the hell was going on?

The rumbling abruptly changed to shaking, unlike anything I had ever experienced. I pressed my hand to the wall on my left, trying to stay on my feet as the quaking worsened and shoes began falling off the shelf over my head. An earthquake in Alexandria, Virginia? Impossible.

The alarms and the falling shoes almost blocked out the sound of something outside of the house clicking and whirring like the innards of a clock. I stumbled back over to the closet doors to see the window on the far wall, ignoring the painful bumps on the head from boxes sliding off the shelf as I saw something amazing.

Huge metal panels shot up from below and clicked into place over the window, swallowing me in complete darkness.

The house was…*transforming.*

It didn't matter if we got caught any more. We had to get out of here. I shoved the closet doors open and turned on my flashlight. Scarlett crawled out from beneath the bed, her eyes red and wet with fearful tears. I pulled her to her feet, my voice nearly giving out because I had to shout so loud.

"We have to get out of here. Come on!"

I went for the door, which had slammed shut after the man and old woman left, but it wouldn't open. I pushed my sister back and kicked the doorjamb once, twice, a third time, but it didn't budge. Scarlett joined me, kicking in unison at the white oak until it splintered. I stuck my hand in the hole we'd made over the doorknob and ripped a chunk of the wood out. The flashlight shook in my hands as metal glinted out from beneath the wood.

Solid steel. Escape was impossible.

We stared at each other, the light allowing me only a glimpse of her face, but I knew our expressions were the same. End of the line.

I wrapped my arms around her and knelt, kissing the top of her head.

"I'm sorry, Lettie. I'm so sorry," I whispered hoarsely, hot tears tracing the lines of my cheeks as the quaking and clicking and screaming alarms worsened.

An explosion rocked beneath the house, and before I blacked out, I felt one sensation.

Flying.

CHAPTER TWO

SCARLETT

I *fucking hated this job.*

I probably should have been more grateful. Not many sixteen-year-olds in Alexandria were fortunate enough to have a job, especially not at a place like Panera. They were usually stuck with unpaid internships. Raking leaves. Mowing lawns. Prostitution. Whatever.

But repetition was repetition, whether you were the President of the United States or just some unlucky bastard working a minimum wage job, and that was why I hated this one. With high school no longer hanging over my head like a hormone-filled piñata after I got my GED, they gave me morning hours and it was the same damn thing day after day. Percy opens the doors, turns on the lights. We count down the safe. I wash the windows. Mop the floors. Turn on the ovens. Turn on all the machines. Wrap my apron around my waist, tie my hair back into a bun, and act like I have no personality. Smile at the creeps who tip me a quarter or check out my breasts as they swipe their cards. The only joy I get is the look on their faces when I tell them I'm only sixteen. Assholes.

Duke hated my job, too, but he knew we needed the money, and being a hot Korean chick usually got me good tips. Not that I really believed I was all that good looking. My claim came from experience more than self-recognition. Older guys treated me as if I were their ultimate fantasy, but only because they knew nothing about me. They knew nothing of my potty mouth, or the illegal tattoo of a butterfly on the inside of my left thigh, or the way I loved the smell of menthols but hated the smell of Marlboros. They only knew what their minds wanted—the stereotypical Asian girl that their TV shows and illegally downloaded porn told them. Obsessed with tiny phones and K-Pop bands and large cocks. The good life, apparently.

Luckily, I charmed my way into getting a night shift. I liked the people who cruised the late hours because they were much more relaxed. They weren't in a hurry to get their food like the morning rush. It was refreshing.

Five minutes before closing time, Percy had gone to the bathroom. I snuck my MP3 player—a birthday present from my big brother—out of my apron and poked the headphones into my ears so I could listen to a song by The Kills. Before long, the broom in my hand became a microphone and I was thrashing around the empty restaurant like an emo kid on a Simple Plan binge. So not sexy. It was mildly reminiscent of someone having a seizure. But I didn't care. I had air conditioning and a few bills in my wallet and frantic lyrics rushing through my veins. That was living in my book.

"Nice moves."

I whirled, popping the headphones out of my ears upon hearing Percy's amused, but authoritative voice. I flashed him an apologetic smile. "Sorry, it...got quiet. I was kinda bored."

He shook his head. "Nah, 's cool. You gotta cut loose every once in a while."

I relaxed a little. "Y-Yeah, I guess so. Is everything ready?"

Percy glanced around the shop. "Yeah, looks like we're good. But...can I ask you something?"

"Yeah, you can ask me anything. You're the boss, after all."

"We've been working together, what? Four and a half months, right?"

"Yeah."

"I don't know about you, but I've always, y'know...kinda liked you. I was wondering if you just wanted to hang out for a while and talk. We never get to talk that much outside of work, and I thought it'd be nice."

My cheeks filled with hot blood. It was easy refusing assholes who knew nothing about me. This was completely new. I had never thought about Percy that way—partially because I wasn't really dating these days. After all, any guy I picked would eventually find out about my parents and how I lived alone with my brother in a crappy loft above a laundromat.

I couldn't look at him while I talked. I just couldn't. So I stared at his belt buckle instead.

"What, do you mean like...now? Like right now?"

He shrugged one shoulder. "I don't have anything better to do. You?"

I shook my head. "Just going home and getting dinner, that's all. Maybe just for a while."

"Cool."

Percy's office was tiny. They had converted an old broom closet from the shop before this one. He sat in his chair, and I sat on the desk, trying my best not to drum my fingers nervously even though the conversation went well. Thirty minutes flew by without my notice, but I still felt on edge about something, and I didn't know quite what it was. Then again, Percy was three years older than me and there was no way my brother would approve. He always had the final say about everything I did.

"I should probably get going," I said with a long-suffering sigh, glancing at the closed door. Chipped white paint, rusted metal underneath. It had been through a lot.

Percy glanced at his watch. "Already? Your brother keeps you on a short leash, huh?"

I bristled. "I'm not on a leash. He's just careful. So am I. Besides, I have to walk home from here. Bus fare's too expensive."

"Fair enough, but you know what I mean. Part of the reason you're so nervous around me—" he held up a hand, noting the offended look on my face. "—yeah, I noticed—is because you're worried he won't approve. I don't blame you."

"Then why'd you ask if you already knew?"

He stood up, surprising me with an intense look. "Cause I do like you, and I think you should decide for yourself if you like me too instead of letting him do it. But for the record..."

He leaned forward, tilting my chin upward. "I think you do like me."

He kissed me. I could have stopped him, but I didn't. Mostly because I wanted to know what being kissed felt like. He tasted like coffee—bittersweet. I didn't know what to do. Should I touch him? Should I open my mouth wider? Should I be a good girl and tell him to stop? What the hell was I supposed to do?

He kissed me softly at first and then moved his tongue into my mouth. I made a noise. It was weird. Heat flared across my skin and part of me knew it wasn't because I was madly in love with Percy or something. He was male, relatively good looking, and tall. I liked tall men. I worked up the courage to lay my nervous hands on his shoulders as he continued kissing me and let it happen for a little while longer, trying to decide if I liked it or not.

I jumped when his hands wandered down to my bare legs and pushed them apart so he could stand between them. I felt his hips press to mine and his hot breath as he started kissing my neck, and knew this wasn't what I wanted.

I pushed against his wide chest, shaking my head. "Um...this is going kind of fast. I think we should stop."

He didn't stop touching me, instead mumbling in a vacant voice, "Just relax. It's okay."

I pushed a little harder. "C'mon, I have to get home. Let go."

His large hands started pushing my t-shirt up. The first stab of fear thrust into my chest.

"I mean it, let go. Seriously."

When he touched my bra, I shoved him away with my feet, holding onto the desk for dear life. He stumbled, his legs hitting the chair with a loud scraping sound.

"What the fuck, Scarlett?" he snapped as he straightened up. "I thought you wanted this."

"I did too, but I was wrong," I snapped back, shoving the hem of my t-shirt down.

"You don't do that. Don't lead me on like that and then just pull out; that's bullshit," he shot back, growing angrier by the minute.

Fear bubbled inside me, spilling outward into my hands, making them tremble. "I'm sorry. I didn't mean it like that. I just wasn't sure. I have to go."

I got up, but he grabbed my upper arm, squeezing. "You're not gonna tell, right? Don't you fucking tell anybody about this."

"I'm not gonna tell anyone, Percy! Jesus, what the hell is your problem?"

"If you tell, I'll lose my job. Do you hear me?" He shook me a little, pulling me closer. I started to panic when I realized how much stronger he was than me.

"Answer me, you little bitch!"

"Fuck you!" I punched him as hard as I could, right in the lip. He crashed into the chair, knocking it over. My knuckles erupted into fire, or at least that's what it felt like. Blood dripped down from the corner of his mouth. He touched his lip, stared at the crimson droplets in shock, and then glared at me. Before I could move, he slapped me. I fell to the floor, clutching one side of my face as it ached. Tears oozed down my cheeks as I looked up at him, unable to stifle a sob. I felt like a child. A stupid little child.

He seemed to realize the enormity of what he'd done, and the anger subsided for a moment. "Fuck. Fuck, I'm sorry, Scarlett, I mean it."

Percy reached for me. I screamed. "DON'T TOUCH ME!"

I scrambled to my feet and threw the door open, running out. He called after me, but I raced out of the restaurant and down the street. My tennis shoes echoed on the pavement and my cheek hurt and my eyes were burning, but I ran until I reached the laundromat. The stairs groaned under my weight and my fingers shook so hard that it took me nearly a minute to unlock the door.

Duke had been asleep on the couch, but my entrance startled him awake. "Lettie, where were you? I—"

He stopped dead in the middle of chastising me when he saw my tears and the side of my cheek. He walked over to me, his face ashen white.

"Lettie, what happened?"

"He wanted to talk. He just wanted to talk." I started to sob, pressing my face against his chest. He wrapped his arms around me, rubbing my back in soothing circles.

"I didn't know that was gonna happen. I didn't know. I'm sorry, Oppa. I'm sorry. You were right. You're always right." Everything came out mumbled through broken gulps of air.

My brother pulled back and held my face in his hands. The whiteness was gone. In its place was a firm resolve, one that nearly scared me.

"Who did this? Who did this to you, Lettie?"

It took me several breaths to answer. "Percy."

He sat me down on the couch and wrapped a blanket around me. I huddled in the cool suede, arms wrapped around my knees, and cried until exhaustion took over. I fell asleep.

I woke up when the front door closed. My eyelids peeled back, sticky from dried tears, to see Duke stalk past the couch and walk straight into the bathroom. His shoulders were shaking. It scared me half to death.

I clutched the blanket around me and wandered into the doorway of our small bathroom. He stood in front of the sink and the water was on. His knuckles were bleeding and so was his nose. He said nothing, but I knew what had happened.

He took a washcloth and started wiping the blood from his nose, wincing here and there when he touched a tender spot. I swallowed twice before speaking, and when I did, my voice sounded hollow and soft.

"Did you kill him?"

He kept wiping and wiping and wiping, but the blood didn't stop. "No."

"Did it hurt?"

"Him."

"I'm sorry."

Duke shook his head. "Don't be. You didn't know. Neither of us did."

"I guess I'm fired, huh?"

"I guess you are."

The bleeding finally stopped. He spat blood into the sink and then began washing his hands. The water turned pink and then slowly faded to clear again.

"I'll get dinner started."

"Okay."

Cold water hit my face. I came out of unconsciousness gasping for air like a fish that had been dragged onto dry land. My wrists were in handcuffs, strapped behind my back, and I could feel the icy metal of a chair beneath me. There was a blindfold over my eyes. My wheezing breath echoed, meaning that the room I was in had to be pretty large. My ankles were chained to the chair as well, and it sounded like tile beneath my boots. These thoughts whizzed through my head for the first few seconds of being awake, and then I realized someone had *tied me up and thrown cold water on me.*

"Who are you?"

A man's voice, frigid, hard, and authoritative. I licked my lips, coughing as the water dripped down into my nostrils. I tried to calm down, but I could feel my body shaking in fear. *So cold.*

"Where is my brother?"

"Answer the question. Who are you?"

"Where is my brother?" I asked, louder this time.

"I'm not going to ask you again."

"Tell me where my brother is first, you son of a bitch!" I yelled at the voice, my anger warming me. I heard movement and then another wave of icy water slapped against my skin, making the tank top cling to my upper body. So cold, so fucking *cold.*

"How did you find out about the Starlight Contingency?"

"What are you talking about? Where am I?"

"Answer the question. Who do you work for?"

"I don't work for anyone," I said through chattering teeth. "I haven't had a job in years."

"How did you find out about the Starlight Contingency?"

Frustration climbed out of my throat. "I don't know what the fuck that even is! Who are you people?"

"Are the Rosewoods part of the conspiracy? Did they promise you safe passage?"

"What the fuck are you talking about?"

Another huge wave of water. I cried out, unable to help it. My skin ached all over.

"I don't know anything! I've never met the fucking Rosewoods and I don't know what a Starlight Contingency is! Let me out of here! Now!" I screamed, hating the sound of my hoarse, grief-stricken voice as it echoed. My chest heaved with every breath, and I couldn't stop shaking. It felt like the tremors were coming from inside my very soul. The voice didn't speak for a long moment. I could only hear my breath and the dripping of the water off my clothes.

Footsteps. I tensed. A large hand grabbed my head and jerked it aside so hard that I thought it would break my neck. I struggled, trying to kick and thrash out of the invisible grip.

"Get off of me! Get off! I'll kill you! I'll fucking kill you!"

Sharp pain in my neck. The cold subsided, replaced with liquid warmth. My limbs went loose and floppy like Nongshim noodles. My lips just barely worked as I started to pass out.

"Where's my brother? Where's *Oppa*?"

DUKE

"How did you find out about the Starlight Contingency?"

"Where is my sister?"

"How did you find out about the Starlight Contingency?"

"Where is my sister?"

"Are you a spy? A mercenary? An assassin? Who hired you?"

"Where is my sister?"

"Were you under orders to kill the Rosewoods?"

"Where is my sister?"

"Is she in on it as well?"

"Where is my sister?"

"The sooner you cooperate, the sooner we tell you."

"Where...is...my...sister?"

"Take him away."

SCARLETT

I woke up on the floor. It was colder than ice, colder than the Arctic Circle, colder than a penguin's ass. Thankfully, my wrists and ankles were no longer in handcuffs, but my head was splitting. Nausea rolled through me in a sickening wave. It took a few minutes for it to pass and that was when I opened my eyes.

The room was white. The walls, the floor, the ceiling, were all blindingly white. I closed my eyes again and pushed up on my hands as slowly as possible. My arms felt like they were gonna fold under me at any second. The room was only about ten feet across from what I could tell with my blurry vision.

I sat up and my back hit something solid. I glanced behind me to see a plain green cot, a white pillow, and a blue blanket. And when I turned my head to the left, I saw a man in black leaning against the metal bars on the far wall.

I scrambled backward on my hands and knees. The man shook his head and spoke with a smoky voice.

"Don't get up too fast. You'll—"

I stood up, walked two steps, and vomited in the corner of the room. My entire body shook, and the headache got worse. It felt like my brain was vibrating inside my skull.

"Told you so."

I wiped my mouth clean and glared at him. "Who the fuck are you?"

My vision cleared somewhat, and I could see him properly. He was white, late twenties, tall, gray eyes, brown hair, goatee, wearing an expensive black suit, tie, and dress shoes. His hands were in his pockets as he watched me.

"Travis Hallstead," he said. "Not that I owe you anything."

"You owe me an explanation," I sneered, trying once more to stand up. This time, I didn't puke and my legs held.

He narrowed his eyes at me. "So do you."

I snorted. "Don't tell me. You're gonna ask me about the Star Wars Contingency."

"It's the Starlight Contingency," Travis corrected. "And yeah, I was."

"I'll tell you like I told the last guy. I don't know what the fuck that is and I don't care. Where is my brother? Where are we?"

He shook his head, smirking. "You're a hard ass, I'll give you that. But that's not gonna get you what you want. If you play ball, maybe you won't spend the rest of your life rotting in this cell, and all the charm and anger in the world won't get you out."

I walked closer, my mouth set in a firm line. He pushed off from the wall, staring me down without an ounce of fear.

"I'm gonna ask you one last time, Mr. Travis Hallstead. Where...is...my...brother?" I enunciated each word with a venomous tone.

"That's the least of your worries right now, trust me."

"Wrong answer." I threw a punch at him.

He ducked and grabbed my wrist, throwing me against the wall behind him. "You really don't wanna do this, little girl."

"Fuck you!" I threw another punch, two more, but he dodged them, stepping back so that they went right past his nose. I switched to low jabs, trying to hit him in the stomach, but he blocked them each time with liquid-fast reflexes. This man was trained, and well. There was no way I could beat him with my fighting skills. But that didn't mean I wasn't gonna try.

I faked a haymaker that made him sidestep, and the back of his legs hit the cot, giving me a couple seconds to move. I shoved him and he fell back onto the cot. I grabbed his tie and yanked him up so that he dangled there awkwardly, raising my right fist.

"Tell me where my brother is or I'll pound that goatee right off your pretty face," I growled.

To my surprise, he offered me a slick grin and then punched me in the right kidney, making me let go of the tie. I fell forward onto his lap, and he grabbed my arms, crossing them over my chest so that I couldn't move.

"You done?" Travis asked in an infuriatingly calm voice.

I struggled, but his grip was like iron. I couldn't move backward out of his lap or to the side, which made me even angrier. "Not by a long shot."

"Well, as much as I've enjoyed playing with you," he replied in a sharp, sarcastic tone, "you need more time to cool off and think about your priorities."

"Oh, I've got those straight. Kick your ass, get out of this cell, get my brother, and get the hell out of here."

He shook his head. "You don't get it. There is no 'out of here.' Like it or not, this place is all you have left now. It's what we all have left."

"What are you talking about?"

His dark eyes searched mine for a long moment and then a look of interest spilled through them. He tilted his head a bit, frowning. "You really don't know, do you?"

"How many times have I said that already? I don't know what happened before we blacked out. We were in the Rosewoods' mansion and then everything started shaking and then we passed out. That's all I know. Nothing else."

His hands loosened on my wrists. "Why were you in their mansion?"

"We…" I bit my bottom lip, choosing my words carefully. "…were on the run. We needed a place to hide and that's where we hid. They weren't our targets—they were just convenient. Nothing more."

His grip tightened to the bruising point. "You're lying again."

"I'm not lying," I snapped. "What do you want me to say? The Rosewoods aren't dead, right? If we had been sent to kill them, then we would have known about their freaky steel doors and magic house vibrator and crazy grandma—"

His eyes widened. "You spoke to Evelyn Rosewood?"

"Briefly. She was just babbling. I figured she was senile."

"What did she babble about?"

"Something about us being chosen, that there was someone waiting in the darkness."

Another look went through his eyes—not fear, but maybe a cousin of the feeling mixed with genuine surprise. Before I could ask him about it, he spoke again. "Last thing—what's your name?"

I eyed him. "Who wants to know?"

His fingers finally went slack around my arms and a ghost of a smile returned to his lips.

"Me."

I stared at him. I couldn't really lose anything by answering him. I was already in a prison. Things couldn't get much worse than that, by my account.

"Scarlett. With two t's."

He glanced at the two streaks of bright red hair at my temple. "Changed your name to fit your hairstyle?"

I smiled. "No, but I get that a lot. It's after my birthmark."

His eyes immediately started searching for a blemish on my skin. "Birthmark? Where?"

My smile stretched. "Not on a first date, Mr. Hallstead. Though I think we're about halfway there anyway."

He then noticed I had been sitting in his lap this entire time and let me up. I flopped against the cot as he stood, letting the humor drain out of me. "I answered your questions, now answer mine."

Travis dusted off his suit and adjusted his tie, then regarded me with a serious look.

"Your brother is being detained and questioned in this facility as well. It's unlikely that the two of you will see each other again any time soon."

His words scared me to my very core. I took a deep breath to calm myself. "Who are you? CIA? FBI? NSA? Division?"

"It doesn't matter. The point is that if your brother corroborates your story, you might have options, but as of now, you're to remain a prisoner."

"For how long?"

He said nothing, only rapping his knuckles against the metal door to his right. A guard dressed in black body armor walked over and unlocked the jail cell, letting him out. He left.

I pulled my legs up to my chest, blanketed in total silence.

"…where do I pee?"

CHAPTER THREE

DUKE

There was a first-degree electrical burn on my left hand.

I had examined the metal bars of the holding cell—slick silver, like a newly minted nickel—and the first touch sent me spiraling backward toward my cot with a shock running through my veins. The hairs on my arm hadn't settled yet and the burn stung in time with my irregular heartbeat before eventually fading away. My captors were very thorough, it seemed. Not a good sign.

The cell across from me was empty, and so were the two next to it. I wasn't sure if this was some sort of trick to make me uneasy, or if I was the only one in this particular prison facility. Every thirty minutes like clockwork, an armed guard wandered past to check on me. They were organized.

I rubbed the burn on my palm again, resisting the urge to scratch it. The nub where my pinky used to be on my right hand had not liked the shock. When I awoke each morning, I had a couple minutes of phantom limb syndrome, and the electricity brought it back for a second or two. It unnerved me every single time it happened, even though it had been years since the incident. The wound was still fresh, raw.

When we decided to start being thieves, I had contemplated this sort of situation. Prison didn't scare me much, but it wasn't something I wanted for Scarlett. She was like a cardinal. The world tried to mute her colors, but she never let it. She sang fiercely and flew where the wind blew. She didn't deserve to be in a cage, even if I did. Every fiber of my being wanted to tear my way out of this cell to find her and make sure she was safe. But I would have to wait. Wait for them to underestimate me. Wait for my chance to escape.

Memories diffused out of my mind and hung in the air like overripe pears. I ignored them. I had to focus, to pay attention to every little detail about this place. The white walls were concrete so there was no way I could burrow out. The floors were linoleum, which made me question what lay beneath them. I suspected we were underground because of the bone-piercing coldness of the floor, but when I inspected the corner, a hole the size of a bucket automatically opened up and it was too dark to see anything. It looked like that was where I was meant to relieve myself. How courteous of them. That, or they didn't want to clean up after me.

My thoughts were interrupted when the guard returned with a man in a black suit: white, 6'0", brown hair, gray eyes, goatee, serious disposition. I remained motionless on the cot with my arms crossed, knees bent, face placid.

"My name is Captain Travis Hallstead. Have you ever heard my name before?"

"Where is my sister?"

The captain shook his head. "You're a very persistent man, aren't you?"

I stared at him. "Where is my sister?"

He sighed and tucked his hands into his pockets. "Your sister is in this facility. She's been questioned. That's why I'm here. Our other extraction tactic didn't work with you, so they called me in."

I narrowed my eyes at him. "How do I know you're not lying?"

He eyed me for a moment and then answered. "Your sister's name is Scarlett, with two t's, and she's named after her birthmark."

I stood up so abruptly that his eyebrows lifted in surprise. "Did you hurt her?"

He held up his hands in supplication. "It's the opposite, actually. She tried to hurt me."

"Tried?"

"I didn't hurt her. Once she realized she couldn't win the fight, she cooperated. Force was not entirely necessary, but you probably already know that, being her brother and all."

I sat down again, letting the tension flow out of me. The captain leaned against the wall, keeping his voice level and conversational. "How did you get into the Rosewoods' mansion?"

I remained silent. He continued onward. "Your sister says you were looking for a place to hide and then everything went crazy after that. Is that true?"

"I'll answer that if you tell me about the old woman," I said, guiding my gaze up to meet his.

He lifted his chin an inch, seeming intrigued. "What did she say?"

"Something about us being chosen. About people waiting in the dark and the cold. Waiting. What did she mean by that?"

"It's classified."

I snorted. "So is how we got to the mansion."

He massaged the bridge of his nose, growing frustrated. I relished the moment.

"Look, I'm trying to save you and your sister from an entire world of pain here. If you don't give me answers now, my superiors will send in the big guns, and they will get an answer out of both of you through blood and tears. Is that what you want? Do you want that to happen to Scarlett?"

"Don't say her name so casually," I replied with a warning tone. "You can't scare me with threats. You're not here to be nice. You're here to make a deal. So make it and get out."

Captain Hallstead ground his teeth before continuing. "If you tell me who you are and how you got into the mansion, then we won't have to torture either of you. Deal?"

I weighed my options. He could be lying. He could kill us right after we told him what he wanted to know. But I wasn't in a position to stop him either way.

"How do I know she's not already dead?"

He reached into his suit jacket. I tensed, expecting him to pull out a gun, but instead he removed a phone from his inner pocket and hit a few buttons. He held it out to me. It was security camera showing a room similar to this one with Scarlett inside, curled up on a cot identical to mine. There were tiny white numbers depicting the time, and I checked the one on my watch. They matched. She was most likely alive.

"Satisfied?"

"No. Why the hell should I trust you? How do I know you won't kill us as soon as you find out why we were in the Rosewoods' mansion?"

"Because, believe it or not, murder is no longer an option. We have to keep everyone alive, no matter how much trouble they give us. Besides, if we were going to kill you, then we would have done it when we found you. No reason to take the extra time to drag you in here and question you."

"I want my sister released."

"I can't give you that. Not torturing her is the best I can do. Take it or leave it."

I closed my eyes and took a deep breath. Fifty-fifty. Might as well get it over with.

"Fine."

"What's your name?"

"Duke Nam."

"How old are you?"

"Twenty-four."

"What were you doing in the Rosewoods' mansion?"

"We were on the run, and we needed a car. We ran in there looking for the garage, but then someone came out into the hallway, so we hid in the old woman's room. Alarms went off and then the house started transforming, somehow. I heard something like an explosion and then we blacked out. That's all I remember."

"We found a duffel bag full of jewelry and cash with you. Are you thieves?"

I gave him a flat look.

A small smile touched his lips. "Yeah, I guess that was a rhetorical question. Thank you for your cooperation, Mr. Nam."

He knocked on the door. It didn't shock him, meaning that there was some way to turn it off from the outside. I logged that away in my mind for later and watched him leave.

Silence folded in around me. I pressed my hands to my lips, replaying our conversation over and over again, noticing his speech patterns, the look in his eyes, trying to decode anything he'd given me.

About five minutes into my thoughts, I realized that I could hear something—not the tiny clicks of my watch ticking or the nearly imperceptible hum of the electrified bars on the cell, but a tapping sound that echoed down the corridor. It sounded as if it were coming from the hallway. I held my breath, listening. It wasn't footsteps or water dripping. They had a pattern. It took me nearly a minute to figure it out.

Morse code.

SCARLETT

My hand had gone numb by the time I repeated the message a tenth time. The heel of my boot made a harsh slapping sound that bounced off the walls and made my eardrums ache, but I knew it was loud enough to hear in other cells. Five minutes of this crap and no response. I couldn't do this forever. Eventually, someone would catch me even though I tried to do it before the guard made his thirty-minute patrol.

As if on cue, the guard walked up to my cell, his voice harsh. "Would you cut out that noise?"

I spat at the bars, nearly hitting him. Goggles obscured his eyes, but his mouth was thin and angry, which made me smile. His gloved hand gripped the butt of the gun on his waist as if he were aching to use it on me.

"You should be more respectful of your elders, little girl."

I spat a bigger mouthful at him that time.

He jumped back, growling at me. "You like picking fights you can't win, huh?"

"Open the door," I sneered. "I'll prove you wrong, old man."

He spared me a nasty smirk. "I saw what Hallstead did, honey. You couldn't handle me if you wanted to."

That stung, but I brushed past it. *Keep taunting. It might give you a way out.*

"Sounds like someone's jealous. What is it? That he's better looking, he has a better job, or that he's not as rock stupid as you seem to be?"

The guard gritted his teeth. *That's it. Open the door. Teach me a lesson.* He gripped his gun again and then let go, stalking off down the hall. Damn.

I resumed the Morse code for another five minutes, but then I heard voices nearby. The guard and someone else. Someone with a smoky voice. *Uh oh.*

"You idiot, that's Morse code she's using!" Travis appeared and opened the jail cell, catching me just as my boot hit the floor again. He snatched it out of my hand and gave me a nasty glare.

"Do you have a death wish? Is that it?"

I shrugged, giving him wide, innocent eyes. "I was just making music. What's wrong with that?"

He let out a haggard sigh. "What were you trying to tell your brother? An escape plan? To continue the mission?"

"There is no mission. All I wanted was something to break up the silence. Looks like it worked since you're in here yapping away at me."

Travis exhaled through his nose. I snatched my boot from him and put it on. He grabbed my upper arm, pulling me to my feet. "Let's go."

"That's the second time you've touched me without my permission," I said in a low voice. "Make a habit out of it and I might have to kill you."

He watched me for a moment and then pushed me face-first into the far wall. "Hands up, palms flat against the wall. Now."

Begrudgingly, I obeyed. The guard handed Travis a pair of handcuffs and he caught my left arm first and clipped the cuff on. His breath was hot against the back of my neck. I couldn't tell if he was doing it on purpose or not. He did the same with my right arm and then tied a blindfold around my eyes.

"I'm not sure if I like where this is going or not," I remarked, only to mask the rampant fears rushing through me at the knowledge that they were taking me out of my safe little cell. This could mean it was the end of the road. Might as well go out like a smart ass.

"You don't ever shut up, do you?" Travis said, kicking my legs a little farther apart. He started patting me down at my right ankle and worked his way up my baggy cargo pants, checking all the pockets and loose cloth. Smart man.

"Not really. You're not giving much to work with, after all. I need a good supporting cast. Can't read lines on my own."

I had to bite my lip when his hand swept past my thighs. "Is this part of my last request thing? 'Cause I have to say this is kind of what I wanted."

He made a noise in his throat that may have been a laugh and placed one hand on my shoulder, shoving me forward to walk. "In your dreams."

I nearly stumbled over the doorframe as I walked, but I kept the conversation going to distract him. "Oh, come on. Don't tell me you're not even a little bit attached to me after all the time we've spent together?"

The guard chimed in. "Would you like me to gag her, Captain?"

"That won't be necessary. Yet."

Genuine surprise struck me. "You're a captain? Why didn't you say that earlier?"

"The psychologist thought that you would respond better to a non-authority figure. Hence, I left out my title when I introduced myself to you."

"Well, then I'm sorry I didn't treat you with the respect you deserve, *sir.*"

"You're a common thief. I doubt you know much about respect to begin with."

The humor died in my mouth. "Who told you that?"

"We found you with a load of cash and jewels. It wasn't hard to figure out."

"You talked to my brother, didn't you?"

No answer. We walked down a short flight of stairs in silence and then took a right turn. I heard a hissing sound of a door sliding open and then a hand on my lower back. Someone's breath brushed my neck again and I heard Travis distinctly say in Korean: "I didn't hurt your brother. You have my word."

Then he pushed me into the room and the door shut.

This room was as cold as the hallway and the jail cell. I could feel the air pushing against my temples from a vent above me somewhere. I started to take the blindfold off.

"Do not remove the blindfold."

A woman's voice, but it didn't sound human. It sounded automated. I licked my lips, taking a gamble. "Will you hurt me if I do?"

"Disciplinary action will be taken if you do not follow instructions."

"Well, shit. I guess I have to do what you say then, huh?" I snapped. This was not what I expected. I expected armed guards, a priest, and a jury of peers. Not VIKI from *I, Robot.*

"Take three steps forward and turn around."

I swallowed and told myself to stay calm as I followed her orders. On the third step, the floor felt different beneath me. Not tile. Something mechanical, maybe. I heard something whirring as if it were being wound up and willed myself to stand still. If they were about to kill me, I would at least die with some amount of dignity.

Two metal bands snapped over my boots, trapping me where I stood. I heard something circling me, some sort of machine, but nothing else touched me. After about a minute, the woman's emotionless voice spoke again. "Analysis complete. You are free to go. Turn around and take three steps forward."

The bands let go of my feet and I walked, completely baffled. No firing squad. It sounded as if they had put me in some sort of X-ray machine.

But why? They already knew I wasn't carrying anything when Travis patted me down.

I heard the door open and footsteps—only one pair this time. "Miss me?"

"Hardly," the guard grumbled, shoving me out into the hallway. We went back the way we came. I listened for voices, signs of life, anything, but it seemed like we were the only people on this level of the facility. However, the alone time was just what I had been looking for. Without Travis—excuse me, Captain Hallstead—shadowing me, I could focus on the hapless guard behind me.

When I was near my cell, I purposely tripped before I got there, landing on my ass. The guard sucked his teeth, telling me to get up. I kicked him as hard as I could in the nuts and quickly slid my cuffed arms beneath my legs to the front of my body. I heard a click and knew that he had unsnapped the holster to his gun, so I visualized how he'd be standing above me and grabbed it, then smashed the butt into his nose. He slumped on top of me, out like a light.

I yanked off my blindfold and wriggled out from under his heavy body. I tucked his gun into the small of my back and crouched there, listening to see if anyone had heard the tussle. Nothing so far. The hallway was long, and there was a total of ten jail cells on each side. I rifled through his pockets and found the keys to my cuffs, unlocking them and stuffing them in my back pocket. I took the walkie-talkie and the key card clipped to his belt and crept down the hallway, checking each cell for signs of an occupant.

"Scarlett?"

Duke gaped at me from the last cell near the wall. A rush of relief went through me, so strong that tears sprang into my eyes.

"*Oppa*, you're alive. Thank God."

He stood, coming as close as he could to the bars without touching them. "What the hell are you doing? How did you get free?"

I examined the lock on the door, digging for the key card I'd gotten from the guard. "Got lucky. The guard is gonna be really mad at me when he wakes up. Might have broken his nose."

"Lettie, you can't do this. Not now. Didn't you hear my message?"

I shook my head, frowning. "They took me right after I stopped using the code. What message?"

"We have to cooperate with them for now until we learn more about where we are."

"Are you insane? The longer we wait, the more likely they are to kill us!"

"No, they won't. That guy, the captain, told me he's not interested in killing us."

"Duke—"

"And I believe him," he interrupted, regarding me with that serious look he almost always wore.

I glared at him. "I'd rather die than play nice with the people who abducted and tortured us."

"Goddamn it, Lettie, listen to me for once!"

"I am listening! All I've ever done is listen to you!" I shouted. "I'm not patient like you, alright? I don't have plans, I'm not smart, I just do what I'm told! Now for once in your life, let me save you."

I swiped the card and the door opened. He stood there, staring at me.

"It's too late."

Then it clicked. I knew what he meant. I turned my head and saw Captain Hallstead at the other end of the hall with four armed guards behind him. He walked toward me, no weapon, because he'd known that he wouldn't need one. I withdrew the stolen gun, not pointing it at anyone. Holding it was enough.

Travis stopped within inches of me, saying nothing. I stared up at him. "This was all a test, wasn't it?"

"Yes. I wanted to see what you would do if given the opportunity. You showed a lot of brains and initiative, but you're still too naïve."

"Looks like you have everything figured out," I said in a mocking tone. "But how do you know I won't lift this gun and shoot you in the face?"

His eyes searched mine. There was intensity there, but behind that I saw a wealth of intelligence. The others might have been mindless drones, but he wasn't. He was dangerous. Like a tiger pretending to be a house cat.

"Because you won't risk dying in front of your brother."

I aimed the gun at his forehead. The men behind him all took the safeties off their rifles and pointed them at me. "Don't act like you know me, Captain. You know nothing about me."

"Lettie, put the gun down," Duke whispered. "Now."

"Why, Duke? You seem to think I don't care about my own life. Maybe I don't. Maybe I should let these guys blow me to kingdom come."

Travis continued staring at me, seeming to ignore the gun entirely. "Do you really want to go down this road? Do you know where it ends?"

I shrugged one shoulder. "Everything ends, one way or another."

"Put the gun down, Lettie. Please." Duke's voice nearly cracked at the end. My throat felt tight, and my arm started to waver a bit as I held the gun on the captain. He was ready to die, here and now.

But I wasn't. Not yet.

I lowered the gun and handed it to Hallstead, brushing past him as I walked back to my cell. One of the guards took the walkie-talkie, the key card, and the handcuffs. I stopped before going through the doorframe, raising my voice so the captain could hear me.

"Thank you."

Hallstead frowned, confused. "For what?"

"For not lying to me about my brother."

I stepped on the unconscious guard on my way in, enjoying the pained groan that emitted from his chest. The guard shut the door and walked away, dragging his senseless comrade. Captain Hallstead retreated as well, but I could feel his eyes on me before he left.

I curled up on my cot and dreamt sweet dreams.

CHAPTER FOUR

DUKE

I was seven years old when I first saw a dead person.

The Nam family had only lived in America for two generations. My grandfather went into the undertaking business because he had fought in a few civil wars during his time and had no trouble with corpses. The business was small back then, but steady.

My father had told me to go get him or we would be late for dinner, so I went inside the funeral home, calling for him.

The boy on the table couldn't have been more than fourteen. I didn't know him, but I remembered his name. Billy Bouber. Hung himself from his bunk bed. His mother found him, nearly had a heart attack. I tried to picture something like that—walking in on a dead family member—but it was too harrowing to imagine so I didn't try.

His skin was pasty and nearly translucent. Grandpa hadn't gotten around to putting on the makeup yet to make him look fresh and peaceful. His lips were dark, almost blue. I bit my bottom lip, my fingers shaking as I reached toward his cheek to touch it. The skin was like wax—almost soft, but not quite.

"Get away from there!" my grandfather bellowed from the doorway. I leapt back, scared out of my wits at his sudden entrance from the bathroom. He marched over and whacked my backside, his gray eyebrows bunched in a scowl.

"Show some respect for the dead, sonyeon."

"I'm s-sorry, hal-abeoji," I cried. "I was just looking."

"You got to treat them well once they're dead. We're all they have left. You remember that, sonyeon." He took my hand and dragged me out of the room, slamming the door shut. His aggression was something I'd never experienced before. He was a very distant man, very traditional, and the only thing in his life that he seemed to take great care of was the bodies. Each one was always flawless, male or female. He took the American phrase "final resting place" to heart, it seemed.

I found it fitting that my father was a mortician. His demeanor was just as cold as the bodies on his slab. My sister used to tell me how much she hated the Asian stereotypes for men—that they were the breadwinners and nothing else, never spending time with their loved ones, never letting them know how much they cared. She wanted to believe that things would be different if we were raised as Americans. Out of the four of us, she embraced the American culture the most. She loved how liberated the women were in this country. The Disney princesses were her role models. She tore pages out of her storybooks and plastered them on the walls. Pretty princesses grinning down at her from every angle, beaming with hopes and dreams and false-hoods. I couldn't bring myself to tell her that she was in love with a fairytale.

My father never said whether he approved of her idols or not. He hardly said much of anything. My mother once told me not to take it personal because he had been a quiet man for as long as she'd known him. Their marriage was arranged. Scarlett used to ask her if she loved him, and she would always smile and kiss her forehead and say, "Of course."

Scarlett believed her. I didn't.

Every Wednesday, my father went straight to the park from work and did ten laps in the pool. I used to ask him if I could go once I got home from school, but he told me he didn't do it for fun, but for work. To keep up his strength and disci-pline. I always found it weird that he cared so much about staying in shape when his life didn't really require it. Most Americans' dads had beer bellies and goatees and big drunken laughs. Not him. Never him.

I only recall seeing my dad smile once. Late afternoon. Bees thudded against the cracked windowsill in the kitchen. Sunlight streamed in unapologetically. He sat at the kitchen table eating Apple Jacks with his stained fingers. My shoes stuck to the floor. I couldn't move. It was everywhere. The entire floor. Sticky like honey.

He looked at my tear-stained face and smiled when I asked him why. He didn't answer. He stood up, dumped the cereal in the trashcan, patted the top of *my head, and walked out the front door. I never saw him again, except in my nightmares.*

I awoke when I heard echoed footsteps. I rolled over on my cot to look at the door. The guard opened it and waved two fingers at me.

"Get up."

I stood, frowning. "What's going on?"

"You're going to be debriefed on the situation. Hands against the wall."

I obeyed, remaining still as he cuffed me and pushed me out the door. No blindfold this time. I logged that knowledge away for later.

At the other end of the hall, another guard hauled Scarlett out of her cell and a small part of me relaxed upon seeing her. She looked small and cold, but her brown eyes lit up when she spotted me. The guards stayed two steps behind us with their guns drawn, ordering us to walk.

"Where do you think they're taking us?" she asked me in Korean, her voice low and filled with trepidation.

"Not sure. It might be more questioning about the Rosewoods or whatever went down last night."

"Stop talking," the guard snapped, jabbing me in the back with his gun. I quelled my anger and continued walking. We turned right at the corner of the jail cell and into a stairwell. I could see an elevator nearby, but they didn't want to risk being in an isolated space with us, so we continued past it. The stairwell's walls were concrete as well, but the floor was metal. Odd.

We went up two flights and entered another hallway. Instead of jail cells, there were what appeared to be interrogation rooms. It may have been the ones they questioned us in right after the abduction. There were large glass windows next to the door, and inside were the same white walls as our prison with metal chairs and a table across from a one-way mirror. My suspicions of being abducted by government agents seemed more and more likely.

They stopped at a room at the end of the hall, and there were two men waiting for us: Captain Hallstead and an older man I had never seen before. He wore an expensive navy suit, and his gray hair was immaculately groomed. They stood in front of a table and two chairs, which the guards instructed us to take.

Scarlett bristled at the order. "I'd rather stand."

"Lettie," I muttered in warning. She glanced at me and sighed, taking her seat. The guards closed the door and stood against the wall behind us.

The older man watched the two of us for a handful of seconds before speaking.

"My name is General Bridgewater. I'm the commanding officer of this establishment. I'm told that you are Scarlett and Duke. Is that correct?"

We exchanged glances and then nodded. He continued. "Normally, our organization is under the kill-first-ask-questions-later policy, but recent events have caused us to reconsider this course of action."

He slid his hands out of his pockets and pressed them against the table, lowering his voice. "However, it would be unwise to take this as a sign of weakness. We are reluctant to kill you, but if necessary, we will. Do you understand me?"

"Sir, yes, sir," Scarlett said with the utmost sarcasm in her voice. I closed my eyes for a second, resisting the urge to kick her in the shin.

Bridgewater glanced at her. "You're the one who's been giving Captain Hallstead trouble, am I right?"

Scarlett's eyes flicked to the captain. "Aw, you told him about me?"

He ignored her. "I wouldn't quite call it trouble, sir."

"Call it what you will. I like your spirit. I've seen many girls like you succeed with that kind of fire, but it won't work here. Here, you either get with the program or you live a hard life. I can wipe your early transgressions clean if you agree to cooperate for the duration of your stay at this facility. That's an offer for the both of you."

"That's very generous of you," I said in a measured voice. "But we'd both be much happier if you showed us the door. "

Bridgewater exhaled through his nose, straightening to full height. "There is no door. That's why we've brought you here. You don't seem to have any more information for us, so it's time to open Pandora's box."

He snapped his fingers. Captain Hallstead stepped forward and placed a manila folder on the table. He opened it, revealing a large photograph.

"Do you know what this is?"

"A satellite. What about it?" I answered.

"It's not just any satellite. This is a deep space satellite constructed to explore galaxies that are too far away for us to reach as of yet. It was put into orbit over twenty years ago. It captured photos of an unidentified planet with qualities similar to Earth. We launched a campaign that year to find out if it had breathable air and other natural resources."

"Yeah, I remember reading about this," Scarlett said. "They were calling it Earth II. The program was canceled for vague reasons. I'm guessing you know why."

He slid the picture aside. This time, it wasn't a satellite. It was something that looked like a giant meteor with spikes coming out of it and an eerie blue glow at the center.

"Earth II was destroyed that same year."

"By what? This meteor?"

"It's not a meteor. It's a ship."

Both of us went completely still.

Scarlett spoke first. "Wait, wait, wait. You're telling us that this thing is an alien spaceship?"

"Yes."

She chuckled, shaking her head. "That's great. Fantastic. It's like we're in *Independence Day*. Where are Will Smith and Jeff Goldblum when you need them?"

Captain Hallstead didn't crack a smile. He kept going. "The ship has a cannon on board that harbors an energy source our scientists call Sorbatium. We believe it's akin to solar energy, as if they are harnessing small suns. They've channeled it into a destructive beam. They fired at Earth II and destroyed it in less than five minutes. The ship then deployed hundreds of smaller vessels to collect the fragments of the planet's core, which we believe they use for profit."

"And who is they?" Scarlett asked, still heavy on skepticism.

"The astrologist who made the discovery was German. He called them the Bergleute des Todes. Miners of death. They travel from planet to planet, destroying them and gathering their core material. We knew it would only be a certain amount of time before they mined all the usable planets in that galaxy and started coming for ours. That's when the Starlight Contingency was put into motion. We selected one hundred million citizens of Earth to be the continuation of mankind if our military force failed against the Bergleute. In secret, their homes were converted into our most advanced space shuttles and outfitted with equipment for an immediate exit of the solar system. The Rosewoods were part of that one hundred million, but your intervention brings that number up to one hundred million and two."

"So what now?" Scarlett interrupted. "We become soldiers in the war against the Bergs? For great justice? Give me a fucking break here. How stupid do you think we are?"

Hallstead's eyes narrowed a bit. "You really don't want me to answer that."

She glared. "Bite me, pretty boy."

"Is there a point to this conversation?" I interjected, trying to stop their squabbling.

Hallstead cleared his throat, taking a deep breath. "Last night, the Bergleute made their way into our solar system. We launched a full assault on them. Every single shuttle was destroyed, and not just ours. France, Germany, Russia, Japan, China, Korea...everyone's. We had no other choice. We launched the Starlight Contingency after the last infantry fell."

"Then what? You need us so you can launch another attack before they blow up the Earth?"

"You don't understand. The Earth was destroyed six hours ago."

My sister couldn't hold it in anymore. She burst out laughing, loud and unbridled. It took her a moment to get it under control, talking through giggles. "This is amazing. I mean, I've never heard such a load of shit in my life. If you want us to work for you, just say so. You didn't have to come up with such an elaborate ruse."

General Bridgewater snapped his fingers again, this time at the guards. "Take them topside. Now."

"Yes, sir."

The guards hauled us to our feet and shoved us out the door. Captain Hallstead and the general trailed us. This time, we used the elevator instead of the stairs. Both men were relatively certain we wouldn't try anything in their presence, it seemed. I could attest to this but Scarlett... not so much. She retained a look of bemusement at the serious expressions on everyone's face. I couldn't blame her. Their story was laughable and had little evidence to support it. I suspected it was part of a larger scheme of brainwashing. I was vulnerable to many things, but manipulation was seldom one of them.

We rose for several minutes. My eyebrow started to lift when I noticed we were now in the twenties. The elevator was all metal, no windows, so I couldn't see the outside. However, the fact that it was about fifteen feet across in both directions certainly roused my suspicion.

Finally, we hit the thirtieth floor and the doors opened. For a second, I didn't move.

It looked like the docking bay of a ship, but not a seafaring ship—a *spaceship.*

There were at least thirty different consoles where men and women in dark blue jumpsuits sat wearing headsets and monitoring digital screens.

Captain Hallstead and General Bridgewater walked in, and the guards nudged my sister and I forward. By now, the skeptical expression on Scarlett's face had subsided and she began to look unnerved.

The two men walked to the front of the deck, and we followed, staring at the sight before us. General Bridgewater brandished a hand at everything before us.

"Welcome to the *Titan*."

There were windows at least twenty feet high in front of us, and beyond them was a sky so black that it felt like night itself stretched across my vision. There was only one thing breaking up the blanket of darkness. To the right, I could see the atmosphere of a moon of some sort —its surface a pale orange. I had never seen anything like it. Stars sparkled out in the distance, but none of it looked familiar. These were not our stars. I had seen them as a child, studying charts in my science classes and naming their patterns while my mother hovered over me, smiling.

"Hey, Duke," Scarlett said next to me in an alarmingly detached sort of voice.

"Yeah?" I whispered.

"This looks kind of...real."

"Yeah."

"Okay. I thought it was just me."

Then Scarlett went limp and started to fall. The guards reached for her, but Captain Hallstead caught her with an expression on his face between surprise and pity. She had actually fainted. Not that I blamed her. The blood had retreated from my face, and I could feel dread filling my stomach like cold poison.

"Take her to the infirmary," General Bridgewater said impassively. "Let me know when she revives." He might have been used to seeing reactions like this, especially if this wasn't an illusion.

Captain Hallstead handed my sister over to one of the guards, his eyes lingering as the man carried her out. I tried to read his expression, but it was like taking impression from stone: flat, lifeless, cold. But there was something there. I just didn't know what.

"Do you have any questions, son?"

I glanced up at General Bridgewater and had to swallow before I could answer. Even then, my voice wavered. "Do you have...footage of Earth's destruction? I'll admit that I am starting to believe you, but this could still be some sort of elaborate ruse."

The general turned and motioned to a wide circular console different from the ones the crewmembers were using. He touched his fingertip to the surface, and an enormous 3D digital map appeared. Briefly, I saw the coordinates for where we were in space and then he switched to a feed from a satellite.

"This is the last footage we received before it happened. It's from one of our satellites. I'm sure other countries have their own versions of it as well. By the time the Bergleute entered the solar system, the ships including the Starlight Contingency had already evacuated the Earth."

The satellite showed the surface of the Earth as I always remembered it—seeming to hang in the darkness of space like a sapphire. The upper corner of the globe began to darken, confusing me until I realized it was a shadow from the alien cruiser. The satellite wasn't facing it so I couldn't catch a glimpse, but I knew it was there. I saw a bright flash and then a red beam burrowed into one side of the planet. My stomach jerked inside me at the sight of the land crumbling and the seas boiling in its wake. It had disintegrated part of Asia already, and there were burning waves climbing outward from the entry point. After a few minutes, the beam burst out the other side of the planet and the tectonic plates of the Earth's surface began to crack apart. Bright yellow and orange spurted from the cracks, evidence of the planet's core peeking through as the weapon ripped it apart from the inside. At last, it exploded, and the satellite feed went to static.

General Bridgewater closed the feed. He showed no emotion at seeing it. I got the feeling he had watched it a hundred times, his pale eyes filling the world just before it turned into nothing more than rocks and dust.

"General Bridgewater," I said. "If this is some sort of trick, understand that I will do everything in my power to end your life."

He nodded. I wiped my eyes and straightened my posture. "Then consider this my agreement to cooperate with your operation. I can't say the same thing for my sister, but I will do what is needed as long as I am on this vessel."

"Good man. Escort him to the barracks."

The guard reached for me, but I held up my hands. "What is going to happen to Scarlett?"

General Bridgewater glanced at Captain Hallstead, and he answered instead. "She needs to be examined for psychological damage, and if she chooses to play ball, she'll be placed in the women's division aboard this ship. You're both going to become soldiers."

"I need to be able to see her. She won't recover as quickly without me."

Captain Hallstead paused, seeming unsure. "We'll see if we can make arrangements, but as of now she won't be released until we're sure she's stable. A lot of people suffer from PTSD after seeing the world destroyed. We'll keep her safe."

I stepped forward, unafraid. "I want your word on that, Captain."

He met my eyes. "You have my word."

I let the guard take me back to the elevator and lead me to my new home. The only home I had left.

God help us.

CHAPTER FIVE

SCARLETT

The first thing I ever stole was a lollipop.

    I was eleven. My mother highly discouraged us from eating sweets before dinner, and she wasn't a fan of American candies, so I took it upon my young self to pilfer an apple-flavored Blow Pop. Nothing tasted sweeter than when I hid in the bathroom sucking on the sweetness of free candy. No one had caught me. No one had thought to look at the little girl hiding behind her mother in the Kroger checkout line, one hand firmly clutched against her jacket pocket. Every second of my mini-heist, I expected to get caught. When the clerk smiled at me, I immediately looked away. When we left the store with my crime undiscovered, I couldn't believe my own cleverness. It was the biggest high I ever experienced.

    I told my friends about it, and they treated me like a goddess. None of them had ever been brave enough to try it. I didn't encourage them to do it. I had just wanted an audience. Someone to shine a light on me and see that I was exceptional. Mostly because in reality, I wasn't. I was just a normal Korean girl whose mother didn't like candy.

    However, the victory was short lived. My friend Bethany tried to steal something—the stupid bitch took a whole bag of marshmallows, what the hell—and squealed on me, saying that I had talked her into it. She lived a block away from me so of course her mother came a-knockin' and told my mom what happened. I got the worst beating of my life, so bad that I had to lie on my stomach that night. One would think I'd never steal again.

I've never been easily discouraged.

I started to steal more because I got in trouble. I had fire under my skinny little butt since my mother had reacted so strongly to my nefarious actions. I stole out of spite, relishing every morning when I walked past her in the kitchen with her none-the-wiser of what I'd done. For once, I held power over a parent.

My father was strict, but he never confronted me about the stealing after Bethany ratted me out. It was my mother's job to deal out discipline in the house. Dad ran things on a higher level—bills, taking us to school, those sorts of things. He felt like a landlord more than a father on some days, but others weren't as bad. When my report card came in and things were good, he would stroke my hair and tell me, "Good job, little one." He never smiled. Value clung to the words, not the facial expressions.

I supposed that was why years later when my brother and I stood in the middle of a bare room with half the month's rent between us, the idea came to me easily.

"What if we stole it?"

He did a double take. "Are you kidding me, Lettie? Do you know how much trouble we'd get in?"

I shrugged. "I'm not talking about a bank vault, Duke. I mean shoplifting to get by. We can fence the stuff to make ends meet."

"Yeah, 'cause we just know tons of people on the black market," he replied, his voice laced with sarcasm.

I crossed my arms beneath my chest. "What do you want from me? We've got two days to get the rest of the rent or we're out on the street. If you've got a better idea, let's hear it."

Duke frowned. I could practically see the gears in his head turning. "I don't want you in any more trouble than you're already in."

I resisted the urge to hit him. "We're in, Duke. Not just me. You don't have to take the responsibility all on your own."

He sighed, shaking his head. "What kind of stuff are you thinking about? Electronics?"

"Among other things. We have to start small since you don't have experience in these things."

Duke scowled. "You're not an expert, you know."

I couldn't help but smirk. "I am compared to you."

He rolled his eyes. "And who are we supposed to contact to sell this stuff to?"

"We go to the inner city and sell it. Word'll get around after a while and then maybe we can find a professional. Someone with connections."

"That's dangerous."

"Not if we travel. We can hop from city to city. That'll keep the crooks and the cops off our trail."

Duke took a deep breath. "Just...let me sleep on it, okay?"

I bit back another argument and nodded. He said good night and shuffled off to his room. I flopped down on the couch, touching my stomach. Butterflies gathered there at the thought of stealing, of being daring, of outwitting the authorities. Each thing I stole replaced that hole inside of me. One day, that empty space would be cluttered, and I wouldn't have to think about the void. Stupid thought, but I hungered for it.

Scarlett Nam, master thief.

I liked the sound of that.

My head ached. My back was sore. There was thin cotton beneath me, itching along my spine. I groaned deep in my throat and rolled onto my side, fingertips skimming my forehead. My eyelids slid back to see a pale green curtain like the ones used in hospitals and a man in black standing in front of it with his hands in his pockets.

I closed my eyes again. "Don't you have anything better to do?"

"General Bridgewater ordered me to make sure you were alright," Captain Hallstead answered in a mild voice. "I don't want to be here."

"And yet you are. I'm starting to see a pattern here, Cap." I felt a pinch in my forearm and noticed that there was an IV in place. It freaked me out. I went to remove it, but Hallstead caught my hand, shaking his head.

"Don't remove it until the doctor comes back."

I shook my wrist loose from his grip, sitting up. "How long was I out?"

"An hour."

I snorted, rubbing my pounding forehead. "Can't believe this. I fucking fainted. How weak is that? I should be in a 1940s horror film."

He made that noise again—the one that was almost like a laugh, but not quite. "You were under a large amount of stress all at once. It's not uncommon."

I shot him a rude look. "How many times have *you* fainted?"

A smirk tugged at the edge of his lips. "Point taken."

I rolled my eyes. "Where's the doc? You suck at cheering up sick people."

"You're not sick. You've just lost your home and every person you know. Everyone on this ship has to face that at some point. Some people can't handle it."

I watched him for a moment, trying to read his face. "You didn't want to do it the way General Bridgewater did, did you?"

He glanced away. "Not really. I thought if we gave you more time to adjust to your surroundings…"

"I doubt that would have helped," I said, my voice soft. He started to say something else, but I cut him off. "Where's my brother?"

"He's been taken to the soldiers' quarters. He's going to start training soon."

My eyes widened. "He agreed to your terms."

Hallstead frowned. "Why do you sound so surprised?"

My suspicions immediately rose. "Why do you want to know?"

He sighed. It made me feel better. My brother once told me I had a sadistic streak. He was right.

The curtain slid aside, and a black man appeared holding a chart, startled when he noticed Hallstead. "Captain, I didn't see you come in."

"I'm on orders," he said, maybe a little too fast. I grinned. He rolled his eyes. The doctor glanced between the two of us, then kept going without mentioning it.

"Well, she's suffered from shock, but there's nothing else showing up in her blood work—"

"You took my blood?" I blurted out.

The doctor adjusted his glasses. "It's standard procedure for unconscious patients on this vessel."

I squirmed in my seat, happy to have been unconscious when it happened. Not that they needed to know that.

The doctor continued on. "She needs some rest and then her psych evaluation will begin."

I stared between them. "Psych eval? You're sending me to a shrink? I thought you said my reaction wasn't uncommon."

The doctor cleared his throat. "It isn't, but your actions beforehand suggest that there are some behavioral issues that should be addressed before you are considered for soldier status."

"Like what?"

"Your temper, your irrational behavior, your problems with authority. Pick a feature."

I glared at Hallstead. He smirked. Jerk.

The doctor gave him a look. "Captain, I would thank you not to purposely agitate my patient."

He cleared his throat. "Apologies, Doc."

"So what? You're going to reprogram me into one of your little drones? That sounds like fun. Just make sure you don't mess up my hair when you give me the lobotomy."

"Scarlett—"

"Save it, Captain," I snapped, crossing my arms and staring at the curtain, watching shadows of other people walking around. After a moment, Hallstead jerked it aside and left. My eyes followed his outline as it retreated. Bastard.

"Get some rest. We'll be moving you in another hour or so."

"Yippeefuck."

The doctor shook his head at me and exited, pulling the curtain back in place. My own little cocoon. I could still hear people talking—mostly doctors and nurses. It sounded like the other patients had problems similar to mine: trauma from the Earth's destruction, psychological issues due to space travel, and even a few pregnant women. I imagined the ride into orbit couldn't be too healthy for a baby. It made me wonder how the hell my brother and I survived without being properly secured or wearing space suits when the shuttle left the atmosphere. I'd have to ask the doc about that when he came back.

My curiosity piqued as I continued watching shadows pass back and forth from bed to bed, attending to people. I calculated that there were about twenty beds on my side of the room and another twenty on the other. This particular wing seemed to be non-emergency patients and there were probably several more of them on this vessel. The sizeable deck and the thirty or so floors made me wonder how many of the alleged one hundred million people were stationed on each vessel. The number sounded more and more preposterous as I thought about it.

An hour later, the doctor came and took me to another bare room with white walls. There was a black woman waiting for me there with silver-framed glasses and her hair in a tight bun. She wore a white lab coat over a dark violet suit. She smiled when I walked in and sat down across from her in yet another cold metal chair. What was it with these things? Did we lose all wooden chairs in the Earth's destruction?

"Hello, Scarlett. My name is Dr. Tiana Warwick. I'll be doing your psych evaluation for the next few days." Her voice was unnervingly similar to the mechanical one I'd heard during my X-ray. A guard had warned me that our interactions were recorded and that if I displayed any overt aggression, I'd be sent back to my cell. Thus, I sat very still with my arms crossed, staring at her with a blank expression. "Why don't you start by telling me a little about yourself?"

I stared at her. The silence stretched for over a minute. Her perfectly arched eyebrows lifted a fraction, and she wrote something on the clipboard in front of her.

"Okay. Would you like to talk about your relationship with your brother?"

Again, I said nothing. She scribbled something else down. I found myself annoyed.

"Is there a particular reason you don't want to talk to me?"

Finally, I couldn't resist. "Oh, I don't know, Doc. Planet blowing up changes a girl."

"This is a very serious loss, Scarlett. I think it would be healthy if you expressed how you feel about it."

I smiled, but it was completely hollow. "I would, but the guard outside told me that I'd be dragged back to my cell if I expressed any 'overt anger' at you."

"So it makes you feel angry?"

"Does it make *you* feel angry?"

Her jaw shifted just barely. I could tell I'd surprised her. "This session isn't about me. I asked you."

"Well, you're the expert. Why don't you tell me how I feel?"

The hostility in my tone made something in her brown eyes light up. She clasped her hands and laid them on the clipboard in her lap. "Fine. If you like, I can do a cold read on you."

I shrugged. "Knock yourself out."

She let her gaze rake over me from head to toe. "You use your anger as a way to get attention. It's not narcissistic—it's compulsive. I'm thinking that you didn't receive a lot of attention from your father as a child and so you developed a problem with male authority figures as well as authority in general. You are very intelligent, based on the way you speak and how you observe everything in a room before reacting to it, and you use vulgarity to make people subconsciously underestimate you so that you have the chance to manipulate them later on. It also means that you're able to keep them from getting close to you. You consider friendships and relationships a liability, so you self-sabotage to make sure you don't bond with anyone except your brother. You're aware of how attractive you are, and you use it as a weapon rather than as a crutch. I was told that you were a thief before entering the Rosewoods' mansion and that leads me to believe you're an orphan. You did not relax around me just because I'm female, so I think that there was some tension between you and your mother figure. You let your actions make you seem like a brat, but it is most likely because you don't want people to be disappointed in your true self, so you act rude in order to keep safe."

I watched her and then nodded. "Very good, Dr. Warwick. Clearly, you went to the School of Blatant Female Stereotypes and got your degree."

She flashed me a thin smile. "Thank you. But the bottom line is this: you will not be released into the women's division of the infantry until I clear you. It would be in your best interest to cooperate."

"You just described me as self-destructive. What makes you think I'll cooperate if I'm just an angry brat?"

"I also said that you were smart. You know the consequences of acting out in here, and they do not outweigh the benefits."

We stared at each other through another bout of silence. I broke it first.

"One condition: you do not ask anything about my brother. Ever."

"Agreed."

"Thank you." Another scribble. Damn her.

"So tell me about yourself, Scarlett."

"My father murdered my mother when I was twelve years old, and I was sexually assaulted at sixteen."

CHAPTER SIX

DUKE

As soon as I reached the dormitories where the soldiers were, I immediately wanted to be back in my jail cell.

The guard explained that I would be arriving a mere ten minutes before the TI ("Training Instructor," he'd answered with an annoyed tone) would call for line formation. The dorms were on the lowest decks of the shuttle, occupying six levels. It turned out that the shuttle that the Rosewoods' boarded was military bound as Mr. Rosewood acted as one of the commanding officers. The elevator usage was restricted for recruits—a precaution in case unauthorized personnel tried to enter certain floors—so we had to walk down more flights of stairs than I cared to count before arriving.

The floors were white linoleum, the walls were dark green, and there were bunk beds lining them from end to end. The room stretched forever. I lost count of how many bunks were on this level. It had to be over fifty on each side.

The guard undid my handcuffs and warned me to be ready. When the doors opened again, it would be the TI. And I didn't want to screw up my first impression with him.

Unfortunately, there were only two doors leading into the dorms: the one I came in through, and the emergency door on the opposite side, which would trigger an alarm if entered. Thus, all the trainees' eyes went to me when I stepped inside. Most of them went back to frantically straightening their bunks, but I knew already that my presence was going to be a problem when I noticed that all of the bunks had identification numbers. I was an uninvited guest, so there wouldn't be one for me. Fantastic.

It also didn't help that they were wearing dark green uniforms that matched the walls and I was wearing the black turtleneck and cargo pants from when we had pulled the heist, so I stuck out even more as I walked down the aisle, trying to figure out where I was going to sleep. It took me nearly two minutes to walk from one side of the room to the other, and I discovered that there was little to no extra space except next to the emergency exit. The guard hadn't said anything about giving me supplies either, so I was completely out of luck.

"And you are?" one of the trainees asked with a voice full of disbelief as I took a seat beside the door. I regarded him with a contemplative look before deciding to reply. He had a bit of a Russian accent that years of English couldn't reprogram, and freckles dotted over his cheeks to match the flaming red hair. I estimated he was maybe two or three years older than me.

"Duke."

"You got a last name, Duke?"

I set my jaw. "Duke Nam."

"Holy shit, are you serious?" A gangly dark-haired boy around my age snorted with a gleeful expression.

"Duke Nam? Do you know who that sounds like?"

I sighed. "Yes, I've heard it before."

The Russian guy looked confused. "Heard what?"

"Duke Nam is kinda like Duke Nukem. He's an old video game character from back in the day. Shit, I wish my name sounded that cool. I'm Sam. That's Han."

Sam studied me. "Where's your uniform?"

"I don't have one yet. I'm…new." Explaining my plight to them would be a mistake. I didn't know if these boys had been selected voluntarily or not. Telling them I was a criminal wouldn't benefit me.

"Sorry to hear that," Han replied with absolutely no sympathy. "Doesn't look like you've got a bunk tonight."

I nearly smiled when I thought about where I had been sleeping beforehand and that it wasn't much worse than this place, but I chose not to reply.

"You'd better get up. We're expecting the TI. Any minute," Sam said, glancing nervously at the other end of the room. I pushed up on my hands, starting to stand, and then the door behind me opened. I froze.

When I turned my head, there was a bald black man standing there in a navy suit much like General Bridgewater's. A bit of gray bled into his goatee around the edges. In an instant, the trainees lined up, and I followed suit, allowing my expression to go blank. He walked up and down the aisle once without saying anything, but I could tell he noticed every object in the room.

"My name…is Staff Sergeant Alexander Rosewood."

Shit.

"I am in charge of every man currently staying on this floor. That air you're breathing? Mine. The blood in your veins? Mine. The artificial gravity, the water you'll get to enjoy every once in a blue moon, the clothes on your back, and the goddamn empty space around you is my world, and you will do your very best to abide by it if you want to live. Do you understand me, trainees?"

Dozens of voices answered, "Yes, sir!"

"Yes what?"

"Yes, Staff Sergeant Alexander Rosewood, sir!"

"That's more like it," the older man mused. "You will address me by my full title at all times. Is that understood, trainees?"

"Yes, Staff Sergeant Alexander Rosewood, sir!"

"Beautiful. You've been on this hunk of junk for a good while now and that was the last vacation you ever got. If you want these alien shit-stains to pay for what they've done, then you will delete every memory in your mind in order to become weapons capable of destroying them all. Is that understood?"

"Yes, Staff Sergeant Alexander Rosewood, sir!"

He walked back over to our area and stood in front of me, sizing me up as I stood there staring at the wall. He crossed his hands in front of him and smiled. "Well, well. Good to see you, trainee. And what might your name be?"

"Duke Nam, Staff Sergeant Alexander Rosewood, sir!" I said at full volume.

He chuckled. "Motherfucker, I *know* your name. But these fine gentlemen do not. Say it again for me, trainee."

"Duke Nam, Staff Sergeant Alexander Rosewood, sir!"

"Nice name. Tough. I'm sure your girlfriends must have loved it."

A couple of chuckles sounded from down the line. If he heard them, he ignored it. Sergeant Rosewood stepped close, hoping that I would flinch, but I didn't. "Let me make one thing clear to you, trainee. You do not deserve to be here. You better thank whatever god you worship that you don't slip up once or I'll put your ass in solitary confinement for the rest of your miserable life or until time stops, whichever happens first. Do you understand me?"

"Yes, Staff Sergeant Alexander Rosewood, sir!"

He turned, glancing at the lines again. "Pick up your skirts, ladies. It's time to get to work. We're gonna play a little game called Thud."

I had played a lot of games in my twenty-four years of living, but none of them were anything like Thud.

For good reason.

We stood at the bottom of the winding staircase that led to the floors above us. The steps were metal, and the stairwell was narrow, meaning that only three trainees could line up at a time.

Sergeant Rosewood stood in front of the first trainees to explain the rules.

"You are going to run up all fifteen flights of these stairs. If any one of you trips or falls, the entire troop will walk back down the stairs and start over. You will continue this exercise until I say stop. Do you understand me, trainees?"

"Yes, Staff Sergeant Alexander Rosewood, sir!"

"Good. Now march!"

We made it four floors up before the first trainee tripped, making a dull sound against the unforgiving steps. There were groans and a handful of curses as we went back down the stairs to start over. Anyone caught talking was forced to do one hundred pushups at the sergeant's feet while we all waited, watching him struggle. The second time, we only made it two flights because the guy who had done the pushups fell. The third time, we made it eight flights. Fourth, five. Fifth, six. Sixth, ten. Seventh, thirteen. Eighth, nine. Ninth, ten. Tenth, twelve. Eleventh, fourteen. Twelfth, thirteen. Thirteenth, fifteen.

By the time we walked back down the final time, my thighs felt like rubber bands that had been stretched across a bicycle from wheel to wheel. The pants chafed against my calves until they were raw and itchy, but I couldn't scratch them while we were in line formation. Sweat poured over every inch of my skin beneath the woolen shirt. I tried visualizing a bathtub full of ice and it helped somewhat. Mind over matter.

"Was that fun, trainees?"

"Yes, Staff Sergeant Alexander Rosewood, sir!"

"Glad to hear it. You have exactly three minutes to hit the showers and another five minutes to get back here in line. Anyone who is late will do another round of Thud. Is that understood, trainees?"

"Yes, Staff Sergeant Alexander Rosewood, sir!"

"Good. You are dismissed."

Pandemonium erupted. Everyone grabbed their individual bars of soap and raced for the stairs. The showers were on the floor below us. I didn't have anything to clean myself with nor did I have a uniform, but I still took a shower anyway to wash away the sweat. Guys tripped over each other toweling off and racing back up the stairs to get back in line. At least twenty people were sentenced to another round of Thud. We all waited for them, slowly dripping on the linoleum and shivering in the ice-cold room. I found myself wishing my hair were shorter. I'd slicked it back in the shower, but the water dripped onto my shoulders and made me want to shiver to warm up.

Just as the last trainee came in from his latest game of Thud, I sneezed.

Sergeant Rosewood's head whipped around—a bizarre movement that reminded me of an owl with a goatee. "Was that you, Nam?"

"Yes, Staff Sergeant Alexander Rosewood, sir!"

"Did you get your germs all over my nice clean floor?"

"Yes, Staff Sergeant Alexander Rosewood, sir!"

"That's a damn fine job, trainee. You're gonna spend the rest of the night cleaning your spot until it shines like the sun." He marched over to someone's bunk and grabbed a shirt, tossing it in my direction. I knelt and began scrubbing the spot, quieting the raging monster of an ego inside me that wanted to tell him to shove this shirt right up his ass.

"The rest of you, head upstairs. Orientation starts in three minutes. Straight line. If I see any of you mess it up or break rank, that's one hundred pushups."

The trainees marched out, leaving me behind. I stayed where I was, polishing the same spot. Water dripped from my hair, giving me new things to mop up every few seconds, and some of it ran into my eyes, making them sting. I stopped, breathing hard, my shoulders and arms shaking like leaves in the wind on a cold morning. Wind that I would never feel on my face again.

I squeezed my eyes shut and told myself not to think about it. *Get it together, Duke.*

The nub on my hand stung from deep within, and I ignored it. It was an ugly little reminder that the past never left me. It clung to my back like a zombie, its undead flesh pressing heavy against my skin, wanting to devour me whole. I had been running from it for as long as I could remember.

When I opened my eyes again, the water had turned a sickening dark red and I scrambled backward, a scream building my throat. Sticky scarlet everywhere. Under my shoes. Splattered on the counter. Dripping from the sink.

I shook my head frantically and the visions stopped, bringing me back to the empty room. My breathing slowed, but the shock raced through my veins for another handful of seconds. I ran a hand through my sopping hair and went back to cleaning.

God help me.

CHAPTER SEVEN

SCARLETT

Dr. Warwick couldn't hide the shock on her face, even though it wasn't the exact same look I was used to when I told people my father had murdered my mother when I was twelve. Some people gawked. Others turned pale and averted their eyes, not wanting to draw attention to the ugly thought. She, however, licked her lips and crossed her legs, seeming to take a moment to process this information, or decide if I was lying.

"Do you want to talk about that with me?"

"Do you?"

She adjusted her glasses. "It may help me to understand you better, but that's your decision to make."

The doctor paused and her voice softened. "Were you there when it happened?"

"No. I walked in after he'd already left. My brother was the first to find them."

Dr. Warwick lifted her pen once more. "How did she die?"

"Stabbed," I said. "Once in the stomach, twice in the chest. My father walked out the front door, got in his car, and drove away. The authorities never found him."

A bitter laugh escaped my throat. "Guess they never will, with the Earth gone and all. Maybe that's the silver lining."

"What happened after that?"

"Social services. The rest of our family lived in Seoul. They are...*were* very poor, so they couldn't afford to keep us. We went to a foster family for a while, but they didn't really care much about us. They just wanted a check from the government. When my brother turned sixteen, we ran away and got jobs to make rent. He started out taking odd jobs outside of Home Depot and then eventually got hired to work there. Once I was sixteen, I got a job at Panera. My boss and I had a...misunderstanding one night."

"Do you feel it's your fault?"

I nodded. "I was stupid. It could have been prevented, but I got curious. With my mother dead, I didn't really know anything about boys and sex."

"How was it resolved?"

I winced and squirmed in my chair. "Not well."

"You're being evasive. That's repression, and repression is not going to help you control your anger."

"How is dragging up my past going to help?"

"We need to get to the root of the problem. Why do you feel so resentful toward men of authority? What's the cause of your impulsive nature? These are the answers I'm looking for, Scarlett. You can't continue on like this or you'll be locked up for the rest of your life."

"Like that would really be a bad thing? I'm not a good person, Dr. Warwick. The army wouldn't be suffering that much of a loss if you didn't clear me."

"So that's it? You'd rather resign yourself to be alone and imprisoned for the rest of your life?"

I stared at her. She shook her head. "What did you do?"

I frowned. "What?"

"You had to have done something awful that you won't admit to that makes you do this to yourself. You're actively trying to sabotage your own life because you think you're inadequate. So what is it?"

My throat felt dry. I swallowed. The answer crawled up the back of my tongue, desperate to find its way out. Just as my lips parted, I heard another sound. A loud whooping, similar to a police siren. A male's voice came over the intercom, startling the both of us.

"*Attention all personnel: please report to your dormitories. All scheduled activity aboard the shuttle has been canceled until further notice. Proceed imme-diately to your lodgings.*"

Dr. Warwick frowned, standing up and heading for the door. I stood, not sure of what to do just yet. The door started to close, and I caught it, trying to listen in as the doctor addressed the guard in front of the room. "What's going on?"

"Don't know, ma'am. But that's a Code Nine, so I'm going to have to escort the two of you out of this facility."

"Lionel, don't you stand here and lie to me," Dr. Warwick snapped, surprising me with the harshness in her tone.

"Tiana," the guard said with a patient voice. "Please just head for your room. I'll tell you what I know after the evacuation is over. I promise."

She gave him a sour look and then beckoned for me to follow her. The guard put my handcuffs back on, much to my annoyance, and we walked at a brisk pace out of the psychology ward. She took the elevator to one of the upper floors, and then the guard and I walked down the stairs to the prison section. I'd gotten a quick peek at the doctor's quarters, and everyone seemed as confused as Warwick had been. My mind instantly started to formulate possibilities: an imminent attack, a mutiny, or maybe one of the ship's systems had started to fail. None of these theories were fun to entertain.

"I don't suppose you've got anything to eat in one of your eight million pockets?" I asked as we walked down the hallway to my cell. The guard didn't reply. I thought about it for a moment and then tried again.

"I haven't eaten in seven hours. I would appreciate it if you found something for me to eat, if you can."

He opened my cell, and I went in without a fight. He paused and then nodded. "I have to check in with my squad, but I'll be back shortly with something."

"Thank you."

The guard's goggles hid his eyes, but I could tell he was surprised. "You're...welcome."

He walked off. I sat on my cot and tried not to think about how much the sirens reminded me of home.

DUKE

"What do you think it is? Engine's gone out? Someone's got Space Madness?"

"Nah, they'd only shut down a section of the ship for that. This is a full lockdown. Shit just got real."

"You think it's the enemy?"

"I dunno, man. Do I look like an intelligence officer?"

"Obviously not."

"Ah, shut up. If we're about to die, I don't want my last word to be with your dumb ass."

"Too late."

The trainees gathered in groups by their bunks to speculate about the sudden order for everyone to return to their lodgings. Thankfully, this rescued me from cleaning duty, as Sergeant Rosewood was called away to meet with the other military leaders.

Han sat on his bed with his large fingers drumming on the mattress while Sam leaned against the post of his bed, chewing one corner of his lapel. I sat on the floor, legs crossed, soaking in the scattered conversations and analyzing them.

"So what do you think this is all about?" Sam asked me, unable to hide his trepidation.

I sighed, annoyed that my concentration had been broken. "I don't know much more than you guys do. Hell, I probably know less."

"Got that right," Han snorted. I ignored the comment.

Sam continued as if he hadn't said anything. "C'mon, throw me a bone here. What do you think it is?"

I went silent, thinking. "They want us out of the way. That makes me think they've made contact with the Bergleute."

Sam's brown eyes widened. "Seriously?"

"You asked."

He glanced at Han. "What about you?"

"He could be right," the big guy said. "Standard protocol is to secure everyone aboard and then construct a plan from there. If it's as serious as we think...we probably won't be briefed on it."

Sam frowned. "That's bullshit. We're already gonna lay down our lives for what's left of the world's population. The least they can do is tell us the truth."

I shrugged. "He's only guessing. They might tell us, they might not."

"Oh yeah? How much did they tell you before they brought you in?"

"Not much," I said, which wasn't a lie. "What about you? How were you recruited?"

"I was set to enter basic training in the fall. They told me this was an early special program they were prepping me for and put me up with other recruits. That's where I met Han, actually. We knew something was fishy based on who they were taking for this program, though."

"How so?"

"People weren't really chosen for endurance or stamina. It's sort of like they were collecting specimens. I mean, look at all the different ethnicities in this room alone," Sam said, gesturing to the other trainees. I glanced around the room, noting that he was right. There were boys from nearly every continent, most of them in their late teens or early twenties. That was definitely on purpose.

"They gave us a speech about how we'd be humanity's last hope and all that stuff, but I didn't take it seriously. I wish I had. I mean, I'm happy to be alive but...thinking about all those people who didn't have a choice. Sucks, you know?"

I lowered my eyes to the floor. "Yeah."

"That's all the more reason for them to tell us," Han insisted, his brow furrowing in anger. "We were chosen. They cannot treat us like children—"

"Truth among the masses almost always leads to panic," I said. "That's why they didn't tell the general public about the Bergleute. Can you imagine what would have happened? Society itself would have collapsed overnight."

"Not them. Us. We have training. We have discipline."

"But that's not what they're looking for. They want obedience. We're not here to be independent thinkers, we're here to follow orders."

"He's right," Sam murmured. "We're soldiers, not leaders. Maybe we should just face the facts."

"That's not good enough."

I arched an eyebrow. "What are you gonna do about it?"

"What if we bribed one of the guards to tell us what's going on?"

"C'mon, money died with the Earth," Sam groaned. "Plus, I left my fifties in my other uniform. We've got nothing they want, unless you can get some keys from the women's dorms."

"What if we figured out a way to eavesdrop on the leaders' meeting?"

"Dude, their conference room is on the fourteenth floor. How the hell would we even get up there without getting caught?"

They stared at each other and then turned to look at me. I held up my hands. "Leave me out of this, Larry and Curly."

"Hey, we didn't say you had to be a part of it," Sam replied with his most earnest look possible. "You could just…y'know…give us an idea."

I fought the urge to roll my eyes. "No thanks."

"What? You chicken?"

I shook my head. "Great reverse psychology there, Sam."

"Damn. He's too smart. Maybe we should just threaten him."

That made me chuckle finally. "Look, I'm not gonna help you get yourselves in trouble. We're probably better off not knowing."

They ignored me and kept going with theories. "What about the trash chute? It connects all the floors together."

Sam scoffed. "Yeah, and it would only work if this mission were impossible, if you catch my drift."

"Ventilation?"

"And *that* would only work if one of us were John McClane. How many American movies have you watched lately?"

I sighed. "You guys are driving me crazy. If you really want to know so bad, you'd have to break into one of the equipment vaults I saw on the way in to get one of those tiny microphone transmitters. Attach it to one of the security guards and that's your ticket in."

They went quiet for a moment. "…why the hell didn't we think of that?"

"No clue."

"Where's the closest guard?"

Han pointed to the exit. "Outside that door. I heard something about them taking attendance in a few minutes. That means we're gonna have to move fast. The vault's on the end of the hall beside the elevator. I can pick the lock, but I need something small and metal."

I tapped the bunk bed. "Mattress spring."

"Perfect."

He lifted the mattress and tore a small hole in the cloth, digging out one of the wires, straightening it out, and then bending it until he had two pieces. "Sam, you'll have to be the distraction. Do something to get the guard in here and I'll go out."

"Got it."

Han started for the door. Once he reached the other end of the room, he gave Sam the thumbs up to create his distraction. The gangly teen looked at me.

"Think the guard knows CPR?"

"Yeah."

"Good." He hit the floor like a sack of potatoes. I nearly jumped out of my skin. It took me a second to realize he was pretending to be incapacitated. Smart move.

The trainees freaked out and crowded around us like little boys around a newly discovered corpse. After they finished gawking, someone had the sense to call for help. The guard appeared within a minute or two, giving Han the chance to slip out. I didn't exactly approve of their plan that I had unfortunately contributed to, but I played along, acting worried about Sam. The guard started CPR and called on his walkie-talkie to request that he be transferred to the medical ward. Curiously, they told him to see if he could get him stabilized and they would send someone if he couldn't be revived. They didn't want anyone in the halls. Interesting.

I wondered if my hardheaded sister had escaped the medical wing, but she wasn't dangerous enough to warrant shutting the entire vessel down. Though I'm sure she would be disappointed if I told her so. She seemed to enjoy being a troublemaker, on some level.

I sidled behind the throng of people to see the door, waiting for Han to reappear. Sam and I hadn't established a sign, but I assumed that he would pretend to come around once his partner in crime came back to his side. He needed to hurry. Sam's ribs were taking quite the beating from the guard's rough resuscitation methods.

Mercifully, Han returned and went to Sam's side, his voice gruff with fake concern.

"C'mon, man, snap out of it!"

Like magic, Sam's eyes pried open, and he let out a dramatic groan that made me stifle a laugh. His audience bought it because they didn't know any better. The guard seemed relieved and instructed him to lie on his bed for a while and let someone know if he felt sick again. We waited for him to go and for the rest of the trainees to lose interest before asking Han how it went.

"Did you get it in place?"

"Yeah, when I patted him on the back and thanked him. Put it right under his collar." Han unbuttoned his shirt a bit and pulled out the radio receiver and began fiddling with it.

"We can't stay out in the open like this," Sam murmured, glancing behind us. "One of the other guys'll catch on and might tell the sergeant. I don't know about you, but I'm not up for another three rounds of Thud."

Han reached into his backpack and handed us both books. Mine was *The Art of War* by Sun Tzu and Sam's was *Leaves of Grass* by Walt Whitman. Interesting choices.

"Here, just act like you're reading. They won't bother us then."

I cracked open the book and leaned my back against the bedpost, doing my best to look casual. Sam did the same. Han grabbed another book and flipped to a random page, keeping his head low so he could hear the receiver. The guys behind us continued talking and paid us no mind.

"Sounds like the guard has reached the meeting room," Han began in a low voice. "I think it's just people on staff in there, no civilians. General Bridgewater's getting ready to speak."

He paused, listening in. "He's saying that the information is completely classified, not to leave the room for any reason. Says anyone who talks will be imprisoned indefinitely. I think he's got some sort of footage to show them."

"Tch. A lot of good that does us," Sam said, but Han shushed him.

"He's saying that the ship picked up an anomaly several miles out from our position. At first, they thought it was a ricochet from one of the other planets the Bergleute destroyed because it was so small, but it was giving off an unusual signature."

He heard something else that made his face go blank. I couldn't help staring at him as his skin paled and the freckles stood out like blots of ink on a sheet of paper.

"What?"

"They said they received a...message."

Shock twisted through my guts like a snake. "What kind of message?"

"Just two words, in very bad English," Han continued, his voice nearly hoarse with disbelief. "Sounded like, 'please help.'"

"Do they think it's a surviving ship from before the Earth's destruction?" Sam asked, but I could tell he didn't really believe his own question.

"No. The ship is unlike anything they've seen before. General Bridgewater says they let it board in the cargo bay and the alien is in custody."

"Shit," I whispered. "They've got one. I can't believe it."

"What are they gonna do with it? Interrogate it?" Sam asked.

I nodded. "And not nicely. They'll get all the information they can, kill it, and dissect it."

"Smart move. It'll help us find a way to kill them," Han replied. The shock was now replaced with a deep sense of vengeance. I didn't blame him.

"But it still bothers me that it came to us looking for help," I said, looking between the two of them. "It has to know we're going to kill it sooner or later. Why take the risk?"

"You think it's a trick?"

"Could be. Or maybe it really does want our help. Maybe it's one of the aliens that survived after they blew up his planet as well. They didn't tell me if they knew what the Bergleute look like. What about you?"

Both of them shook their heads. "What's he saying now?" I asked.

"Be on high alert for an attack. Regular scheduling will commence in 24 hours. That means we're stuck here until then."

The doors to the room opened, and Han stuffed the receiver back in his jumpsuit, buttoning it up as we hurried into line formation. I wondered why this guard hadn't been briefed at the meeting, but then I noticed that he had an earpiece and had probably been listening to it. He went down the line with a clipboard calling names. When he was about halfway down, I noticed a low murmur coming from Han's shirt. A horrible realization came over me: *he hadn't turned it off.*

Sam mouthed frantically for him to turn it off, and he glanced at the guard as the man got closer. Sweat started to bead on his forehead as he lifted one arm and reached inside his jumpsuit. I tapped him on the left leg and opened my palm as he pulled the receiver out. He dropped into my hand just as the guard got over to him and called his name. I slid it into my pocket and continued standing at attention as he came to me next.

"Nam, Duke!"

"Present, sir!" I bellowed, hoping he wouldn't be able to hear the faint murmur coming from my pants. He gave me an odd look and then shrugged.

"Nice set of pipes you got there, son."

"Thank you, sir!"

"Your clothes aren't regulation, so I'm gonna have to have you change out of them." He handed me a folded-up uniform, and I subsequently started having a heart attack as I undressed. His attention went back to the clipboard, and I tried to figure out a way to get the receiver out of my pants pocket without him noticing. I pretended to drop my shirt and picked it up, but as I went, I slipped the receiver out of its hiding spot and kept it in my palm. I put the uniform on and managed to tuck it in the band of my boxers as I finished buttoning the pants.

I handed him my old clothes, and he went on his way. A relieved sigh escaped me. We were safe for now.

"Your orders are to study the materials you received during orientation and to stay in this room. If you disobey, you will be subjected to punishment directly from Staff Sergeant Rosewood. Instructions for bathroom breaks and lunch will be given later."

The guard closed the door, and I heard it lock behind him. Trapped. Fantastic.

Han let out a long rush of breath, glancing at me with a grateful expression. "Thanks."

"Forget it. At least we have a link to the outside. We just have to be a little more careful." I handed it back to him once the guys broke out of line.

"Agreed. I'm sure a lot has happened during the attendance. He's probably no longer at the meeting. I'll keep an ear open to see if anything else comes up. For now, we just have to wait."

"My favorite game," Sam said with a dry voice, climbing the ladder up to his bunk above Han's. I resumed my spot on the floor, trying to ignore the cold linoleum underneath my ass, but then Han tossed me his blanket. He gave me a small smile when I sent him a questioning look.

"You've earned it."

CHAPTER EIGHT

SCARLETT

S o," I said through a mouthful of ham sandwich, "I don't suppose you can tell me what's going on?"

The guard stared at me and then smirked ever so slightly. "Sorry. Not my department."

"Not even if I ask nicely?"

"Afraid not."

I shrugged. "Well, you do what you can."

My casual words were nothing more than an act. I was trying so hard not to stuff the sandwich in my mouth in one bite that my hands were shaking. I hadn't really realized it had been hours since my last meal. We ate before the heist back on Earth, nothing fancy, just a bucket of KFC. He'd gotten me something from the break room—thin slices of ham, a layer of mayo, a piece of American cheese, all on two pieces of wheat bread. It was like a meal of the gods to me.

I licked my fingers and nibbled on any crumbs I found, which caused the guard to chuckle. "You really were hungry, huh?"

"Starving," I sighed as I leaned my back against the wall. They had taken my sweatshirt sometime after my brother and I arrived on the shuttle, and I honestly missed it. The blanket could only do so much against the cold. Still, I wrapped it around my shoulders and noticed that the guard didn't immediately leave. He didn't seem to be in a hurry. It had been about three hours since the lockdown. Only the guards were allowed out and about.

"Can I ask you something?"

"Sure."

"Why…are you being so nice to me?"

He seemed to think about it. "For one, you stop being such a hard ass and asked nicely for the food."

He had a point. I let it slide. "Two, I've got nothing better to do right now. There's no activity, and I'm on duty for the next eight hours."

The guard stepped a little closer, lowering his voice. "And three, between you and me, you gave Simmons a bloody nose. I hate that guy. He's such a pain in the ass."

I giggled. "Happy to help."

He grinned. "Though, I'd be careful if I were you. Because of his failure to keep you contained, he's been reassigned to another division. If he sees you again, I'm sure he'll be holding a grudge."

I snorted. "Well, I doubt I'll be out and about any time soon, so I think we're safe."

The guard stepped back, leaning against the bars on the opposite cell. "So what's with you, anyway? All they told me is that you snuck aboard the Rosewoods' shuttle and that's what landed you here. Standard procedure would have called for your release after interrogation."

"I have…problems with my temper," I admitted, letting some of the humor drop out of my voice. "And that's putting it nicely. They want my behavior adjusted before I join the ranks."

"You okay with that?"

"Don't really have a choice."

"Point taken." He reached into his pocket and withdrew a quarter. I watched with interest as he pulled off his glove and started to flip it across his knuckles. At first, I wondered if he were trying to impress me, but then I picked up on the fidgety nature of the movement.

"You used to smoke, didn't you?"

He lifted his goggles to look at me and I could see his eyes—brown. He looked to be in his mid-thirties, and I could tell he was of Middle Eastern descent, though he didn't have an accent. "How'd you know?"

"You look like you're the kind of smoker who needs something to do with his hands. They won't let you smoke out here because of the limited oxygen supply, I'm guessing."

He nodded. "Yup. Hardest thing I ever had to do was give 'em up. But I also did it for my baby girl, so it's not all bad."

"How old?"

"Three. She's on one of the other shuttles. They're set to transfer over here when we reach the rendezvous point."

"Where's that?"

"Not far from here. They want us at a safe distance in case the Bergleute feel the need to pick a fight. Doubtful, but better safe than sorry." He then frowned. "I probably wasn't supposed to tell you that."

"I'll pretend you didn't."

"Thanks," he grunted.

I hid another smile. "So what are you allowed to tell me? Can I ask anything about the ship?"

He eyed me. "Depends. I can't tell you anything that would help you escape your cell again. I'd rather not get reassigned."

I grinned, holding up my hand. "Scout's honor, I won't try again. I meant about the technology. The stuff in here—artificial gravity, traveling at the speed of light…this is all stuff I've seen in sci-fi movies. How did we get this advanced?"

"Truthfully? This tech's been around for longer than you think. Thirty, forty years, actually."

My jaw dropped. "You've gotta be kidding me."

"Nope. It's called hiding in plain sight. The government knew people wouldn't really get suspicious about things they see in movies, so we put it all out there. They didn't release this stuff to the public because most of it would be used for the Starlight program. We couldn't risk it coming to light, so all the tech was strictly utilized for the Contingency only."

"Damn shame. I could have used a jetpack back on Earth."

He chuckled again. "Flying cars and jetpacks were pure fantasy. They never intended to actually make them. People have a hard enough time not killing themselves on the ground, forget the sky."

"So the Contingency was a worldwide agreement instead of just the United States?"

He nodded. "I was stationed in Pakistan. The idea originally came from Germany, and they reached out to all the other nations for suggestions about what to do. Things got pretty ugly, but as time went on, they put their differences aside. Those space stations that they made a big deal about were fronts for the military spacecrafts. We sent the parts up and then built them in deep space to avoid suspicion."

"How many battle fleets were there?"

He shook his head. "Can't remember. Hundreds."

I winced. "Jesus. I can't believe they didn't make it."

"Yeah. We had a hell of a run, though."

He sighed, flipping the coin into his palm and closing his hand around it. "It's hard thinking about the Earth not being there anymore. No more Sunday walks, no more Saturday nights at the bar, no more ocean, no more sky. Shit. I don't know how people are getting by these days."

"Not thinking about it helps," I murmured, resting my chin on my knee.

"It won't work forever."

"It doesn't have to."

He met my eyes and smiled again. "Y'know, you're alright."

"I try."

"Uh-huh. I've got to go check in. Don't go anywhere."

"I wouldn't dream of it."

He started to walk away, and I called out to him, "What's your name?"

"Evans."

"I like it. See you around, Evans."

He left. I lay down on the cot and tugged the blanket around me. I was still alone, but for the first time, it didn't feel quite so terrible.

The water was cold, ice cold, so cold that my skin went numb. It was at chest level, lapping against my breastbone and making the tank top stick to me like glue. I had never seen this room before—the walls were white as chalk, but the water was tinted blue. The pool had to be about twenty feet across, and my feet touched the bottom, so it wasn't very deep.

A strange gurgling sound made me turn. To my horror, there was someone at the deep end of the pool with his thin arms thrashing as he tried to stay afloat.

"Hold on, I'm coming!" I shouted, plunging in. I swam quick, strong strokes over to the boy and grabbed him around the midsection. As soon as my hands went around him, he clung to me, coughing mouthfuls of water out of his lungs. I waded over to the pool's steps and climbed out, sitting him down. He was so small and thin, with brown hair plastered over his eyes, and his lips were nearly purple. He would have died in seconds if I hadn't gotten to him. He continued coughing up water while I rubbed his bare back in calming circles.

"Just keep breathing, you're alright," I said in my most soothing voice. When

all the water was gone, he looked up at me with large brown eyes that were red in the corners, as if he had been crying.

"Can you help me get it off?"

"Off?" I asked, confused. That was when I felt it. When I drew my hand away from his back, his pasty skin came off in wet clumps, sticking to my hands. I should have panicked, but I didn't because he wasn't upset by this bizarre development. I crawled behind him and found that there was a strange greenish brown skin poking through the hole I'd made, almost the color of a turtle's shell. I stuck my fingers into the hole and continued peeling off the layer along his back. The skin came off easily, almost like a snake's yearly shedding. I removed all of it from his back and shoulders, moving on to his arms next. He had four fingers on each hand with black claws at the end and a hard exoskeleton covered everywhere else.

Eventually, the only thing left was his face, and I carefully pulled off the skin from his neck upward, revealing his head. His nose and mouth were like a hawk's beak, curved with two pinpricks as nostrils, and each of his four eyes had a thin film over them like a frog's rather than an eyelid. His eyes were completely black with a tiny dot of white in the middle. The top of his skull formed a point, and there were two oval-shaped ears on either side of the sharp angle.

I dropped the skin and stared at him in wonderment. "What are you?"

"In trouble," he whispered. The creature reached up and touched the side of my face. The clawed hand was surprisingly delicate against my skin. "Please help me. I'm the only one who got out. They need us. They need you."

"Who does?"

"Shasar. My people. They're dying."

I shook my head. "I don't understand. Why do you need my help? I have no power."

"You have the power to hear and to speak. Do not underestimate them."

Before I could answer him, there was a sharp tapping sound that nearly deafened me.

I came out of the dream gasping for air like I had been the one drowning. My eyes focused to see the guard, Evans, tapping on the bars. It took some effort, but I managed to sit upright and rub my eyes. "I'm up, I'm up. What is it? Do I get a shower break?"

"You've been summoned."

"By whom?"

"Captain Hallstead."

My eyebrows shot up so high that they almost vanished beneath my hairline.

"Um…why?"

"He didn't specify."

"…I can't say no, can I?"

"Not really."

I tossed the blanket down and stood as he opened the door. That was when I noticed the solemn expression on his face. His entire posture and demeanor changed. Something was wrong, very wrong.

He put the handcuffs on me and then we walked to the stairs. "How many floors up?"

"We're going to the fourteenth floor."

"What's up there?"

"Conference rooms."

"Oh, good. I thought it was the dorms."

He made a noise. "It's not *that* kind of summon."

"Hey, you never know. We are on a military vessel populated mostly by men."

"Point taken." As we walked, I tried to come up with a reason why he wanted to see me but couldn't theorize anything logical, especially since the lockdown was still enacted. I had only been asleep for roughly four hours. Something must have happened. For a second, I thought about Duke. Panic gripped me. What if he was hurt? What if he had gotten sick? What if I lost him?

I clenched my hands into fists and told myself to calm down. Duke could take care of himself. He had proven that time and time again.

We opened the door to the fourteenth floor, and two more guards greeted us. They gave me suspicious looks until Evans explained that the captain wanted to see me, and then they relaxed and let us by. The hallway was wide, unlike the interrogation and therapy wards, and there were closed doors everywhere. At the end of the hall was a set of double doors guarded by three armed men. Evans showed them his entry card, and they let me in while he stayed outside.

The room was an auditorium with stadium seating. Cushioned seats all faced a large console like the one on the deck of the ship. A huge holographic projector was lit up with security camera footage that Captain Hallstead was rifling through when I walked in. The eerie blue screen cast pale light over his face, and I realized how gravely he seemed, as if he hadn't slept in a while.

"Scarlett," he said.

I walked over to him, cautious but civil. "Captain. I understand I've been summoned."

"Yes, you have," he replied, giving me nothing but that intense stare of his. I fought the urge to squirm under the weight his heavy gray eyes.

"Did I do something wrong?"

"No. In fact, it seems like you've done something very useful. I don't know how you did it, either, which is the amazing part."

I couldn't hide my confusion. "What are you talking about?"

"Before I explain, I need you to understand something." He started touching panels on the holographic projector as he spoke. "What you're about to see is classified. If you tell anyone about it, anyone at all, you will be put in solitary confinement for the rest of your life with no chance of release. Is that clear?"

"Crystal."

Hallstead took a deep breath. "Several hours ago, we received a message from a small craft pleading with us for help. At first, we thought it was an escape shuttle from Earth, but when it got closer, we realized the ship was not from our world. It was alien."

My eyes widened and my mouth tumbled open in shock. He continued. "We let the vessel dock with our cargo and went to apprehend what we thought would be one of the Bergleute. We assumed they were trying to set some sort of trap, but what we found inside was not one of them. It was a completely different type of alien altogether. We took it to the interrogation room to get some answers, but it didn't understand what we wanted. The alien's English seems very limited, and it could only say a few words. It kept asking us for help."

A cold feeling slithered up my spine as he went on. "General Bridgewater thought it was a trick of some kind to catch us off guard, but his tactics scared it so badly that it wouldn't talk to him any longer. Instead, it asked for you."

My mouth fell open. "*Me?* What the hell do you mean it asked for me?"

"It said your name, Scarlett. First and last."

"That's *impossible*, Captain."

He touched one last panel and brought up a picture of the alien. I stumbled backward.

It was the creature from my dream.

"Shit," I whispered. "Holy *shit*. That wasn't a dream. It was...contacting me."

"I figured as much. I looked at the security footage in your cell. You were tossing and turning in your sleep right when we think it made telepathic contact. A few hours ago, it retreated into some sort of catatonic state, and we think that's when it somehow connected with you in your dreams."

I regained control of myself enough to ask a question. "What do you want me to do?"

"Talk to it. Find out what it wants."

I shook my head frantically. "You can't be serious. I don't know how to negotiate—I can't even communicate properly with human beings! That's why you put me in therapy!"

"You have to."

"There's got to be someone more qualified. It's a mistake. It probably didn't mean to contact me. You can get my brother to do it; I'm sure he'd be better at this—" I babbled as he stepped toward me. He reached out and I flinched, half-expecting him to hit me, but instead he laid his hands on my shoulders.

"Scarlett, you're the only one who can do this. It doesn't matter if you're ready or not. It chose you. Just you."

"But what if I fail? You can't put all your hopes on me. I'm not...I'm not..." I pressed my lips together, glancing away.

"You're not what?" he snapped, forcing me to finish the sentence.

"Good enough," I whispered, staring at his chest because the eye contact was too much for me to handle in my current state. "I'm not good enough. I never was. I was just lucky. That's all I've ever been."

He didn't say anything for a handful of seconds. Then he lifted my chin and made me look at him. "There were 7.3 billion people on the Earth before it exploded. Seven *billion*. Now there are only one hundred million and two left. You are one of those fortunate few for a reason, Scarlett. What are the odds that you and your brother made it into a shuttle literally moments before everyone else died? A million to one? Well, guess what? You're the one. Literally."

A choked laugh escaped my dry throat. "That's pretty corny, captain."

A smirk tugged at the edge of his lips. "Maybe so. But I'm still right. You wouldn't have survived if you weren't good enough. So suck it up, get in there, and do your job."

I took a deep breath and straightened my shoulders. "Yes, sir."

In a miraculous rare moment, Hallstead actually smiled. Not a smirk but a smile. It was like seeing a solar eclipse—a once in a lifetime phenomenon. I caught myself wishing he'd always look at me like that before reality returned in the form of the door opening and the guard telling us that General Bridgewater was waiting. Captain Hallstead quickly dropped his hands from where they had rested on my shoulders, and I remembered how cold it was without them. Damn.

They led me out of the auditorium into one of the bathrooms. The guard gave me a more streamlined version of a hazmat suit, complete with piped in air for me to breathe. After all, it was an alien. It could have viruses, bacteria, or other contaminants.

After that, they took me to a conference room near the end of the hallway. Hallstead opened the door, revealing that there was a separate room with a one-way glass that looked into the main room. It had been completely sealed off like a clean room with a gap for entry and sterilization afterward. Inside, there was an oak table and four chairs—three behind the table and one where the alien sat. My breath caught in my throat.

At first, it didn't even look like the alien I'd seen in my dream until I stepped a little closer and peered through the mirror. What sat on the chair appeared to be a huge greenish brown pod shaped like a pistachio. My eyes traced the seams in the shell and then I put it together. It could apparently curl up almost like a turtle and pull its limbs to its body so that they fit like puzzle pieces. Interesting survival tactic. Still, I realized it was probably scared.

"Go on," Hallstead said. "I'll monitor from here. You'll be safe."

I nodded and took a deep breath, opening the door into the conference room.

The alien didn't stir when I walked, slow and steady, over to its chair. Tension sang up and down my arms, in my shoulders, in my spine, and I had to force myself to take even breaths. Each footstep felt absurdly loud, even for hazmat boots. When I was about a foot away, I bit my bottom lip and tried to think of what I should say.

"Hey there," I said softly. "It's Scarlett. The girl from the dream."

No response. "You contacted me a few hours ago. You asked for my help, so I came to talk to you."

Still nothing. I pulled up a chair. The entire situation was surreal enough, but I still couldn't wrap my head around the fact that I was talking to a gigantic nut-shaped alien.

"It's okay if you don't trust me," I continued. "I don't blame you. The men who took you in aren't very nice. They probably tried to hurt you like they did me when I was brought here. I'm sorry you had to go through that. I know it doesn't mean much, but we're not all like that."

There was no way to tell if he even understood me, but once the words started, they flowed out of me like water.

"In case you're wondering, we call ourselves 'human beings.' We're from Earth. Well...we *were* from Earth. The Bergleute destroyed it, so we're homeless now. Is that what happened to you?"

Silence. I nodded. "Yeah. I figured as much. I guess we're both orphans."

"What does orphan mean?"

I jumped right out of my seat.

A dreamy, child-like voice had spoken, but the alien hadn't moved. Stranger still, I hadn't exactly heard it with my ears but rather *in my head.*

"What did you say?"

"Orphan. What does it mean?" the alien spoke again. I reminded myself to calm down and lowered myself back into the chair.

"It means someone who has lost their mother and father."

"Those words mean 'parents' in your language, correct?"

"Yes."

I paused. "How are you doing that?"

"Our minds are linked. I am not speaking in your native tongue; you are understanding what I say in your language through mental manipulation."

"That is really confusing."

"Shall I explain it further?"

"Only if you want to. I'd just feel better if you did it out loud, so the men watching us don't think I'm talking to myself."

"I am frightened to show myself again. They will hurt me."

A wave of sympathy rolled over me. "They won't hurt you again. That's why they came and got me. They realized they were wrong and shouldn't have treated you that way."

"You promise they won't hurt me?"

"I promise."

Slowly, the little cracks in its shell widened and it unfolded its body from its protective state. Its head slid upward, and its limbs stretched until it sat mirroring me with its clawed hands on its knees, blinking at me with a curious expression.

"Does this make you more comfortable?"

"Yes, it does, thank you. I'm Scarlett. Scarlett Nam. Do you have a name?"

"Yes. Hatwer."

"Nice to meet you, Hatwer." The pronunciation of its name was interesting—the h had an underlying w-sound to it and the "wer" was pronounced like "where." The way it talked made me wonder how old it was in their concept of age, but that could be discussed later. The voice also made me think it was male, which also explained the little boy I saw in my dream.

"So why did you come to us? Why do you need our help?"

Hatwer's head tilted downward, and he stared at the floor as if saddened. His beak did not move when he used his telepathy, but I assumed he could say a few words in English since Hallstead and the others had interrogated him earlier.

"My people are dying. They cannot escape the ones you call the Bergleute. I hoped you would be able to free them."

"Where are they?"

"Aboard the ship. The one that darkens the sky. The one that destroyed your home and mine."

"They're prisoners?"

"Worse. They are slaves. The Bergleute discovered our technology—the bright light that pierces the souls of planets. On our planet, we used it for digging new homes. We lived underground. The Bergleute invaded our colony and killed many to harvest the weapon for their own gain. But they could not use it well, so they enslaved the rest of my people to serve them always."

"God," I whispered. "I'm so sorry."

Without thinking, I reached out and touched his right hand. His shell was moist and solid like a crab's. He cocked his head slightly to the left, watching me.

"What are you doing?"

I withdrew my hand. "Sorry. I was trying to comfort you."

"I see. Is that what contact means in your culture?"

"Sometimes, yes."

"Oh. Is there anything your people can do to help us?"

I felt at a loss for words. The Bergleute had killed nearly our entire race, and this poor alien's as well. Realistically, we wouldn't be able to fight them and free his people, but I wasn't about to tell him that. Not if I had a choice.

"I hope we can, Hatwer. We are training people to fight them. Do you know anything about them that can help us? Their weaknesses? Their strengths? What they look like?"

"I am afraid I do not know much, but perhaps I can share with you what they look like."

He hesitated before speaking again. *"I must warn you. It will be... unpleasant."*

"Don't worry—I'm used to that feeling," I admitted with a sad smile.

"Very well." All four of his eyes closed, and I felt something curl through me, like a feather along the edges of my brain. My eyes closed, and in the darkness, I could feel Hatwer's mind connected with mine like links snapping into place.

At first, I saw and felt nothing. Then the images smashed into me like an eighteen-wheeler, and my senses drowned in a sensation that could only be described as agony.

There were bright green electrical chains hanging from my neck, and they were linked to the two aliens on either side of me. We were all connected standing before a huge metal table, our claws buried in the entrails of a dead beast from light years away. The Bergleute considered its intestines to be a delicacy, and the young aliens of my race had small enough hands to remove them without damaging them. We removed the guts and placed them in buckets on the floor, which others picked up in pairs and brought to the washroom. Many of them were smaller and weaker than me, frail from lack of nutrition and having been beaten for not working fast enough. A large conveyor belt above us dropped a new animal every few moments and we had to salvage all the usable parts or we'd be electrocuted by our collars.

One of the smallest aliens standing across from me fainted after the next beast fell, exhausted from hours upon hours of labor. We all froze in horror as the ground beneath us trembled.

It was approaching.

A looming shadow fell across our table. I cowered in my spot, not daring to look up and attract its attention. My eyes were downcast enough to see its four bent legs supporting a powerful frame. Two razor sharp claws lay at the end of each foot, tapering up to a huge muscular torso with two arms on each side. Its skin was dark gray with black spots, and it wore some sort of armor over its chest. A whip hung from its belt right next to a gun modified with our technology—one that could vaporize an enemy over a hundred steps away.

The Bergleute picked up the youngling, which shivered and came awake all at once, screaming for his parents as the predator lifted it and turned off its collar. I could not resist looking up into its horrible face. There were six milky white eyes, as thin as slits, and the mandibles housed four overgrown canines for tearing apart any meat it wanted to devour. A forked tongue dangled out one side of its mouth and globs of spit rolled off. It was hungry.

"Too tired to work, little one?" the alien purred in our language. The young one cried and begged for mercy, but the Bergleute merely chuckled.

"Don't be so modest. You need rest. Come. I will show you to your eternal resting place."

He bit clean through the young one's head. I covered my eyes, trying to block out the sight of its skull crushed into only meat and blood. The horrid crunching sound made me want to vomit and cry until there was nothing left in my glands.

The Bergleute marched away, continuing to feast on the remains of the worker and leaving us all to ferment in the misery and death it left behind.

All at once, my eyes opened and I fell to my knees, gasping for air. Tears streamed from my eyes. God. *God!*

The door burst open behind me. I could hear Hallstead calling my name. Hatwer went back into his shell as they came over, yelling for him not to move. Hallstead knelt beside me, touching my back and trying to make me look at him.

"Scarlett, are you okay? Say something! Can you hear me?"

My chest had constricted too tight for me to speak, and all I could feel was Hatwer's fear. It suffocated me like an invisible hand over my nose and mouth.

Hallstead held my face between his hands, searching my eyes for answers. "Scarlett, answer me! What happened?"

I took several gulping breaths and managed to stammer out something. "Not his f-fault. He d-didn't hurt me. Showed me what the Bergleute did. Fucking horrible monsters."

"It's okay. Put your guns down. She needs a break. Leave the alien alone."

"Hatwer," I muttered. "His name is Hatwer."

The captain cast a confused look over my face but nodded anyway. "Hatwer, then. Let's go."

He helped me stand and led me out into the observation room with the one-way mirror. I couldn't stop shaking even though the memories were already slipping back into the dark recesses of my mind. Out of courtesy, the guards stepped out, leaving just the two of us. I took off the Hazmat suit, glad to breathe freely again. Hallstead cursed under his breath as he saw me trembling and took off his suit jacket, draping it over my shoulders. I pulled it around me as much as possible, still shaking from the images lingering in my thoughts.

"Jesus, you're scaring me," Hallstead murmured, rubbing my shoulders. "What the hell did they do to him?"

"T-They're keeping his people as slaves to make the weapon work," I whispered in a hoarse voice. "God, one of them ate a child in front of him. He was so afraid. I can't even put it into words."

Hallstead pulled me into his arms, stroking my back. "Take a deep breath. You're safe. It didn't happen to you. Keep repeating that to yourself."

After a while, the shaking subsided, and I could breathe normally. Hallstead's warmth seeped into me and helped stave off the nightmarish visions I'd seen. Too soon, I remembered that he was a military officer and I was a dumb ex-thief. We were not supposed to mix.

"Won't you get in trouble for being nice to me?" I mumbled against the cotton of his button-up shirt.

He made that almost-laugh noise again. "No, I won't. I'm not all bad, you know."

I forced myself to move away, wiping my face clean. "Maybe you're trying to lure me into a false sense of security."

Hallstead smirked. "Maybe. Or maybe you're just afraid to admit you don't hate me as much as you wish you did."

I scowled, though it was hard because I wanted to smile. "You're a very smug man."

"Thanks." He adopted a more serious look. "I know this is a little sudden, but do you think you could work with a sketch artist to get us a drawing of what the Bergleute look like? We only got small glimpses of them during the solar system assault."

"Yeah. That shouldn't be a problem. But what's gonna happen to Hatwer in the meantime?"

"We'll keep him here."

I narrowed my eyes at him. "I promised him no more enhanced interrogations. I meant it."

He nodded. "You have my word. We won't lay a hand on him."

"Thank you."

"You're welcome." He started to move past me, but I touched his arm, and he stopped as he saw the expression on my face.

"I mean it. Thank you."

His gray eyes met mine for a long moment and he nodded once, understanding what I meant. He opened the door, and I walked out, still holding on to his jacket for warmth. Hallstead followed me, talking to one of the guards.

"Get me Toshida."

CHAPTER NINE

DUKE

"**G**et your fucking hands off her!"

My muscles popped and strained and screamed louder than my voice. For a fleeting moment, I wished I could slip my skin like a poltergeist to get to her. Scarlett looked frail—like a doll—in the grip of the flunkies. Her bare legs twisted and struggled against the hardwood floor. The side of my head was bleeding from a splinter that had jammed into my skin when they forced me to the floor. I could still see the knife underneath her chin, glinting, winking at me like a playful scoundrel.

"Tsk, tsk," Andy clucked his tongue. His voice held enough arrogance to drown in. "You shouldn't be so rude. We haven't even done anything to her."

He let out an ugly snort. "Yet."

"I'll kill you," I spat. "I'll fucking kill you!"

"Aw, you don't mean that. You're just worried about your little sis. I can see why. She's pretty hot." He strolled over to her, and the boys stretched her arms between them so he could touch her. He caught her face in one large hand, squeezing so that her lips pursed a bit. Tears leaked from her eyes, but they were brown orbs of fire.

"Get off me!" she shrieked, but he only squeezed harder.

"Why are you raisin' such a fuss? You came on to my brother. You're a tease. Admit it."

He shook her a little, and she winced. "Say it. Tell the boys what a slut you are."

She spat in his face. He let go and wiped it away with his sleeve. "That's not nice. You should be nice to people who are about to do you a favor."

"What favor?"

"I'm not gonna carve you up like the skinny little chicken you are. Instead, I'm gonna be nice and let you stay as pretty as you want to be."

Andy walked back over, pointing his knife at me. "But your big brother here? He's gonna take one for the team."

"No!" Scarlett screamed, thrashing to get loose. One of the guys behind me handed Andy a cleaver—the kind that usually hung in the window of a butcher's shop. My body shook all over from pure, unadulterated fear, but my mind was strong. I would not fail her like my father failed her. Scarlett was my blood, my flesh, my sacrifice.

Andy lifted my chin with the heavy blade, making me look him in his pitiless blue eyes.

"Are you okay with that, big bro? Taking the fall for lil sis?"

"No! Let him go! I did this, not him. I came on to Percy. I rejected him. Duke didn't do anything wrong, please! Take it out on me!" Scarlett sobbed. I stared at her, not the violent freak of nature before me, and spoke the word.

"Yes."

"So be it."

"No! Duke, please! Tell him it was my fault! TELL HIM!"

The boys grabbed my right hand and stretched it out on the floor. A huge foot stomped down on my wrist, keeping it in place as Andy knelt, selecting a finger. Scarlett kept screaming my name, screaming for help, screaming for anyone to save us. My mind went blank, and a white space filled my insides. This was her price. Mine to pay. Mine to keep. Mine to save.

Out of the corner of my eye, the cleaver bit through the darkness.

I came awake gasping for air in the cold darkness, the nub on my hand itchy and irritated. It took me a second to realize where I was; the dream had been so vivid. The borrowed blanket had tangled around my arms and neck, which probably tricked my body into believing I was back on Earth, back in the second worst moment of my life. I slowed my breaths, and a fluid calm seeped through my veins. But I knew sleep wouldn't return for quite some time.

The trainees' room was populated by the snores of the exhausted boys. Sam in particular was pretty loud and sounded like an elephant inhaling honey through his trunk. A tiny sliver of light trickled in from the emergency entrance to the barracks, and it was just enough for me to see so I could take the receiver out of my pocket.

I checked to make sure there were no guards around and switched it on. Judging by my watch, I calculated I'd been asleep for four or five hours. For a while, the trainees had stayed up studying and talking, but then the guards insisted we pipe down and get some sleep since we would be rising early to continue our studies. Whatever happened seemed to have tapered off at some level, so they were going to let us into the computer lab, which I hadn't been to on account of my "cleaning duties."

I held the receiver close and adjusted the volume, listening in to hear the guard talking with one of his friends.

"So where is it now?"

"Same room. They've got the girl nearby talking to Toshida."

The other guy groaned. *"Anything but that kook. They'll be lucky if she's still sane by the time he gets through with her."*

"You know him?"

"Yeah. Toshida's what you call a Jack-of-All-Trades in this business. He worked at MI-6 for a little while, and they've been bouncing him around different agencies for being a troublemaker."

"He's a sketch artist?"

"Among other things. So what's this girl like?"

"Skinny thing. Drinking age, but only just."

"Hot?"

"Smokin' hot, but in that damaged sort of way, y'know? Like maybe she grew up in a rough part of a foreign country so she doesn't like men very much."

"How'd Hallstead feel about that?"

"You know him. Stone-faced. But I can kind of tell he doesn't hate her. Especially not when you consider how she got here."

"How?"

"Word is that she and her brother snuck into the Rosewood mansion right before it launched into orbit."

My blood ran cold. Scarlett was involved? How the hell had that happened? Even in outer space, the girl was still getting in over her head.

"No shit! That was pretty lucky."

"Yeah, almost too lucky. Bridgewater thinks it was some kind of set up, like maybe they're spies, but Hallstead seems to think they're on the level. I dunno. Sounds too convenient to me, y'know."

"Yeah, 'specially with this alien showing up outta nowhere. Where's the brother?"

"He's down in the dorm with the new meat. A real hard ass, or so Hallstead says. Sergeant Rosewood's got his number, though. He took the break-in pretty personal."

"Wouldn't you?"

"Good point. Ah, hell. Here comes Simmons, better shut up."

I shifted, listening with bated breath to faint footsteps. A muffled voice spoke, sounding like he had a cold or something else stuffed up his nose.

"Fellas."

"How ya holdin' up, Simmons?"

"I'm fine," the guard grumbled, clearly irritated. I recognized his voice. He was one of guards who escorted Scarlett and me around the ship. By the sound of things, he was the one she knocked out during her escape attempt.

"The psych ward is a pain in the ass. There's nothing to do with everyone on lockdown. Can't believe I let a ninety-pound girl get the drop on me."

"Hey, nobody's perfect. I heard she got the drop on the captain, too."

Simmons snorted. "Yeah, right. She probably just wants to fuck him, the little slut."

My blood boiled. Simmons was going to have another injury to worry about if I saw him again. That was a promise.

"C'mon, man, you know the rules. No messing with the new recruits, no matter how tempting they are. Hallstead's not gonna give in even if she does want a piece."

"Yeah, yeah, I know the damn rulebook. Still, I'd like to see someone take her off that high horse. She isn't any better than the rest of us. We're all bums now, nowhere to live, nowhere to go."

"You're just a ray of fuckin' sunshine, y'know that?"

"So I'm told. I've got to get back." I heard movement and then a brief pause.

"That guy's such a tool."

A snort escaped me. My experience with the guards had been limited, so I tended to forget that they were just regular guys with military training. Still, my mind kept circulating around the new facts I had discovered. Why had Scarlett gotten involved? It sounded like they made contact with one of the Bergleute, so why would they need her? Bait? Payback for her difficult behavior? No, that didn't make sense. There had to be a logical explanation for what was happening, and I needed to find it.

"Hear something interesting?"

I jumped, glancing upward to see Sam leaning part of his skinny torso over the bunk bed to whisper to me. No wonder I'd been able to hear the soldiers so well. He'd stopped snoring.

"A bit," I said. "We were right about the contact. They've got one of them on board. Probably questioning it as we speak."

"Good. I hope they give the bastard hell. Maybe we can figure out how to kill 'em all."

"Maybe," I muttered. Of the many problems occupying my brain, the new one would be figuring out how Scarlett tied into this mess. I was nothing more than a scrub down here. Hallstead claimed he would keep me in the loop, but there was no way to contact him. Asking Rosewood for help was just as useful as stuffing a gun barrel down my throat. He wouldn't help me. I'd have to do this on my own. No surprise there.

"You'd better get some sleep, dude. If they catch us, we'll have to do pushups. And I'm already worn out," Sam advised, yawned, and rolled over. He had a point. I decided to give it another five minutes in case the guards had anything else useful to say, but they started reminiscing about baseball and I eventually drifted off.

A short, loud blast from a whistle jolted me out of sleep so hard that I thought I got whiplash. The lights came on, nearly blinding me as I sat up, kicking off the blanket tangled around me. When my eyes adjusted, I could see Sergeant Rosewood standing in front of the door with a silver whistle clutched between his lips. The trainees scrambled out of bed to line up, some of them falling from their bunk beds with heavy thuds.

"Morning, trainees! Did ya sleep well?"

"Yes, Staff Sergeant Alexander Rosewood, sir!" we chorused. He nodded as he started down the line, yelling at certain soldiers to straighten up. I took the opportunity to smooth my hair down and brush off my uniform before he got to our side of the line.

Sergeant Rosewood stared me up and down, smirking. "Oh, I see you got your new threads, Mr. Nam. You must think you're one of us now, huh?"

"I wouldn't presume so, Staff Sergeant Alexander Rosewood, sir!" I replied.

He adopted a mockingly impressed expression. "Eloquent scrub, aren't you? Guess you have opened a few books in your time. Would you like to tell these gentlemen what your favorite book is?"

"*Native Speaker* by Chang Rae-Lee, Staff Sergeant Alexander Rosewood, sir!"

"Ooh, that sounds like a good one. How much of the *Air Force Training Handbook* have you read, trainee?"

"The first hundred pages as requested, Staff Sergeant Alexander Rosewood, sir!"

"Is that right? So tell me, what are the three things required for an effective soldier, if you don't mind?"

I cleared my throat, which gave me a couple seconds to remember. I had speed-read through one of the trainees' books when I had been assigned cleaning duties. My recall abilities were pretty good, but I would have loved to have a photographic memory.

"One: discipline. Two: perseverance. Three: obedience, Staff Sergeant Alexander Rosewood, sir!"

He snorted. "Not bad. Maybe you're not such a screw up after all."

"Thank you, Staff Sergeant Alexander Rosewood, sir!"

He turned on his heel and headed back down the line. I breathed normally for the first time in almost a minute.

"Alright, trainees, we are heading into the computer lab to get you reacquainted with your curriculum. You will be expected to remember every little detail you see, and you will be tested frequently. Do not treat this like some public school class. If you fail the test three times, you will be a janitor for the rest of your lives. Do you understand me?"

"Yes, Staff Sergeant Alexander Rosewood, sir!"

"Good. Now march!"

We all pivoted and started filing out of the door. I snuck a glance at my watch. It had been roughly twelve hours since the lockdown. I guessed they had gotten some kind of handle on the situation if they were letting us get back to work, or they wanted us to be prepared for a battle a little early. Even in space, time was still valuable.

Tempus fugit.

SCARLETT

"Can I ask you something?"

"*Hai?*"

"Is it really necessary for you to sit this close?"

Toshida glanced at me, deadpan. "Absolutely necessary."

I arched an eyebrow. "How so?"

"I get a better idea of what you mean if I can feel the vibrations from your voice."

"Uh-huh," I said, unconvinced. Toshida was five foot nothing, skinny, and chewing vigorously on the strawberry Bubblelicious the military vessel inexplicably possessed. He definitely wasn't anywhere near my age. I guessed he was about sixteen years old. Thus, I wasn't thrilled about him squished next to me in the small conference room. Still, I couldn't deny that his skill with a sketchpad and pencil were otherworldly.

"And you're sure these suckers didn't have tails or extra heads or nothin'?" he asked, popping a large bubble with his teeth.

I resisted the urge to sigh. "Yeah. That's pretty much what it looked like in a nutshell."

He sat the pencil down, whistling. "Ugly bastards. Maybe they're traipsing around the universe killing every species that looks better than them."

"Interesting theory," I replied with a flat voice.

He grinned at me then, coffee-stained teeth and all. "I'm annoying you, aren't I?"

I held my thumb and first finger an inch apart. "A little bit, yeah."

"Excellent."

I stared. "Why is that excellent?"

"If I annoy you, you'll be thinking about me when I leave. Then eventually you'll start to dream about me and attach attributes to my personality that you think I possess since we've only known each other for—" He glanced at his watch. "—thirty minutes and fifty-seven seconds. After you have an unconscious connection to me, you'll start to fall for me and it's a done deal."

I continued staring. "...you've done this before, huh?"

"Yup."

"And it works?"

He shrugged, bumping my shoulder with his. "More or less."

The door opened and Hallstead appeared, clearing his throat. "Done?"

Toshida pouted. "You're such a cockblock, Hallsy."

I coughed hard into my hand, trying to mask laughter. Hallstead flashed Toshida an annoyed look. "I thought I told you to cut back on the nicknames, kid."

"The military is the most humorless industry there is. Someone's gotta lighten up the place, Hallsy," Toshida replied, handing the older man his sketch.

Hallstead took a long look, examining the drawing. "Thanks. You're dismissed."

"No, I think I'm comfortable right where I am," Toshida said, wiggling his narrow hips with emphasis so that he'd rub the left side of his body against the right side of mine.

Hallstead glared. "Out. Now."

"Oh, I get it…" Toshida said with a nod. "You're trying to steal my girl. Not gonna happen."

Hallstead sighed. "You can either walk out of this door or I'm going to kick you through it."

The Japanese boy groaned, standing. He made the "call me" motion with his hand as he exited, prompting me to bite my bottom lip to hide another laugh.

"Weird kid," I admitted once the door was shut again.

Hallstead shook his head. "You have *no* idea. So this is what you saw?"

I winced as he flipped the sketch toward me. "Yeah. Not good news for us. From what I saw, it had to be at least seven feet tall. I don't know how your boys'll handle them."

"We will," he assured me. "Nothing's indestructible, not even them."

I folded my hands, growing serious. "So where do we go from here?"

"We need to keep talking to Hatwer about the ship itself. Vulnerabilities, how he escaped, the works. Anything and everything you can learn from him."

I nodded. "And where are you going to keep him after we've gotten all the information? In a cell like mine?"

"Something a little more secure, but yes. And…" His expression lightened somewhat. "I think your cooperation has earned you something other than a cell."

"Really?"

"Really. You'll still have a guard present, but you'll be staying in one of the extra rooms with the employees until Dr. Warwick clears you from psych evaluation. Then you'll be moved to the dorms with the other female soldiers."

I tried not to let that fact dampen my relief. "Thank you."

"Careful," he mused. "You almost sounded like a normal person just then."

I flashed him a sarcastic smile. "Oh, forgive me. I retract my statement. Go to hell, Captain Hallstead."

He chuckled and I let the sound fold over me before continuing. "How's my brother doing?"

"I haven't heard from Rosewood yet, but I'll ask. He should be fine."

My mouth dropped open. "Rosewood? You mean as in one of the Rosewoods whose mansion we broke into?"

"Yeah."

"Don't you think that's a horrible idea? The guy's got to be holding a grudge!" I protested, but Hallstead shook his head.

"It'll be good motivation. If Sergeant Rosewood has a chip on his shoulder, he'll work your brother harder than anybody else. The more work, the more likely your brother will become a great soldier and you won't have to worry about him protecting himself."

"I've never been worried about him protecting himself," I said. "It's others that I'm worried about."

He frowned. "What do you mean?"

"My brother has something of a hero complex. He would much rather take the blame for someone else's mistake than let others get hurt. He's been like that since we were kids."

"Some people would consider that admirable."

"He's not your brother," I replied, a little softer than I intended. The subject matter made me uncomfortable, so I started to play with the hem of the jacket sleeve. I'd had to roll them up a few times to use my hands as it was about three sizes too big. But at least I wasn't cold anymore.

Hallstead started to say something else, but there was a knock at the door. Evans appeared, glancing between the serious looks on our faces.

"...am I interrupting—"

"No," Hallstead said. "What is it?"

"The general wants to speak with you. Now."

"I'll be right there." Hallstead crooked a finger at me. "Let's go. I'll walk you over. The guards'll be watching in case anything happens. If it does, get out of there. Got it?"

"Got it."

He opened the door for me and Evans, and I went inside. There was another guard already waiting. I climbed back into the hazmat suit awaiting me on a hook by the door and walked back into the conference room.

"Hatwer?"

At the sound of my voice, the alien poked his head out of his protective pod state.

"Scarlett?"

"Hey," I said in my kindest voice, pulling my chair closer. "Sorry about earlier."

"Am I in trouble?"

"No. I explained what happened, and they know it wasn't your fault."

"I am sorry. I did not think you would respond so strongly to what happened."

"You warned me. I should have prepared myself better," I admitted. "But now I need your help. What can you tell me about your escape?"

"It was very difficult. I am lucky to be alive."

"I'll bet. Start from the beginning."

"The Bergleute are assigned in pairs as the overseers where I was forced to work removing the organs of their food source. Once, I heard two of them talking. I had been imprisoned for a long time, so I learned enough of their language to understand basic conversations. They were talking about the next planet they wanted to harness—one that had life on it. It had been a long time since they found a world with intelligent beings, so their commander was considering sending out a probe. Before the probe reached your planet, it found one of your satellites. This discovery informed the Bergleute that your race was more than simply sentient. They also saw your space station and figured you would most likely try to defend yourselves if attacked. They viewed you as a threat, and I thought that maybe if someone told you what they were doing, you would fight back and set us free."

"So what did you do?"

"There is a gland in the dead beasts we disassembled that causes instant death if swallowed. The Bergleute know what it looks like and so we could not poison their food, but I saved one. Ingesting the entire gland will kill you in seconds. I had seen some of my people take them to escape our miserable life, but I calculated that if I took only a few drops, it would put me into a catatonic state instead of killing me. When we die, the Bergleute do one of two things: if the body is relatively healthy, they will eat us. If the body has been tainted, they throw us out with the rest of the garbage, which is emptied every so often. I chose one of the

days where there was not much trash and took the poison. My body was taken to the trash chute and left there. When I regained consciousness, I climbed back up the chute and snuck onto one of their escape pods. The Bergleute's attack vessels have security codes and clearance requirements, but the emergency pods do not, so one can quickly escape if the ship were compromised. My limited under-standing of their language allowed me to use their technology, and I escaped just before the Earth was destroyed. The explosion damaged my ship, so I sent out a distress call to the nearest vessel. Yours is the one that found me."

"You're very brave to have done that, Hatwer. I hope you know that."

His head tilted downward. *"I had no other choice. My parents are still aboard that ship working endlessly...suffering. I must save them."*

"I know how you feel. If I had a chance to save my parents like you, I would have done the same thing. My mother died when I was twelve, and my father probably died in the Earth's destruction."

"I am sorry. It is my people's creation that has caused this destruction."

"No, Hatwer. You and your people are not responsible for this. It's the Bergleute. They took something harmless and turned it into a weapon and you can't blame yourself for that."

An inky substance began to leak from the corners of his eyes. Tears. *"You are too kind."*

I laughed, though the sound was hollow and bitter. "You say that only because you don't know me very well. There are far better people out there than me."

"That is untrue," Hatwer insisted, wiping his eyes with the back of his wrist. *"I was only able to make contact with you because you are Huswan."*

"Huswan?"

"I believe the word in your language is an Empath. You are sensitive to the needs and feelings of others, though it is subconscious. That is the only reason why I was able to get through to you. The others cannot hear my thoughts."

"That can't be right," I insisted with a frown. "I'd have to be telepathic for that to be true."

"Telepathy among other human beings is impossible. Most do not possess the right genetic makeup, but you do. It is a very rare trait."

"How do you know so much about human beings?"

He tapped one claw against his skull. *"When I shared my memory with you, other information was exchanged on a subconscious level. Nothing private, but general things you know, I know as well."*

"Wow," I muttered to myself. "The one thing that makes me useful is something I have no control over. Fantastic."

I raised my voice to address him again. "Is there anything else you remember about the Bergleute? Weaknesses? Vulnerabilities?"

"*I am afraid I do not know anything else about them,*" the alien answered, crestfallen.

"Don't worry. You've done great so far. They can take it from here."

"*Who is 'they'?*"

"The people that built this ship to save us. They knew the Bergleute were coming, so they made hundreds of ships and put people on them to escape."

"*I see. You were able to save many. I wish we had known about their arrival before they descended upon us.*"

"Did you fight them?"

"*We Shasar are a peaceful race. Outside of law enforcement, we had no training for war or battle. Our technology was advanced enough to make our lives comfortable, but nothing more. The Bergleute outmatched us in size, and they were ruthless.*"

"I don't get it. How did they even know about the weapon? I thought they just went from planet to planet gathering the core material."

"*They sent out a probe first, and they noticed the power and accuracy of our drilling equipment. That is when they descended and kidnapped hundreds of us to build them a weaponized version of it. Afterward, they tested it by destroying our world.*"

"Why didn't they do the same thing with our planet? Don't we have valuable technology as well?"

"*Perhaps it was not what they wanted. Perhaps they thought it would be too dangerous for them to take human slaves. I am not sure.*"

"Do you know what they do with the core material?"

"*The slaves speculate that they use it to make things: armor, ships, weapons, and such. It is easier than taking over a planet and mining it.*"

"What can you tell me about the ship? How much of it did you see while you were escaping?"

"*Not much. The ship draws its power from an infinitely renewable energy source. I believe your people call it Sorbatium. However, I believe that the main supply is in one particular location.*"

I nodded. "I see. So if we were able to somehow board the ship and confiscate it, we would have a better chance of killing them and freeing your people."

"*It will not be easy. There are sentries on all levels of the ship. I eluded them*" *because they were all busy preparing the weapon. It is the only time when they leave their posts."*

"Where did they keep your people when you weren't working?"

"The lowest level of the ship. The children are kept in one large cell, separated from the adults. Our electrified chains never deactivate. We must be taken off of them, like I was when the Bergleute overseer thought I had died."

I sighed. "That won't be easy. We'll have to find out how they are controlling the collars. It could be hand-held devices or from a control panel. You told me that the children dissect the animals for food. What are your parents doing?"

"I have heard that the adults maintain the weapon and work on upkeep of the energy source. If they refuse, they are killed immediately and replaced with others. Once, there was an escape attempt by a large group, but they were caught and executed to make an example. The last time I saw my parents was when we were abducted from our world."

I paused to shuffle through my thoughts for any other questions. "When you left...are you sure they didn't follow you?"

"Yes. They would have noticed that one of the pods was missing, but by then I had already gotten relatively close to leaving the solar system."

"Do you think it had some sort of tracking device?"

"Perhaps."

I stood. "I'll be right back."

I hurried to the door and opened it, looking for the guards. Before I opened my mouth, Evans said it for me. "We're contacting the team examining the ship as we speak. Nice catch."

"Not really," I admitted. "It's been hours. I hope your team already found it, or the Bergleute definitely know where we are."

"Relax. Even if they do, what reason would they have to come here?"

"They might not want us having access to their technology," I said. "Or they might want to silence Hatwer. They already consider us to be some sort of threat, even if it isn't a large one."

Evans eyed me and then nodded. "Point taken."

He glanced at his partner, who had one hand up to the communication link in his ear. "Anything yet?"

"Waiting for the report. They've been running diagnostics non-stop since it arrived and they're still finding things."

We waited a minute or two before getting a response. The guard glanced at Evans. "He says he thinks they found some sort of tracking device in the ship's console about four hours ago. It's been disassembled."

I let out a relieved breath. "Then let's pray they lost the signal before they got anywhere near us. Where are we, anyway?"

"That's classified."

I rolled my eyes. "Oh, right. Forgot about that. Thanks anyway, boys."

I started to open the door, but Evans caught my arm. "I think that's enough for now. Say goodbye and we'll escort you to your room."

"I'd feel a lot better if I could go with Hatwer to wherever you're keeping him."

"You're not authorized to be in that part of the ship."

"Technically, I'm not authorized for anything. Just give me a break, will you?"

They stared at me, uncooperative and silent. I sighed again. "C'mon, Evans. You've got a kid. From what I can tell, Hatwer is just a child. You can't even imagine what he's been through, and he needs to feel like he has someone he can trust."

Eventually, Evans just heaved a sigh. "Fine. But don't mention it to the captain or he'll get sore about it."

"My lips are sealed."

CHAPTER TEN

DUKE

I had never spent more than two hours on a computer at a time—which I'm sure is shocking when one considers the Asian nerd stereotype—so the intensive six-hour training session we spent staring intently at our screens gave me a headache. The massive headphones canceled out any sounds around me and made my ears sweaty. Several times, I rubbed my eyelids to cajole them into producing more tears. Time slipped into oblivion as I watched video after video of instructions on how to be the perfect soldier, the perfect weapon, the perfect hero. Part of me wanted there to be an updated version of this fallaciously hopeful virtual manual—one that didn't have as much emphasis on being a hero because our world was dead. We were no longer heroes. We were walking gravestones. Memorials with pulses.

After the videos ended, we were thankfully dismissed for lunch in the mess hall. We marched up three floors to the cafeteria—which looked like the one in my old high school—and went through the line and sat down at the long, bolted-down tables to eat. Thankfully, we didn't have to deal with dried astronaut food as the technology had advanced to where they no longer needed to vacuum seal everything. It was, however, rather simple. Meatloaf, peas and carrots, mashed potatoes, and your choice of water or vitamin water. The vegetarian trainees were given tofu meatloaf instead. I found that amusing.

"Y'know, there are some days when I think we're in prison," Sam mused, letting his runny mashed potatoes slop from his spoon onto his tray. "And there are some days when I *know* we're in prison. This is one of them."

I shrugged, taking a sip of my vitamin water. "No sacrifice, no victory."

"Thanks, Mr. Witwicky, but I thought sacrificing women would be enough. I didn't think I'd have to make my tastebuds suffer as well."

Beside me, Han let out a derisive laugh. "What women? In all the time I've known you, you haven't talked about a single girlfriend."

Sam became very interested in examining his peas. "I've had girlfriends. Plenty of 'em."

Han rolled his eyes. "Like?"

"Tina."

"Tina who?"

"She's from my hometown in Colorado. We went out for a year, but I dumped her when I got accepted into the Air Force. Couldn't have her waiting around for me."

"Uh-huh," Han said, fixing him with a disbelieving stare as he ate. I shook my head, biting my lip to hide a smile.

Sam seemed to notice and switched his attention to me. "What about you? Any girls on your end?"

I shook my head. "Not really. A couple here and there, but no keepers."

"Hmm, that's boring. You got a sister?" Sam added, wiggling his eyebrows.

"Younger. Her name's Scarlett. With two t's," I added, smiling out of habit. She always insisted that people spell it the way our mother spelled it.

"Oh," he faltered. "I didn't mean anything by it. Did she...y'know... make it?"

I chose my words carefully. "Yeah, she's in the women's division here."

"Is she anything like you?" Han asked.

I almost laughed. "Complete opposite in every way."

"Those are sisters for you. Their entire existence is to get their brothers in trouble. Anya was like that." Sam shook his head, smiling fondly. Earlier, I had noticed a picture clipped to the outside of his duffel bag in the dorm. A girl with dirty blonde hair and dark eyes like his. She looked a little older than him.

I swallowed another mouthful of my drink, lowering my voice. "Did she...?

Sam's face sobered. He shook his head once. I closed my eyes. "Sorry, man."

"S'okay. At least I've got something to live for, y'know? Making sure I kill every goddamn one of the Bergleute," he said, his voice filled with a quiet, ugly promise. A reverent silence fell.

Before anyone could say anything else, two guards entered the cafeteria. I expected them to call us to attention, but they continued walking along the tables until they got to me.

"Mr. Nam, was it?"

"Sir?" I asked, confused.

"Come with us."

My blood ran cold. I stepped away from my seat, and they motioned for me to walk ahead of them. There weren't many reasons why they would come for me, and none of them made me feel reassured. I'd left the receiver wrapped up in my borrowed blanket for safekeeping, but it wasn't impossible to find. If that were the case, I'd be thrown back in my cell for stealing, which was exactly why I didn't want to help Han and Sam in the first place. Nothing I could do about it now but accept my fate.

They took me to the interrogation rooms and a guard kindly opened the door. Captain Hallstead and Sergeant Rosewood were waiting for me —the former seated in front of a table and the latter leaning against the far wall with his arms crossed. I arranged my face into a placid expression, glancing between the two of them.

"Have a seat," Captain Hallstead said. I pulled out the chair on my side and sat down, folding my hands in my lap. The rule in Sergeant Rosewood's presence was not to talk until I had been addressed, but I wasn't sure if the same went when there was someone else with him.

"Do you know why you've been brought here?" Rosewood asked in an unnervingly calm voice.

"No, Staff Sergeant Alexander Rosewood, sir."

"Fancy a guess?"

I hesitated. "No, Staff Sergeant Alexander Rosewood, sir."

"Don't be so modest," Rosewood continued with the utmost snark in his voice. "You seem like a smart guy. Why do you think we brought you here?"

I cleared my throat. "My sister, Staff Sergeant Alexander Rosewood, sir?"

He shook his head. "Good guess, but no. Take it away, Captain."

Hallstead reached into his pocket and dug something out. He placed a tiny black device on the table in front of me. My fears were confirmed, but I kept my face blank.

"Any idea what this is?"

"No."

Hallstead's eyes narrowed the slightest bit, but he continued without acknowledging whether he thought I was full of shit or not. "It's a radio transmitter, built to listen in on conversations with minimal chances of detection. One of our guards found it underneath his collar just a few minutes ago. We found the receiver in the trainees' bunk."

He folded his hands and laid them on the table beside the transmitter. "There are a lot of theories we could come up with right now, so I won't bore you with details. I'm just going to ask you a few questions and you're free to go after that."

Don't fidget. Don't blink. Just answer. "Yes, sir."

"How much do you know about Han Blankenship?"

Shock rolled through me in waves, but I kept it under control. "Not much. He was in the same infantry as Sam before they left Earth. And he's got some sort of Russian background from the sound of his accent. That's all I know."

"That's a shame," Hallstead replied. "Because we found the transmitter in his blanket. We have reason to believe he might be some sort of mole."

I couldn't help looking surprised then. "A mole? For who?"

"We're not the only ones out here, Duke. The world's governments came together to invest in the Starlight Contingency, but there was also an opposition movement from a small faction. We have not confirmed that they died with the rest of Earth in the explosion, so it's possible they're out there spying on us and plotting revenge. That's why we've got you here. We need answers. Is there anything about Han that would suggest he is untrustworthy or working for someone else?"

I couldn't answer him at first. If I said no, they would keep digging. The problem is that they wanted to find the mole, not to find out if there was one at all. I held both of our lives in my hands. Keep one, drop the other. Han was guilty of being curious and nothing more. But what if they figured out what we had done? All three of us would be thrown in a cell for the rest of our lives, or at the very least, punished within an inch of our lives. These people had already shown that they had no problem with getting their hands dirty. If I gave up Han, that would be the end of the issue. A practical choice.

He is not your sister. You owe him nothing. The little voice in the back of my head whispered in its silky, persuasive tone. *It's easy. Just say the words.*

"I…"

"You what?"

"I would like to continue observing him for any signs of disloyalty," I said finally, unable to make the decision. At least this would give me time.

Hallstead stared me down and then nodded. "You have one week to come up with something concrete. If he's innocent, we'll continue investigating elsewhere. If he's guilty, then he'll be interrogated. You already know what that's like, so don't screw this up or you'll be subjecting an innocent man to torture."

"Yes, sir."

He stood. The sergeant pushed off from the wall, heading toward the door. I stopped Hallstead with another question.

"How is Scarlett?"

He paused, giving me an interested look. "Fine, from what I hear."

"I would be grateful if you'd allow me to see her."

He cleared his throat. "Well, she's still deep in session for her anger problems, but I think I may be able to arrange something for you in the near future. In the meantime, stay focused. You've got quite a task ahead of you."

"Yes, sir." Hallstead exited, and the guards beckoned me to go in front of them. Lunch had concluded by the time we rode the elevator down, so I was taken back to the computer lab where the trainees had already begun the introduction to the next section we'd be learning. Just before we put our headphones back on, Han leaned across his desk, his face serious.

"What was that all about?"

I opened my program and slid the sound-canceling headphones on.

"Nothing."

SCARLETT

"Welcome back, Scarlett."

"Doc." My hostility levels were much lower than they had been before, but I couldn't help my tense posture of crossed arms and a blank expression as I stared back at the russet eyes of Dr. Warwick. They had finally announced an end to the lockdown, so I was booted right back to our formerly interrupted therapy session, much to my dismay.

Before they escorted me to the psych ward, I had seen Hatwer's lodging for the time being. They put him in a cell, which I didn't like, but I could live with it because I knew the alternative would have been leaving him in that room all alone without even a bed. That is, if he slept at all. They didn't know much about his physiology, and I suspected that as soon as I left, they would take him to the X-ray machine as they had done to me. I only hoped he was being treated well. I hadn't been so lucky.

"I understand that you've been cooperating with your superiors in the last few hours," she continued in that endlessly patient voice. "Is there a reason for that?"

I shrugged one shoulder. "You catch more flies with honey than vinegar."

"I see." Her eyes slid from my face to my upper body. "And…if I'm not mistaken, that is Captain Hallstead's jacket, is it not?"

I self-consciously tugged at the hem, resisting the urge to scowl. "I was cold. He offered; I didn't ask for it."

"I didn't say you did." Was that a smile? Damn this woman. She knew exactly how to make me uncomfortable.

"How would you describe your relationship with Captain Hallstead?"

"Have you ever seen the old Tom and Jerry cartoons?"

"Yes."

"I'm Tom and he's the dog, Spike."

Dr. Warwick smiled then. "I see. Is this common in your relationships with men?"

I snorted. "What relationships with men? The only man in my life that I'm close with is my brother."

She raised her pen, glancing down at her clipboard. "So you've never had a boyfriend or a significant other of some sort?"

I thought about it. "Not really. Unless you count the guy I lost my virginity to."

Dr. Warwick jumped a bit, blinking at me. "Pardon?"

"What? Am I going too fast?"

She pushed up her glasses, clearing her throat. "No, it's just…you mentioned that you had a near-rape experience. Did it happen with—"

"No. God, no. Wally happened about a year and a half after that. He lived in an apartment complex next door. Friends with my brother." I stopped, unsure where this conversation was going.

Dr. Warwick tilted her head as she watched my growing discomfort. "Forgive me, but I find this a very odd occurrence. Most women with sexual trauma tend to avoid situations that could lead to sex. Were you in love with him?"

I choked on a laugh. "Hell no."

She frowned at my reaction. "Then why?"

"Why do we teenagers do anything stupid? Because we don't know any better. I didn't. He seemed nice, and he was. He never said out loud that he wanted to take the next step with me, but it was always there, under every conversation. Finally, I just gave in. I rationalized it, actually. I figured that being with Wally would erase my mistake with Percy. I needed a new memory. I needed someone else to fill the hole, no pun intended."

"And did he?"

Memories crashed against the surface of my mind. Lumpy pillow. Salty tears. Whisker burns on my thighs, right above the fresh tattoo. Aching birthmark. Flat beer.

"No."

She hesitated before speaking. "I'll be honest with you, Scarlett. I think this decision has a lot to do with why you have self-confidence issues. Many girls experience low self-esteem if they think they let go of their virginity too soon. You try to hide it by seeming arrogant and rash."

"Oh, is that what I'm doing?" I let my voice come out harsh and sarcastic. I didn't like that she was digging up my faults and dissecting them one by one.

"Hostility is not going to work against me, Scarlett. I'm not going to get angry with you and you know that. I know that you're trying to stall me so you don't have to join the Air Force and we're going to have to address it at some point."

"Awesome."

Dr. Warwick narrowed her eyes at me. Ha. Maybe I was getting under her skin. I wondered if she would say something rude and prove that she was actually human; instead, I got:

"Tell me about your mother."

A hurricane of thoughts and feelings rose to the surface of my skin for the first few seconds after she asked the question, and then the storm quieted as I continued taking slow breaths.

"What about her?"

Dr. Warwick shrugged. "Anything."

"She was a seamstress. Worked from home. Best in the city. Had her own business."

"Did you like that she was a stay-at-home mom?"

"Didn't have much of an opinion on it, really."

"I don't believe that," she said. "You seem fiercely independent. Being a seamstress is often considered a domestic job. You must have thought so at a young age."

"Well, what do you want me to do? Just stay home all day like you? Why is it so bad that I want to do something else, Mom? Do you even have a reason?"

"A direction would be nice, Scarlett. You're all over the place. Your grades are slipping, and you've been in three fights this year. Why should I even trust you to go out by yourself when I can't even trust you to behave at school?"

"I didn't ask for your trust!"

"Not really."

The therapist fixed me with a probing stare. I did the same. Eventually, her expression softened somewhat.

"I'm sorry about your mother, Scarlett."

"Everyone's sorry. Doesn't change anything."

"You must have asked yourself a thousand times why your father did it. Do you blame yourself?"

"Yes."

"Why?"

"I should have killed him first."

The employee living quarters I had been put in appeared to have been altered. It felt too empty and there were little holes in the floor indicating that they had unscrewed something—maybe a dresser or a table. Still, I couldn't complain because instead of a thin cot, I had a mattress complete with a bed frame, a tiny closet, and an even tinier bathroom with a toilet instead of a hole that opened up in the floor whenever you got close to it. Naturally, the door wouldn't lock because there was no knob on my side.

It ran on electricity and swooshed open and closed like the doors in the old *Star Trek* series. There was a handprint console to the left that controlled it, but it had been disabled.

They had also been kind enough to return my sweatshirt that they took when they found Duke and me in the mansion, and it lay over my lap at the moment, warming my legs. I considered taking off Captain Hallstead's jacket, but it had conformed to my curves and warmed me up enough that I left it on.

Time slid off its axis as I stared up at the ceiling, my thoughts runny like the way my mother used to make scrambled eggs. Where was Duke right now? Was he okay? Was Rosewood tormenting him at every turn?

The movies always had the stereotype of siblings with telepathy or that shared pain, and for the first time in my life, I wished I had those silly powers. Before this little adventure, the longest time Duke and I were ever apart was at birth. My mother used to call him "jikineun-gae," the Watchdog, after I was born. He would always crawl over to wherever I was sleeping and stay there, making sure I was breathing. The air always felt a little thinner when he wasn't around me.

I had nodded off at some point when I heard someone knock and then the unmistakable swoosh of the door opening. Groaning, I rolled over onto my stomach, barely conscious as someone flicked on the overhead light.

"Five more minutes…" I mumbled. "Having a good dream."

"About what?"

I sighed, recognizing the voice. "Annoying captains who don't let me sleep." I tilted my head to the side and raked a handful of hair out of my face. "Don't you have minions who can run your errands for you?"

The edge of Hallstead's lips twitched upward. "Yes, but the general instructed me to keep the gossip to a minimum. If we keep sending guards, there's a chance that word will get around about Hatwer, and we don't want a panic on our hands."

"Uh-huh. Why don't you just admit that you're attracted to my magnetic personality and be done with it?" I challenged in my most mocking voice.

He started to say something but then shook his head, shoving his hands into the pockets of his black slacks. "You're the one who's still wearing my jacket."

Damn him. "There is a completely logical explanation for that."

"And that would be…?"

I scowled. "Black is my color."

Hallstead smirked. "Right."

I pushed up into a sitting position and stifled a yawn with my hand. "Other than the verbal sparring, what can I do for you, Captain?"

In an instant, the amusement on his face vanished. "Roughly an hour ago, we launched a probe to find out where the Bergleute are heading. The probe was destroyed when it entered the space where Jupiter used to be."

"Shit," I murmured. "What do you want from me, then?"

"We need you to talk to Hatwer and ask him if he happens to know where they were headed last. Hopefully, away from us. Our instruments can only detect the Bergleute from a certain distance, and we need to see them coming."

"Got it." I stood up, and as I did, he took a step back and cleared his throat.

"What?"

"You seem to be having a wardrobe malfunction."

Frowning, I glanced down and discovered that in my fitful napping, the hem of my tank top had gotten caught beneath one of the cups of my bra. Hot blood filled my face, and I quickly adjusted the shirt to its proper position.

"How long ago did you notice that?"

Hallstead stared at me. Then, he gave me a very slow and secretive smile before he walked to the door, saying nothing.

He didn't take me to the interrogation room this time, but rather the cell where Hatwer now resided. It had been changed into a clean room and sealed off with an entryway. I changed into the suit again before getting ready to see him.

Hatwer looked small and unnatural against the sterile white walls, especially in his pod form. Hallstead said he'd go for a walk, which was code for "I'll be in earshot but out of sight." Very polite for a covert pervert.

"Hatwer?"

He emerged from his pod state, blinking up at me. *"Scarlett? What are you doing here?"*

I knelt in front of him. "Sorry, were you sleeping?"

"I was meditating. It keeps me calm."

"Oh. I'm sorry to bother you again, but I need you to do something important for me."

"What?"

"While you were escaping, did you happen to catch a glimpse of where the Bergleute were going? Directions, coordinates, anything you heard or saw that might tell us where they were headed?"

He lowered his gaze. It was hard to read Hatwer's face because of his hard skin and lack of facial movements, but his eyes always gave him away. They were cat-like ovals that changed with his mood—widening when he was upset or curious and narrowing when he was pensive or confused.

"The ship's console had coordinates in its database that I had to disable. The Bergleute seem to keep the escape pods synchronized with the main battle cruiser. Do you think that might be the information you need?"

"Yes, that's perfect."

He hesitated. *"I feel uncomfortable sharing my memories with you again because you had such a strong reaction to my emotional state. Perhaps I can illustrate these coordinates for you instead?"*

I nodded. "That could work."

I stood and called for Hallstead, asking him for paper and a writing utensil. He disappeared down the hallway for a couple minutes and then returned with the items. Hatwer unfolded his body and sat on the floor, taking the pen between his clawed fingers rather delicately. I watched with fascination as he started to draw in careful, almost practiced movements.

"This is your solar system. They were just outside of the Earth's orbit when I escaped. I believe they were working their way from the outer planets to the inner planets."

"Do they harvest stars?"

"No. The weapon is powerful, but collapsing a star would result in the death of everything in the solar system. Theoretically, your sun's explosion would cause a supernova, which would destroy everything in the vicinity and then the remains would be absorbed into a black hole. I believe that once they have finished with the rest of the planets in this solar system, they will simply move to another."

He finished the drawing, which depicted the ship's position outside of the Earth and a woven path leading to Venus, Mercury, and then past the Sun to another part of the solar system. It made me wonder if they tested a planet for the core material before they blew it up since there were many theories about Venus' inner core—that it may have been completely liquid or that it had hardened and contained no liquid at all, at least according to my astronomy teacher back in middle school.

"But that was before you escaped. We're worried that the Bergleute might seek us out in order to..." I stopped, restructuring my sentence. "...keep you from talking to us about them."

He stared up at me. *"You mean kill me."*

I didn't respond.

"It is alright. I knew there was a chance that they would come for me, but I hoped that they would think you weren't much of a threat now that your home planet is gone. I was wrong."

"You did what you thought was right, Hatwer. You can't blame yourself for that."

He pushed the paper toward me after writing several coordinates in shaky but legible English. It looked as though he had a photographic memory. I'd kill for one of those.

"Thank you, Hatwer. I'll be back as soon as I can."

"You are welcome, Scarlett."

I left, waving at the alien. He mirrored me and then stared at his raised hand with that curious look in his eyes. It almost made me smile.

After I stopped to get out of the suit, Hallstead led me down the hall to talk, inquiring about the map Hatwer had drawn. I stuffed my hands in the pockets of the borrowed jacket. "What do you think? Would they change directions to come get us?"

"I doubt it, but that's not what we were worried about."

"What do you mean?"

"The main ship would take too much time to turn around. They would deploy their smaller defenders like they did when we launched an assault on them as they entered our solar system."

My eyes widened. "Evans told me it was a massacre. What happened?"

"Their weapons are too advanced. We couldn't fire shots quickly enough to keep up with them, so they slaughtered all of our infantry in only minutes. We were never able to recover one of their vessels to study and find the weaknesses."

"But what about Hatwer's escape pod? What if we trained someone to fly it back to the mothership and board it?"

He gave me a surprised look, but it disappeared behind his normal stoicism. "That's a suicide mission, Scarlett. General Bridgewater would never authorize something like that."

"What if they do send a smaller defender to destroy the *Titan* and we capture it instead of blowing it up and make it seem like it was escorting the escape pod back to the mothership?"

"Too risky. Orders are to destroy any enemy aircraft on sight if it comes within range of our instruments. Doing otherwise would endanger the passengers and we can't afford that."

"But think about the alternative: what if we did sneak aboard their ship?" I argued, starting to get frustrated. "We could plant an explosive and nuke all of those bastards."

"But you're forgetting about Hatwer's family. We wouldn't have the means of getting them out."

I bit my bottom lip as I thought it over. "What if they used the escape pods as well? We could lead them out."

"Scarlett, stop. There are too many factors that could go wrong with that plan."

I stepped back. "What are you saying, Hallstead? That you don't intend to rescue those innocent aliens who have been slaves to the Bergleute for years and had their home world blown up just like ours?"

"It's more complicated than that."

"What's complicated about doing the right thing?"

"I'm not talking about this with you here," he said, grabbing my upper arm and pulling me out of the hallway and into the elevator. We rode up in a stagnant silence and neither of us spoke until we returned to my borrowed room.

"The kind of jailbreak you're talking about would be impossible without an extensive knowledge of the ship's interior," Hallstead explained. "Our survival is the number one priority right now and what you're suggesting would put the people aboard this ship in jeopardy."

"I can't believe this," I spat. "Do you know what he's sacrificed by coming to us for help? Do you even care? Or are you just a thick-headed soldier who can do nothing more than follow orders?"

He shook his head. "Scarlett, we don't have the resources to save Hatwer's people. I'm sorry, but we don't. I know that the two of you share a connection, but this is the way it has to be. You can't let yourself be emotionally compromised by him."

"How can you say that? I told you what those bastards did to him and you expect me not to be emotionally compromised?"

Hallstead stepped close, lowering his voice, and the anger in it nearly scalded my skin. "Several hours ago, you didn't even know he existed.

Now you're willing to sacrifice your own people to help him. If our roles were reversed, how would that sound to you?"

I ran my hands through my hair, trying to stay calm. "I'm not saying it makes sense. I'm saying that it needs to be done. It won't be easy or pretty, but we still need to do it because it's possible to do the right thing. It's not probable, but it's possible. I couldn't live with myself knowing that we had a chance to help someone in need and didn't take it because it wouldn't be the safe option."

"You're asking me to put my men on the line for a bunch of aliens who may not even exist," he hissed. "For all we know, Hatwer projected false information into your mind in order to lure us into a trap."

"Fine."

He stopped in the middle of ranting at me, growing suspicious. "What do you mean 'fine'?"

I brandished my hands at myself. "Send me. I'm expendable. I should have died when the Earth exploded, but I didn't. If I die trying to save them, it won't affect things on this ship."

"You don't have the proper training. You're twenty-four years old, for Christ's sake."

"Then train me. Teach me to be a good little soldier like you and I'll go on the mission. You'll still have your hundred million people safe and sound and I can have a clear conscience."

He let out a harsh snort. "Wow. I figured you were irrational, but this is an entirely different level of illogical."

"Why?" I asked, lacing every word with the utmost sarcasm. "Would my death make you feel guilty, Captain? Would you mourn me?"

He glared at me. "I don't call the shots on this ship. General Bridge-water does, and I am telling you now that he won't approve a kamikaze plan like yours. I do want to help Hatwer, but what happens to him isn't up to you and me."

He turned his back on me, walking toward the door, but my words stopped him.

"Then what am I going to tell him?"

His shoulders tensed, and the black cotton shifted over the muscles, the only physical sign of an emotion other than anger that I had drawn from him during this argument. He tilted his head until I could see the profile of his face.

"Nothing."

"What do you mean 'nothing'? He's going to ask the next time I see him. He's a telepath; he'll know that I'm lying."

Hallstead didn't reply. He just kept standing there, as if rooted in the spot by my words. My anger grew and another onslaught of words bubbled inside my chest, but then, slowly, it hit me. His husky whisper held more importance than anything else he had said to me in the last five minutes. Nothing. He didn't mean that I would lie to the alien.

He meant that I wasn't going to see Hatwer again.

"You're gonna kill him, aren't you?"

Hallstead didn't speak, but as I stared at him, his hands balled into fists.

"You son of a bitch," I whispered. "Why?"

He turned around stiffly. He wouldn't meet my eyes as he explained in a detached voice. "General Bridgewater gave the order a few hours ago. In order to understand more about alien anatomy, he wants to do an autopsy on Hatwer and to make sure that he isn't a mole sent to trick us. It's been scheduled for early tomorrow."

Silence buzzed in my ears. Autopsy. Like he was just a frog in a science lab, not a young child, not a soon-to-be-orphan, not a son.

"Say something," Hallstead murmured, sounding so out of character that I almost thought he hadn't said it at all. I couldn't recall how long I had been standing there, staring at the floor, trying to remember to breathe.

I punched him in the jaw.

He stumbled backward a couple of steps, touching the back of his wrist to his mouth as a trickle of blood appeared. I slumped down on my bed, my arms loosely hanging in my lap.

"Get out."

The command was no more than a whisper because my throat had tightened to nearly the choking point. He didn't yell at me, didn't hit me back, didn't say anything. He just walked out and left me empty and cold. It was at least a minute before I realized that there were tears on my face and that he could have easily dodged my punch. He wanted me to hurt him. He hated himself as much as I did right now.

I threw his jacket on the floor and pulled my knees up to my chest, wishing my brother were here.

CHAPTER ELEVEN

DUKE

After the four-hour block of computer-based learning, we were dismissed for a short break before starting the next cram session. As we exited, one of the guards pulled me aside and told me I had somewhere else to go. My first thought was that Hallstead wanted something, but that seemed strange since he would know that nothing could have happened while we were stuck in the computer lab. Still, I didn't complain because he didn't put handcuffs on me—meaning that I had earned some level of trust to walk through the *Titan* without being restrained.

He took me to one of the upper levels of the ship, and it was nothing like what I had seen before. When the elevator doors opened, I saw a hallway with dozens of doors with numbers on them. It took me a moment to realize that these were apartment-style rooms where the employees stayed. I hadn't gotten a good look at the entire vessel, but I predicted that there were hundreds of occupants, considering how many floors there were.

The guard led me to a room and slid his keycard through the slot, giving me a serious look as he spoke. "Fifteen minutes."

The door slid open, and I walked inside, confused. As I entered, a light overhead flickered on, and I could see that I stood in a small bedroom with a dresser, bathroom, and closet. There was a bed pushed against the wall to my left and on it lay a dark-haired girl, curled up on her side in the fetal position. The willowy limbs and jet-black hair were a dead giveaway.

I walked over to my sister, peering over into her face. She was asleep. I touched her shoulder, whispering, "Lettie, wake up."

Her brows furrowed. She rolled over, blinking up at me. It took her a couple of seconds to recognize me and her sleep-muddled voice made memories rush through me. Time couldn't change the childish look on her face whenever she woke up.

"*Oppa?*"

I smiled. "Yeah."

She sat up and threw herself at me, almost knocking us off the bed as she hugged me. I wrapped my arms around her back, squeezing her.

"I was scared I'd never see you again," she whispered against my neck, her voice thick.

I rubbed her back in slow circles. "Me too."

After a moment, she let go and wiped her eyes. "You look stupid in that jumpsuit."

I grinned. "I know. But it makes my ass look awesome."

She laughed. "Same old Duke."

Our smiles started to fade around the edges as we stared at each other, happy to be together but unsure of how to proceed. She broke the momentary awkward silence first. "I don't understand. Why'd they let you see me?"

"I made a deal with Captain Hallstead to come check on you. Don't worry, I'm as shocked as you are that he held up his end of the bargain."

At the mention of his name, a hard look slipped across her face. Her eyes were red at the corners as if she had been crying, and I got the sinking sensation that he was the reason why.

I tilted my head slightly, starting to frown. "What's that look for? Are you and he still butting heads?"

"If that's what you want to call it," she muttered, pulling her knees up to her chest and wrapping her arms around them. It was a classic Scarlett pose: small, protected, and unreadable.

I paused, trying to figure out how to proceed. "Look, I don't know what's been happening with you in the past couple of days, but he seems to be the only decent person on this ship. Maybe you should give him a chance. He might actually want to help you."

She shook her head. "You don't get it."

"No, I don't. So explain it to me."

"I can't. I'm not supposed to talk about it with anyone or they'll throw me right back in my cell."

I scooted closer, dropping my voice and switching from English to Korean. For all I knew, there may have been security cameras or listening devices, but I had to risk it.

"I know you're involved with the alien on board."

Surprise flooded her features. "How...?"

"Long story. I need you to tell me what's going on. They keep the trainees in the dark, but we managed to spy on them enough to get some details. They caught one of the Bergleute, right?"

She glanced around the room and lowered her voice. "It's not one of the Bergleute. It's another alien enslaved by them. He escaped their battle cruiser and came looking for help. For some reason, he contacted me telepathically asking me to tell the general what was going on. He wants us to free his people and kill the Bergleute."

"How did they know it wasn't a trap?"

"He showed me what happened while he was a slave. It was very... convincing." She glanced away, seeming to hide a reaction to whatever had happened.

"What do you mean 'showed' you?"

"We shared memories."

My eyes widened. "Scarlett, don't you think that's a little dangerous? What if he tried to take you over and make you his slave?"

"No, you..." she sighed. "If you met him, you would understand. He's just a child. I know it sounds suspicious, but I trust him and I believe what he showed me."

"Why did he pick you? Why not someone else?"

"He said I was an Empath of sorts. No one else can hear his thoughts and he speaks very little English out loud."

"Is that why you're upset? They've decided not to help him?"

"No. I'm upset because they're gonna kill him."

I grimaced. "Shit. I got the feeling that they would in order to make sure he's not a threat. I'm so sorry, Scarlett."

"Don't be. I'm not going to let them murder an innocent creature."

A wave of worry rolled over me. "Lettie, what the hell are you talking about?"

"I'm going to get out of here and I'm going to set him free," she said with absolute resolve, as if what she was talking about wasn't completely insane.

"That's impossible," I replied in my most patient voice. "And even if it was, they would imprison you for the rest of your life."

She let out a dry chuckle. "Duke, we're already prisoners. You know that. We can never leave, we can never make another decision on our own, and we can never go home. If they lock me up or kill me, at least I can accept it knowing that I did the right thing."

"But you *don't* know that it's the right thing!" I snapped in frustration. "The alien could be lying, trying to lure us out to help the Bergleute. You'd be risking your life for no reason, or you could doom everyone on this ship. You've got to think this through or you'll end up dead."

"Duke, I know how it sounds. I really do. And you're right, I could be completely wrong." She bit her bottom lip and then took a deep breath. "But what if I'm right? What if we launch a bomb and kill the Bergleute and an entire race of completely innocent aliens? They're not that different from us. They're orphans too, and we'd be condemning them to die alone and helpless. I would never forgive myself, just like I don't forgive myself for not spending every waking second of my life looking for Dad."

I stopped breathing for a couple of seconds. She *never* talked about what happened to our parents. "Is that what this is about? This reminds you of Mom and Dad?"

She wouldn't meet my eyes. I sighed. "Lettie, it's not the same. There was nothing you could have done to stop him. Me neither. Helping this alien isn't going to change what happened."

"I know it won't, but this is the only chance I've got to make up for every shitty thing I've done in my life. To Mom, to me, to you..." Her eyes wandered to my right hand, and I could see that she was resisting the urge to cry.

I touched the side of her face, making her meet my eyes. "Scarlett...I can't let you do this." She closed her eyes and the tears streaked down her cheeks. "...alone."

My sister looked up at me, a question embedded in her face. "What?"

"I'd be a horrible older brother if I let you do this by yourself. Besides...I fuckin' hate this jumpsuit."

Scarlett wrapped her arms around me, crying and laughing as I held her. Same blood, same heart.

Some things never change.

HALLSTEAD

"Hungry?"

I shook my head. Truth be told, I was starving, but the smell of the seared ribeye in front of me made my stomach churn. Few military men were vegetarian. They liked their protein. I took supplements and got along fine.

He sliced the steak into neat little pieces and dipped them in a small puddle of sauce, eating a couple of mouthfuls before addressing me. "Do you know why I've called you in?"

"No, sir."

Bridgewater wiped his mouth with a napkin and then sat his dining utensils on his massive oak desk. He laced his fingers together and regarded me seriously with his pale blue eyes.

"I'm worried about you."

I couldn't stop the look of surprise from overtaking my face. "Worried?"

"You're extremely competent, Hallstead. That's why I recommended you to be in charge of the *Titan* and to keep things running smoothly should anything happen to me. However, there's another reason that I picked you: your rationality. It's practically unmatched."

He took a sip of the wine. Red, not white. The dim lighting made it look like blood. *General Vampire*, my mind mused before I could stop it. "However, I can tell that this business with the alien is getting to you."

"Sir," I began. "I assure you that there's nothing wrong with me. I agree with every decision we've come to regarding the alien. I've followed every order to the letter."

"Yes, you have. But I don't believe that you want this alien dead like the rest of us."

I started to protest, but he held up his hand. "Captain, you can be honest with me. It won't leave this room. Speak your mind."

I stared at him. He stared at me. A little itching feeling started to develop between my shoulder blades. Discomfort. I didn't want to tell him the truth, but nothing ventured, nothing gained.

Sighing, I shoved my hands into my pockets and spoke the truth. "I just think that he would be more valuable to us alive. We need to have a longer period of time with him in order to determine if he's really innocent or if he's a threat. Besides, he might know more about the known universe. That's information that could give us a huge advantage in the long run. Especially if the intention for us is to colonize a new planet before we run out of resources."

He nodded. "Good. Those are all perfectly logical reasons."

Somehow, I didn't like the way he said that. "But you're still not going to consider letting him live."

General Bridgewater sipped his wine again. "You're well aware of our 'shoot first, ask questions later' policy."

"I am. But we don't always need to use it. It was my suggestion to let the Nam siblings live, and they turned out to be more useful than either of us ever imagined."

Something went through his eyes at the mention of the Nam siblings. That too made me suspicious. He stood up, stepping around the desk to face me. "Excellent point. Without the Nam girl, we wouldn't have been able to make effective contact with the alien. She's quite valuable, wouldn't you say?"

I eyed him. "Sir?"

"Oh, you and I both know we wouldn't have had the breaks we've had without…Scarlett, was it?"

"I'm not following, General." Yes, I was. But I wanted to hear him say the words. Out loud. No more bullshit implications.

"Captain, every decision you have made under my command has been beneficial to this vessel. But there's a bit of an asterisk next to that statement. That asterisk is Scarlett Nam."

I cleared my throat. "You think she's a threat, sir?"

"No. I think she's a distraction."

I took a deep breath through my nose. "General Bridgewater, that girl is impulsive, rude, emotionally unbalanced, and stubborn. She is not distracting me."

He crossed his arms. "How long have you been working for me, son?"

"Two years."

"And in that time, how many women have you been involved with?"

I gritted my teeth. "None, sir."

"So you don't think that the amount of time you've spent around this girl is unusual?"

"She's the only method of communication we have with the alien. How is it unusual that I directly interact with her?"

"It's unusual when she's starting to influence how you think," he said, his voice switching from conversational to cold so fast that I thought I'd get a brain freeze. "It's not a person, Captain Hallstead. It's a *thing*. A species. Not a 'him.' It's given us everything we need to eliminate a threat. Think of it as ammunition. When the clip's empty, you throw it away. The bullet's already hit. You just haven't noticed yet."

He walked back over to his desk and sat down, resuming his meal. "Trust me, Captain. Less contact with the girl will make you see things in a whole new light. She'll be just another pretty face in the ranks soon enough, so get her out of your system as soon as possible. Understood?"

It physically hurt to answer without growling. "Yes, sir."

I turned and exited the office. My hands were balled into fists inside my pockets. I had been taught as a child to channel my anger, to control it and not let it control me, but somehow that leaked out of my head in that one moment. I began to forget that he was my superior and instead thought of him as a pompous asshole. Though I didn't know what pissed me off more: that he acknowledged my argument and then completely ignored it, or that he implied that I was lusting after Scarlett.

I had two hours before I would have to resume my duties on deck, so I headed to the gym to vent my frustrations on inanimate objects. The other four people gave me a wide berth when I stalked in from the locker room, heading straight to the mat to stretch. We were allowed a few luxuries and one of them happened to be music. I plugged the wireless headphones into my ears and let the music flood across my neck, over my shoulders, down my arms, my chest, and my legs, helping me breathe out my irritation.

General Bridgewater had always thought of me as the perfect soldier. Loyal. Obedient. Competent. But his words bothered me, especially the bit about ammunition. Did he see everyone as disposable? If I crossed him, if I disagreed, if I defied him, would he throw me away as well? How could we trust someone so callous to lead us?

Hypocrite, the little voice in the back of my head snorted. *Isn't that callousness what saved humanity? If we had alerted the general public to the Bergleute, there would have been mass panic and hysteria. It was better for them to die ignorant than to know that their doom was coming.*

Which was true. It was a mercy kill of sorts. Not everyone could be saved. It just wasn't possible. But...was it our right to make that decision for them? If I had a choice to face my death or remain ignorant, which would I choose?

The practice dummy was made of rubber. It bounced against my knuckles with every punch: placid, emotionless, just like I was supposed to be. I wished that every blow took a little more of the anger away, but it didn't. It festered inside me like a disease. Doubt. A soldier couldn't afford to have doubts. Doubt made you sloppy. Unsure. Weak. Maybe he had been right. The alien was affecting my judgment, and so was Scarlett, despite my previous unwillingness to admit it.

Earlier, I had read the initial analysis that Dr. Warwick had kindly made a copy of for me. She inferred that Scarlett's traumatic experience of her mother's death was what motivated her to be so aggressive and non-compliant. The anger acted as a cover for deeper feelings of inadequacy. Though I didn't really need a report to tell me that. It was in her eyes—the rawness that came with seeing death firsthand, being close enough to touch it. She seemed to not give a shit about how her actions affected others, but in actuality she controlled every little bit of how people saw her. Every word that came out of her mouth was calculated, precise, to convey a headstrong young woman and cloak the intelligence and vulnerability underneath.

Like the others, I thought she was just a brat when I first met her, but after Hatwer shared his memories, I could see the layer beneath her bravado. She was a girl scared of her own potential. Scared of her self-worth. Scared of both failing and succeeding.

Like me at twelve years old, holding my father's gun, pointing it at the man who had broken into our home. Defiled it. Smeared the walls with sin.

I stopped and breathed deeply, calming my thoughts. By now, I had worked up a sweat and would need to cool off soon. I glanced at my watch. My timing appeared to be working. When Bridgewater called for me, I sent Duke to his sister. She needed comfort. Someone to get through that thick skull of hers. Only her brother could do that. It wasn't my job to care. I had my orders. Another mercy kill.

Click, click, boom.

The muffled sound of the gunshot still didn't knock me out of my thoughts. There were far more advanced weapons on the *Titan*—automatics, laser rifles, even Toshida's prototype for a lightsaber—but the only thing that felt reliable to me was a handgun. Something about the weight in my hand, the metal resting so perfectly in my palm, was something the other weapons couldn't capture. The precision involved with shooting always calmed me down better than physical combat, better than alcohol, better than sex. Well, maybe not better than sex. Though I hadn't had it in quite a while. Sometimes I worried I'd forgotten the enjoyment of the act entirely, as some military men do. What a depressing thought.

I lowered the gun and pressed the button on the console. The paper fluttered as the conveyor belt reeled it in, and I could see the neat little holes my bullets had made in the ten-ring. I took it down and put up a new one, sending it back out onto the range. Just as I raised the gun again, someone tapped on my shoulder.

I took out my earplugs and turned to find one of the guards saluting me—Evans, I think was his name. Decent guy, good soldier. "What can I do for you?"

"Just thought you'd like to know that the package has been delivered," he said. A generic code, as there were other people in here practicing and none of them needed to know our business. I nodded and shoved the gun back in its holster at my waist, following him out into the hallway.

After making sure it was empty, I continued with a question. "Did Duke make any mention of Han to her? Any suggestion that he knows more than he's letting on?"

"No. For the most part, they just started catching up."

"Well, that's disappointing."

"I said for the most part." He held up a small compact disc. "The rest is in Korean. I don't speak Korean. But I believe you do."

I slipped the disc into my pocket, checking once again to make sure no one saw us. "No one needs to know about this."

"Yes, sir. Happy to help."

"And he's back in the ranks?"

"Yes, sir."

"Good man. Keep an eye out for both of 'em, will you?"

He smiled. "Not that they need any more help."

He saluted and walked off before I could ask him what that meant. Figures. Half the people in this place never said what they meant anyway.

I heard a short beep and touched the link in my ear. "Hallstead."

General Bridgewater's voice came out sharp and brief. "Get up to the deck. We've got something."

I hurried to the elevator and rode it up to the main deck. When the doors opened, I went to the primary console where General Bridgewater was already waiting for me.

"Sir?"

He touched the console and brought up a map of our current position.

We had been cruising at a good pace through the Milky Way Galaxy and had just reached an unmapped quadrant.

"We've got a hit on one of the probes."

"What kind of hit?"

For the first time in a long while, General Bridgewater smiled. "The good kind. It's showing signs of a planet that may support human life."

For a moment, I couldn't speak. I had to clear my throat twice before I could. "Sir, that's…amazing. Where is it?"

He expanded the map with his fingertips, pointing to a planet with three moons, hovering toward the middle of a small solar system.

"Our computer calculates it would take about 48 hours at our current speed to reach it. I'm thinking we should send a team down there to gather information before the rest of the vessels converge on that same place."

He lowered his arm and the smile faded. "However, this would mean that we would have to move up our assault on the Bergleute. We can't occupy this planet until they have been eliminated; if they do decide to follow us as a result of the alien we found, they would destroy this new place as well."

"Do we have any indication that they've changed course?"

General Bridgewater brought up an image of a security camera feed from one of the probes. "This is the Titan Probe 4X51. We left it stationary at a checkpoint outside of the forty-seventh quadrant. Take a look."

I watched the camera, expecting a looming shadow like the one that had appeared over the Earth before it was destroyed, but I didn't see anything like that. Instead, I caught a flash of movement, then the feed cut to static.

"What was that?"

He slowed down the footage to a mere crawl and made it a little bigger. This time, I could see an angular shape with an odd blue tint to it fly past the probe just before the footage stopped.

"Our analysts seem to think that this is something the Bergleute sent after us. The probe clocked it at a speed I don't think any of our vessels can approach. It emitted some sort of electromagnetic pulse as it passed, which killed the feed."

"So she was right," I muttered. Louder, I asked, "Is it just the one?"

"Appears to be."

"I'm guessing it's a search-and-recover effort, then. If they wanted to kill all of us, they would have sent more than one. It's going to take out Hatwer so he won't give us any more help. We've got to get him off this ship, sir. Now."

"I thought we already discussed this, Captain."

I paused long enough to keep my temper in check. "I understand that, sir, but maybe this would be how we could draw them away from the *Titan*. We're too close to finding a new home to risk it now."

"How would you suppose we do that? We don't know if they're tracking the alien or tracking their ship."

"But what is the alternative? Wait for it to get close and hope we can obliterate it? That didn't work with over one hundred of our best battle-ships, so why would it work with the *Titan?*"

He narrowed his eyes at me, and I saw a muscle in his jaw twitch. "What would you suggest then, Captain Hallstead?"

"Lead it away. Find a vulnerability. If we mount an assault now with these untrained soldiers, all we would be doing is wasting their lives. We can't afford to do that."

He massaged the bridge of his nose. "Or we can just kill the damn alien and jettison his body into space for the Bergleute to find. Problem solved."

My hands formed fists. I breathed deep to calm my nerves. "There's no guarantee that the ship they sent won't continue tracking our movements. The Bergleute aren't stupid. They might figure it's easy to just follow us to the new planet and blow that up too. Things have changed, General Bridgewater. We can't think short term. We need a plan, not another massacre."

He stared me down for a long moment. "One hour. That's all you get. You take off and you come up with a plan that makes sense. And if I'm not impressed, we're sending the corpse out there and that'll be the end of it."

"Thank you, sir." The words were bitter in my mouth, but I swallowed my pride and left the main deck. When the elevator doors closed, I exhaled and ran a hand through my hair. Things were spinning out of control, minute by minute, second by second. We wouldn't last much longer like this. I knew that for sure.

My bedroom looked like a hotel or a hospital, to be honest. Other employees had stashed posters in their luggage to decorate, but my walls were bare, sterile. The bed was pushed against the far wall so I could face the door, a compulsive need I had ever since I was a kid, and the white was broken up by two bookshelves and a computer desk. Books were crammed into every available inch of the shelves and populated about 70% of my computer desk, the laptop taking up the remaining space. I'd done my best to fill in the gaps from my education regarding astronomy, environmental science, geology, biology, and microbiology.

I flipped the computer open, digging the disk out of my pocket. Evans' words had me spooked. The fact that Scarlett and Duke had started conversing in Korean meant they were trying to hide something. I got the feeling that maybe even Duke wouldn't be able to talk Scarlett out of her protectiveness of Hatwer.

I drummed my fingers on the desk as I waited for the disc to load. A pencil and paper lay beneath them to help me remember every detail of what was said. My Korean was just below fluency—courtesy of my traveling days in the military. I'd picked up several languages during my career: Spanish, French, German, Vietnamese, Korean, and Japanese. I knew it was a long shot trying to glean their conversation from the recording. There was no guarantee that I would even be able to hear every word. They may have been ex-criminals and impulsive ones at that, but I found myself admiring the level of intelligence each of them possessed. Sure, Duke was the mastermind, but Scarlett wasn't that far behind him. The fact that they had both learned Morse code proved that they knew it could come in handy someday.

Finally, the footage started. I watched them hug and listened to their conversation in English, making a few notes on my paper about exactly what was said while I could gather it with ease. Then they switched to Korean and I had to increase the volume and pause every so often to write out a sentence and translate it so that it made sense to me. After all, it had been a while since I had spoken or listened to any Korean.

Scarlett had taken a huge risk telling her brother about Hatwer. The security cameras were an insurance policy against mutiny or other problems the employees might try to hide, but the bug had been my idea. If General Bridgewater found out about this, both of them would be tossed right back in their cells until further notice. Normally, I would weigh the decision to turn them in against letting it slide, but Bridgewater had pissed me off and so it was going to stay a secret unless they revealed something dangerous.

Toward the end of the conversation, Duke surprised me. His decision to help her instead of trying to stop her struck me as odd because of his calculating nature and the fact that it would be a nigh impossible feat. Then again, I'd underestimated the bond between family members. I was an only child raised by my stepfather. I didn't know what it meant to share blood and to put myself in danger just because of that.

After Duke agreed to help her, a new problem arose. The two of them sat Indian-style on the bed facing each other and effectively blocking my view since the hidden camera was mounted in the wall behind a fake electrical outlet. They appeared to just be staring at each other, but I zoomed in a little more when I saw Duke's shoulder moving just slightly. I leaned in, peering at the screen, trying to figure out what was going on. Then it hit me.

He had taken her hand and started using Morse code on her palm.

I pushed my chair back, plunging a hand into my hair in sheer frustration. What the hell was I going to do about this? Bridgewater would know something was wrong if I brought one of them in for questioning. As much trouble as the two of them were causing, I didn't want them tortured again. It hadn't been my decision the first time. It wasn't probable that they came up with a plan that would work and free Hatwer, but it was possible. A one in a million chance. Make that two in a million.

Duke wouldn't break. Not unless I threatened Scarlett again, and I got the feeling he would know I was bluffing. She was a chronic pain in my ass, but I didn't want to hurt her. I would get better results if I tried to get an answer out of her instead, but Bridgewater didn't want me anywhere near her because of his "concerns" about our interactions. It wouldn't be easy, but there was no other choice.

I picked up my personal internal-network phone on the desk and dialed. It rang about four times and then an authoritative yet clinical female voice answered.

"Hello?"

"Dr. Warwick, I need a favor."

CHAPTER TWELVE

SCARLETT

"S o...why am I being taken to the infirmary?"

"Just a routine check-up," Evans replied. "Nothing major."

"...it doesn't involve needles, does it?"

He chuckled. "Not that I know of, no. Shouldn't take long."

I sighed. "Good. It's hard to be a tough guy when you're in the fetal position."

He snorted and swiped his keycard. "I'll be right outside. Behave yourself."

I fluttered my eyelashes at him. "Don't I always?"

The door swooshed open. I stepped inside, finding a tiny patient room with the green curtain drawn around the bed and an empty desk against the adjacent wall. I suspected a computer used to be there, but it had been taken out for whatever reason. Maybe the doctor would bring the equipment with him.

I noticed a shadow beyond the curtain and sighed, pulling it aside.

"What's this all about, Doc?"

I jumped when I saw who was sitting on the bed, moving back a couple of steps in alarm. Hallstead met my eyes with a steady gaze and didn't bother answering my question. "I'll make this simple. Tell me what you and your brother are planning, and I won't throw you in jail for the rest of your life."

I took a deep breath, trying to remember those anger exercises that Dr. Warwick had taught me. None came to mind. Great. "What plan? What are you talking about?"

He held up a small disc. "You used Morse code for exactly four minutes and fifteen seconds. I guessing you weren't trading secret recipes."

I crossed my arms and arranged my face to be completely blank. "What we talked about has nothing to do with Hatwer or you or the Starlight Contingency."

He stood up, stepping close enough to invade my personal space. "Then tell me what he told you."

"How to make the best chicken dumplings," I replied with the utmost sarcasm possible.

Hallstead shook his head. "One way or another, you're going to tell me, Scarlett. You can do this the easy way and that'll be the end of the issue. Stop being difficult for once in your life."

I smiled. "Why be difficult when you can be impossible?"

Anger darkened his face. "You really don't want to do this with me."

"Oh, trust me, I really do," I sneered, not backing away like I was sure he wanted me to. "So what are you gonna do? Water-board me until I spill the beans? Threaten my brother? Staring contest? Mud wrestling? I'm sure I can find a swimsuit in a jiffy."

"No," he answered. "I'm just going to tell you the truth."

"What truth?"

"The truth about who you are. Dr. Warwick says you've been evasive about whatever it is that makes you hate yourself."

I gritted my teeth. "And you think that's going to make me give up our plan?"

He ignored the comment and instead brushed past me. He put his hands in his pockets, speaking in a casual tone.

"You did something that caused your brother to get hurt."

I froze. How could he possibly have figured that out? I hadn't told anyone, not even Dr. Warwick. Still, I pressed my lips together to stop the question "How did you know that?" from spilling out and confirming his accusation.

"You don't have to admit it. It's in your eyes. It's on your face every time you're around your brother. It's guilt. The way he treats you is like he's your bodyguard, like you can't get along without him because of what happened. You let him take on this role because you feel like he earned the right to be in charge of you. You need him, but you don't need him that much, and your guilt makes you stay silent and obey his every command."

I closed my eyes, taking slow breaths. *He's trying to provoke you. Don't react. That's what he wants. Stay calm.*

"The missing pinky on Duke's hand isn't a birth defect. The scarring suggests that it was severed, not burnt or smashed. I bet you know the exact date and time when it happened too. He lost a little piece of himself that day and you lost a little piece of you as well."

My breathing started to pick up and my hands curled into fists. He was unraveling my past one thread at a time, picking at me like a bug in a Petri dish, laughing as my wings were plucked off and nailed to a wall in his office.

"That's why everything you do isn't good enough. You pretend not to care about what people think of you, but deep down you just want to cover up your mistake—the mistake that your brother paid for in blood. He took your place, and you feel like he took your identity when he made that decision for you."

"Shut up," I whispered hoarsely, attempting to control the panic attack trying to spew out of my chest, my lungs, my limbs.

"That's probably what led you to stealing. It gave you a false sense of superiority over others. Made you feel special, strong, clever. On some subconscious level, you know it's not going to make your problem go away, but it affords you a different identity. You can be someone else instead of the Scarlett who made the mistake."

"Shut *up*."

"I'll bet if we dug deeper into your past, we'd find something wrong between you and your father. That's why you hate men of authority. They remind you of him, and what he did to your mother. The ultimate dominance. Murder."

"Shut your fucking mouth!" I threw a punch, sloppy, unfocused, filled to the brim with sorrow and rage and other stupid emotions that had no business being there. He knew I was coming and sidestepped, grabbing my wrist as my fist went past him. I tried to hit him with my other one, but he caught that one too and kicked my legs out from under me. I thought I would hit the floor, but the mattress was right behind us. He pinned me beneath him, and I struggled uselessly against his iron grip. He hovered there, staring into my eyes and never once raising his voice.

"I can do this all day, Scarlett. Unearth every single one of your insecurities and make you face them. You can't stop me, and you know you can't, so why don't you just give me what I want and we don't have to do this."

My breath came in ragged pants that just barely hid the sobs growing in my throat. I had tried so hard to bury my past, to keep the dirt from clogging my nose and suffocating me, but it was always there, ready to swallow me up like quicksand. The anger burned through my gut, but it was only a front for the agony of realizing that he was right about me. Every goddamn word.

"Just kill me. Just fucking kill me," I rasped, shaking my head. "I'm not giving you what you want, you bastard. I won't give you that satisfaction."

He squeezed my wrists and narrowed his eyes at me. "You think I like doing this? You think I get some sick kick out of treating you like this? I don't, Scarlett. But I'm a soldier. I do what I need to do to get the job done."

"How is that any different from me? Maybe I do hide from who I really am. Maybe I do let my brother run things because I screwed up, and he had to pay for it. But that's the only thing that keeps me from slitting my goddamn wrists. I do what I have to do to survive. So let me have it, Captain Hallstead. Tell me more about what a piece of shit I am. I don't care. I'm not telling you a damn thing no matter what you say."

He leaned in closer, dropping his voice to a dangerous hiss. "I don't believe you."

"Tough shit."

I waited for him to continue ripping me to metaphorical shreds, but he didn't say anything. He just kept glaring down at me and that was when I felt it. An odd electric buzz that started in my feet and crawled up my legs to my thighs and over my stomach. Our breathing had unconsciously synchronized, and I could feel every hot burst of air across my neck. Something changed in that millisecond. An invisible force tugged at my core and whispered the impossible in my ear. No. Couldn't be.

The next second didn't quite feel real. One moment, my eyes were wet and I wanted to scream at him to let me go and tell him what a fucked-up person he was and then my lips were sucking his bottom lip between them. He made a sound against me, like the echo of a groan, and I swallowed it, sliding my tongue past his teeth. He tasted of mint. I lifted my knee and ran it down the inside of his thigh. He shuddered, kissing me harder, using his teeth.

Then, he pulled away and snapped: "What the fuck are you doing?"

For a second, I wasn't sure he had been the one to say it because I found myself wondering the same thing. "I…"

"You what?"

I licked my bottom lip, trying to wipe away the taste of him, but it clung. "I don't know. I just…felt something."

He jerked against me when I rubbed my knee closer to his crotch and I lifted an eyebrow. "And apparently, so did you."

Hallstead glared at me, but I could see that the kiss had affected him as much as it had affected me, maybe even more so. "Nice try, but this isn't going to work, either."

"Then it looks like we're at a stalemate. Sort of."

My knee went upward another inch, and he made a strangled sound, pushing my leg aside. Before I could move, he nudged my thighs apart and knelt between them, planting his large hands on either side of my hips without touching me, but the implication was clear. He dropped his voice to a tone between irritation and arousal, which was quite devastating from so close.

"You have a knack for getting in over your head," he growled.

I smiled again, but it was a little unsteady for reasons I didn't want to admit to myself. "So do you. You can see right through me, but you failed to realize that I've seen who you really are underneath the soldier persona."

His gray eyes searched mine and he didn't deny it, so I kept going, my confidence growing as I went. "The reason why you want to know our plan so desperately is that deep down…you want to help us. Maybe because it's the right thing to do or maybe because you just want to defy your boss. You're a better man than this and you know it, but you can't be because of your duty. And that's also why you can't admit that you want me."

"Fraternization is strictly forbidden. Did you ever stop to think that had something to do with it?"

"Not really. It bothers you, but not that much. You hate that we're attracted to each other because it makes you look like you're taking advantage of me, though we both know that if it ever happened, it would be the other way around."

A dangerous look went through his eyes then. It was so animalistic that I couldn't help but shiver a little. "Is that right?"

I let my smirk widen. Part of me knew better than to provoke him, but I couldn't help myself. This was not the typical socially appropriate Hallstead. The man before me had shed his skin to reveal his primal side. No more suit and tie, no more protocol. Just sex and violence.

I looped my arms around his neck, continuing in a low murmur. "It's a shame it'll never happen. I wonder what would happen if that guard wasn't outside. Who would be making the other person scream first?"

"Careful, little girl," he whispered, a guttural sound. "You might not like the answer to that question."

"I don't recall you complaining a minute ago."

He frowned harder. "Did you have a point somewhere in this speech?"

I quelled my desire to tease him more and pushed up to a sitting position. He mirrored me, staying just out of touching range but only by inches. "I think we can help each other. You don't want Hatwer dead any more than I do."

"I—"

"Save it. I'm hardheaded, not blind. I'll make it simple—my brother and I can work outside of the military regulations because we weren't part of your ranks to begin with. There's no need to risk your own men. They don't owe Hatwer anything and they wouldn't understand even if I tried to explain it to them."

"What are you saying?"

"I'm asking you to give us one chance to save his people. Just one. If we fail, then that's the end of it and you can do whatever you want. You and I both know that the Bergleute will send an assassin for him, and we'll use it to return to their mothership. Once we're inside, we can shut it down and get his people out of there. Then you send your boys to take them out."

"How would you even know how to pilot that thing? We're talking about advanced alien technology. You're an ex-thief. How are you anywhere near qualified?"

"I shared memories with Hatwer. I know how to pilot the escape pod, and I'm guessing he can help us figure out how to pilot the ship the Bergleute sent. He'll be our guide."

"And what if you get compromised while on the mothership? We can't send someone to get you out. They'll see us coming."

I took a deep breath. "That's why you're going to send a bomb with us. If we can't get them out, at least we can damage the damn thing."

He stared at me. "Are you out of your mind?'

"I'm not going to die alone, Captain. If I die, I'm taking as many of those bastards as I can with me."

Hallstead shook his head. Something in his expression gave me the impression he didn't approve, but he didn't protest aloud. "How could we communicate with you once you're on the ship? The one they sent to kill Hatwer can disable our signals."

I tapped my watch. "Time. Duke calculated how long it would take to reach them and you have to follow it to the very second. If your men don't see us leaving the mothership, they can still get out of there without getting killed."

"This is insane. We don't have enough room on our ships to support the Shasar. We don't know what they eat or even how to talk to them."

"If I survive, then I could translate for them. It would only be temporary. We'll find them a nearby planet that can support them. If we start to run low on supplies, they could take the other vessels from the *Titan* and search on their own."

He glanced away and I paused, growing suspicious. "You know somewhere they can go, don't you?"

"That's classified," he grunted at me.

I rolled my eyes. "Don't be a dick. If you've found a hospitable planet, there's no reason we can't share. I don't think there'll be that many of them left anyway."

"Fair enough, but there's no way that General Bridgewater is going to agree to this."

"Exactly."

He gave me a confused look. "What?"

"What the general doesn't know can't hurt him. That's where you come in. You're going to pretend that you didn't know about any of this and work behind the scenes. That way you won't have to risk getting fired or locked up if you pitch the idea to him. I'm sure he's scheduling Hatwer's autopsy pretty soon, so we'll ambush the guards and take him and the ship."

He shook his head. "You'll never be able to hold off all the guards between the morgue and where they're keeping the escape pod."

"True, but if you pull some strings, I'm sure we can make it happen.

We'll make a big show of leaving and Bridgewater will send someone after us whose ship will 'conveniently' break down while chasing us."

Hallstead arched an eyebrow. "You've really thought this through to the minute details, huh?"

"Yeah, I feel very Lex Luthor right now. Thank you for noticing."

He shook his head. "This isn't going to work, Scarlett. There are too many things that can go wrong."

"But what's the alternative? Let them die, let Hatwer die, and hope that the Bergleute don't decide to come after all of us? You know we have a chance. That's all I'm asking for. I have to make this right. You said yourself that Hatwer chose me. There's got to be a reason for that."

The silence stretched a mile wide. I wanted to shake him, to make his answer fall out so I wouldn't have to keep waiting.

Finally, he sighed. "If you don't pull this off, it's my ass."

"Don't worry, Captain Hallstead," I replied in a deadpan voice. "Your ass is in our hands."

Hallstead rolled his eyes at me, and I couldn't help but smile. He stood and checked his watch, adopting a more serious look. "We've got three hours before Hatwer's autopsy. How is your brother planning on getting out of the dorm?"

"He said he was going to give the guard a message saying that he had important information on one of the trainees, some Russian guy. You'll have the guard escort him to the interrogation level and that's when he'll make the escape."

"What about you?"

I shrugged. "I've always been good at picking locks."

He snorted. "Figures. Here."

He tossed something at me, and I caught it on reflex, glancing down to find a phone resting in my palm. "That's my personal phone. It's got the coordinates to the new inhabitable planet we're heading toward. Arrival is set for less than 48 hours from now."

"What if they ask you how I got it?"

"I'll tell them you lifted it off me after the last time we interrogated Hatwer together. You were a thief, after all. I'll slip three space suits into the escape pod. They've got roughly five hours' worth of air, so be mindful of the time."

Another awkward silence started to descend, but I quickly filled it.

"Guess this is goodbye." I bit my lower lip, not sure of what to say at first. "Thank you."

A bit of surprise crept into his features. "For what?"

"This. For not being as much of a bastard as you could have been. For not taking advantage of me." A small laugh escaped me. "Come to think of it, you're probably the closest thing to a nice guy that I've ever known. Isn't that sad?"

He allowed a smile to touch his lips. "Incredibly. It's been a pleasure, Miss Nam."

"Goodbye, Captain Hallstead."

"Travis," he said softly.

"Goodbye, Travis."

He turned, then hesitated.

"What?" I asked.

Hallstead grabbed the side of my face, yanking me up toward him. He kissed me, hard. It was passionate, exciting, scary, and undeniably sexy. I didn't resist it, gripping his shoulders and pressing myself up against the firmness of his chest. He felt good, solid, smelled like aftershave and gunpowder.

When he let me go, I stood there for a couple of seconds and then opened my eyes to see his flushed face up close, his eyes half-lidded, filled with want. "Why?"

Hallstead smirked. "For luck. Besides, might not get to do that later."

I allowed a wolfish smile to cross my lips. "Not if I have anything to say about it. Good luck."

He brushed a lock of my red hair behind my ear. "Good luck, Scarlett."

Hallstead walked out. Some part of me left with him. I'd have time to deal with that later, God-willing.

I checked my watch. Three hours.

Tempus fugit.

DUKE

"Need a spot?"

I craned my neck to see Han behind me with both of his enormous hands resting on the barbell I had loaded with thirty-five pounds on each side. Time dripped off the clock on the far wall, and it was hard to think about anything else. Every other scheme we had concocted was usually only possible because I could control all the factors involved. Not the case here. I'd always thought that Scarlett had unbelievable luck, but this was the first time I hoped that it was actually true.

"Uh, sure," I said once I realized I'd been sitting there for a couple seconds, distracted by my thoughts. Sergeant Rosewood had set up a rotation system for the trainees in the gym. We would spend twenty minutes rotating from spot to spot using different equipment. My partner had gone off to the bathroom and we weren't allowed to lift weights on our own.

I lay back and wrapped my fingers around the bar. It was cold, much like the floors, and walls, and everything else on the *Titan*. Before all of this, I had belonged to a gym so I could stay limber and healthy. Scarlett had preferred doing her workout at home, but I liked the public setting.

I did five reps before Han said anything. "So you gonna keep lying to me or what?"

I adopted a confused look, pausing with the bar held high but parallel to the floor. It always took some effort to keep one end from tilting.

"What are you talking about?"

He narrowed his eyes at me. "Sam might not notice everything, but I do. Why did they call you out of training?"

"It was my sister," I lied through several deep breaths. "She's sick. They just wanted to let me know."

"Still lying. I've seen the way you look when you talk about her. You'd be more worried if it was about her. So that leads me to believe that they asked you about the bug."

I risked a glance up at him and his frown was deep and bitter. No point in denying that since he had proof. They had taken it with them before they came to collect me.

"What happened? Did they ask you about it?"

I shook my head. "You're being ridiculous. If they thought you were involved, they would have questioned you by now. It has nothing to do with the bug."

"Not true. Sergeant Rosewood has been watching me more closely ever since they took you. It can't be a coincidence."

"Sergeant Rosewood hates everyone," I said with a snort. "That's not unusual, that's just the way he is."

I finished my last rep and sat up, mopping the sweat off my forehead and the back of my neck while Han replaced the barbell.

"I am not stupid, Duke. You know more than what you're saying, and

I'm going to find out what's going on, one way or another. This is your last chance to come clean while we are still friends."

I turned around and left my face blank. "I already told you, Han. This is not about you."

He nodded. "Very well. But remember that I gave you a choice."

Han walked away just as my partner returned, staring between the two of us with a confused look, as if the air held static that he could feel. Maybe it did, maybe it didn't. I hadn't wanted things to go this way, but it was still my fault. I could have told them it was my idea and taken the heat, but then I wouldn't have been able to see Scarlett and come up with a plan to save Hatwer. Then again, letting Han take the blame didn't feel right because he was a good soldier and a decent person. Damned if I do, damned if I don't. The story of my life.

Eventually, Sergeant Rosewood called us to attention and dismissed us to the cafeteria for lunch. I maneuvered myself to the back of the line and stopped in front of him before leaving the room, clearing my throat.

"Staff Sergeant Alexander Rosewood, sir, may I have a word with you?"

"Oh? About what, Mr. Nam?"

"I have information about Han that I think should be reported to Captain Hallstead, Staff Sergeant Alexander Rosewood, sir."

"The captain's indisposed. You can tell me what's so important, though. I'm all ears."

Panic gripped me. I hadn't realized until now that my entire plan hinged on the fact that they were going to escort me out of here. If he didn't take me to see Hallstead, Scarlett would be on her own.

I tried again. "I would rather not discuss it here. We don't know who might be listening, Staff Sergeant Alexander Rosewood, sir."

He crossed his arms, fixing me with a hard, suspicious glare. "Are you saying you don't trust me, trainee?"

"I trust you, Staff Sergeant Alexander Rosewood, sir."

"Then you can tell me now and I'll take the message back to Captain Hallstead."

Shit. "Forgive me, Staff Sergeant Alexander Rosewood, sir, but I am under direct orders not to talk about anything I find without the audience of the both of you. According to the Air Force regulations 7560 column B, subsection 15, I am not authorized to disobey a direct order from a commanding officer above Staff Sergeant."

He glared at me. It took all of my will power not to glance at the clock, knowing that my precious minutes were ticking off of it one by one. Finally, he nodded. "Very good, Mr. Nam. Glad to see you've memorized your manual. Maybe you're not such a screw up after all."

He motioned to the guards to follow us and touched the link in his ear, calling Captain Hallstead. I trailed behind him, waiting to overhear the response. Scarlett had told me she would try to convince Captain Hallstead to help us—a pipe dream at best, but I decided to have faith in my sister. A moment later, Rosewood got the go ahead for the meeting and the plan was set.

We went up several flights of stairs to a floor with the elevator and boarded it. I mapped out my assault in my head. Sergeant Rosewood would not be an easy takedown. He was much stronger and taller than me, but I did have the element of surprise.

Then, the elevator stopped and I opened my eyes, not realizing that I had closed them as I visualized my escape route. Sergeant Rosewood stepped off, glancing at me over his shoulder. "I've got a quick stop to make. Don't start without me."

"Yes, Staff Sergeant Alexander Rosewood, sir," I replied, trying not to frown. Where the hell was he going? And why? Then again, he had just eliminated my most prominent problem in the escape route, so there was no reason to worry about where he was going.

The elevator continued upward for several floors until we reached the interrogation level. Two guards flanked me as I walked, checking the rooms to make sure they were all empty. The hallway was also empty, but my new problem was the alarm button positioned at the end of the hall. If one of them got to it, the jig was up. I'd have to take them down quickly and quietly. No second chances.

I glanced upward at the ceiling and frowned, stopping dead in my tracks. "What the hell is that?"

Both guards looked up. I thrust both elbows into their throats simultaneously, momentarily paralyzing their vocal cords. I turned to the man on my right and punched him as hard as I could in the solar plexus, winding him. When he bent over to wheeze, I slammed my knee into his forehead. He dropped like a sack of hammers.

The man on my right grabbed his gun and I caught his wrist, twisting his arm so the gun wasn't pointed at me and kicking his legs out from under him. He went down and I fell on top of him, leaning my forearm on his throat so that he couldn't breathe. He started to squeeze down on the trigger of the gun, so I broke his wrist and threw the gun away. He punched my kidney with his free hand. I grimaced through the pain, pressing harder on his throat as gurgled screams tried to escape. Seconds later, he couldn't lift his arm to hit me anymore and his eyelids fluttered shut. I immediately let go and crawled off of him, panting from exertion and the aching pain in my side.

After I caught my breath, I took both of their guns and stuffed them in the loose pockets of my jumpsuit. I used one key card to open an interrogation room at the end of the hall and dragged both of them inside, laying them flat on the floor directly in front of the window so that no one would see them until they literally walked in the room. I took a moment to strip them of any useful equipment. One of them had a taser. Bingo. That was the kind of thing that could come in handy.

I made sure to check their pulses, in case I needed to send for a doctor on my way out. Both were still alive. Thank God for that.

I took one of the guns out of my pockets and checked if it was loaded and the safety had been turned off. Then, I cracked the door to see if anyone had heard the commotion. The gun felt foreign in my hands as I closed the door behind me and crept down the hall to the elevator. I hit the button and waited with the gun aimed for it to arrive. The bell sounded and the doors slid open, revealing only one man, who was already pointing a gun at me.

"Hello, Mr. Nam."

"Hello, Sergeant Rosewood."

He stepped out of the elevator, and I backed up, keeping my arm steady as I aimed the gun at his forehead.

"How'd you figure it out?" I asked.

Rosewood snorted. "You must think I'm a fuckin' moron, huh?"

I smirked. "You're an asshole, but you're not a moron. I just want to know exactly what tipped you off, is all."

"You're a pretty good liar, Mr. Nam, but you're not perfect. You pushed so hard to see the captain that I could tell something was wrong."

A creeping sense of dread crawled up my stomach. "That was about five minutes ago. I'm assuming you've called Hallstead and General Bridgewater to let them know I'm a traitor."

"Nope."

Shock rolled through me.

Rosewood flashed me a nasty smile. "Went to get my good gun. You broke into my house. You could've hurt my family. I'm gonna take your ass down myself and enjoy the look on your face as I throw you and your rotten little sister in jail for the rest of your lives."

The surprise abated, leaving my face cold with anger. "Why not just kill me? Don't want to get your hands dirty?"

"That'd be too easy, son. I want you to be alive to remember that I did this to you."

"Guess I was right. You are an asshole."

He smirked. "And don't you forget it."

"I don't want to kill you, Sergeant, but you're standing between me and my sister. I'll ask you only once to get out of my way."

"I'll have to decline that offer. You want me to move? Shoot me."

We were at a stalemate. He and I both knew it. But we couldn't stand here forever comparing dick sizes. The autopsy was approaching and Scarlett needed me. I'd have to do something or all three of us would be dead.

But could I do it?

"You got the balls to kill me, son? I don't think so. You're gonna put that gun down and accept your fate like any other man would do. You can't help your sister if you're dead."

A long silence spilled between us. I stared at the cold chunk of metal in my hands. Then, slowly, I lowered the gun.

"You're right, Rosewood. I can't kill you."

He kept the gun on me and reached for the handcuffs in his pocket. He reached for me. I smiled at him.

"But I have no problem tazing your sorry ass."

I took out the taser and shot it at him.

He screamed and the gun went off. The bullet went straight through my right shoulder. It felt like someone had taken a red-hot poker and plunged it into my skin—a horrible pain that spread from the wound to the tips of my fingers.

I managed to push myself off the bloodstained wall behind me to look down at the paralyzed, twitching man on the floor, his eyes wide as plates and bloodshot. I kicked the gun across the linoleum and grabbed the handcuffs, adding it to the collection I'd gotten from the guards. I mustered one last comment before I got onto the elevator.

"*Now* I think you're a fuckin' moron."

The elevator doors slammed shut, and I rode up floor by floor to the level where they had taken Hatwer to be killed. Blood dripped down my arm in thick rivulets. I tore off one sleeve of my jumpsuit and tied it over the wound, slowing the blood flow. A puddle formed under my feet like morbid graffiti. I couldn't seem to catch my breath. The pain flickered through my upper body with every beat of my heart. It felt like life itself was oozing out of me. *No, don't think about it. She needs you. They need you. Be strong.*

The bell rang again and I lifted the gun in my left hand, trying to steady my breathing so that the barrel wouldn't shake as I aimed. The doors slid open and I tensed. The hallway was empty. It made sense; no one knew about the autopsy except the higher ups, but I didn't like it. Something felt wrong. Very wrong.

My boots made tiny echoes as I walked toward the only laboratory with light peeking out from beneath the double doors. I used one of the guards' key cards for entry and kicked them open.

Inside, I found a team of four doctors crowded around the alien, who had been strapped to an examination table. Their heads all whipped around when I entered and I could see the surprise on their faces even through their hazmat face masks.

"Hands in the air! Now!" I commanded in a harsh voice, pointing the gun at each of them in turn. One had been lowering a mask attached to a tank of what I assumed to be some sort of gas onto the alien's beak and he let it go. The alien blinked at me with four black eyes and there was a thick goo oozing from each of them. Jesus. It was...*crying.* My heart crumpled inside my chest like a piece of paper.

"Do not move unless I tell you to. If you try to run or set off an alarm, I'll shoot your kneecaps off. Nod if you understand."

They all nodded. I pointed the gun at the two doctors closest to me and then gestured at the alien. "Untie him."

They shuffled forward and started undoing the straps keeping the alien hostage, which allowed me a moment to take a good look at him. His body seemed encased by a shell much like a crab, but it had a humanoid fashion to it. He was very small, about four foot flat, and had insect-like qualities. It was hard to find him as endearing as Scarlett did, but she had always been able to see greatness in the seemingly ugly.

After the doctors got him loose, I reached out a hand to help him down. Hatwer stumbled a little as he got off the gurney, but his legs held. I pushed him behind me and then took two pairs of handcuffs from where they hung on my belt like heavy jewelry. I tossed it to the nearest doctor. "Sit down and cuff yourselves around the table in a circle."

Again, they obeyed me without question. I still didn't like how easy this felt, but I let it go as they finished and stared at me for further instruction. Though I felt a little bad for them. They were just following orders. "Someone will come get you as soon as I'm gone. Don't try anything funny or I'll be back. Come on, Hatwer."

I pulled the doors shut and ran for the elevator. Hatwer followed me on his odd bent legs, a little shaky but mostly stable. I had arrived just in time. Big damn hero, that's me.

I hit the elevator button several times, even though I knew it wouldn't make it go any faster, and tried to ignore the pain lancing through my right arm.

"Thank."

I jumped, glancing to my right at the alien. He blinked all four eyes at me, wiping the dark liquid away from them.

"What did you say?"

"Thank," Hatwer croaked again from his beak-like mouth. He sounded like an old man with a breathing disorder, but the meaning was clear.

I offered him a kind smile. "You're welcome, Hatwer."

He lowered his gaze from my face to my arm. "Hurt."

"It's okay. We'll be alright. We just have to make it to your escape pod and we'll be fine."

He tilted his head at me, and I realized he probably hadn't understood me. I thought about what to say that would be familiar to him.

"Scarlett. We're going to see Scarlett."

At the mention of her name, his eyes widened and he seemed to regain some of his strength. I figured it would have that effect on him.

The elevator doors opened and we rushed inside. I hit the button for the right level and took a deep breath. Almost home free.

The cargo bay was on the lowest level of the vessel and that was where Scarlett was supposed to meet us with the supplies we needed for the mission. Anticipation rode high in my throat as I watched the digital numbers drop lower and lower until we hit the very last floor. The doors opened for the last time.

And all hell broke loose.

CHAPTER THIRTEEN

SCARLETT

Fifteen minutes.

That was how long I had to get to the escape pod before it launched. Too bad I was still stuck in my room trying to undo the locking mechanism on the door.

I had taken a leg off the bed frame and jammed it into the drywall until I could see the circuits. Being a thief, I was well versed in electronics, but this circuitry was unbelievable. Now I understood what they meant when they told me that our technology was far more advanced than they let the general public know about. Everything had a backup system. Every wire I cut had one to replace it, and I was running out of time and burnt fingertips.

Earlier, I had tried the sick patient routine but no one responded: meaning that either the guards had gone on break or they were simply ignoring me. I believed the former rather than the latter because no one came to look in on me after I cracked a hole in the wall.

"Shit!" I grimaced as another tiny shock went through my hand, and pressed my head against my forearms, breathing slowly. *Calm down.* No one said this would be easy, or sane, for that matter. I'd gotten myself into this mess and I had to fix it somehow.

As I lifted my head, a couple strands of hair got trapped in my watch and I accidentally ripped them out, wincing. I growled curses at them, but that was when the idea hit me. I had been so busy trying to disable certain systems that I hadn't considered merely redirecting them. One of these combinations would yield the automatic open system if I did it carefully enough.

Rejuvenated, I put down the makeshift blade I had fashioned from part of the bed frame and examined the wiring I had already snipped. Pretty soon, I could see the patterns emerging and went to work reconnecting them in the right sequence until at last, I heard something click and the door slid open. Joyous, I straightened up and started to walk through the entrance only to bump into a guard.

"Guess I'm a bit late," Evans mused. I mouthed uselessly for a moment, not sure of what to say, but then he interrupted. "It's okay, I'm in on your plan. Captain sent me to get you clear as soon as possible. You're under a pretty big time-crunch, after all."

"Understatement of the century," I said as we hurried toward the elevator. Luckily, it was in the later hours aboard the ship; it ran on a military time schedule of "daylight" and "nighttime" hours, so most people were asleep right now, leaving the hallway empty. The doors opened and the two of us stepped inside.

Evans pulled his backup gun out of its holster and handed it to me. "If we're gonna make this look realistic, you're gonna have to pop me one. Big bruise'll convince the guys above us that you got the drop on me."

"I figured I'd have to do that," I admitted, a little crestfallen. "Where do you want it? Left or right temple? Forehead? Cheek?"

"Temple looks more dramatic. I'd aim for the left one."

"Got it." I paused, glancing at him with a sheepish look. "I'm sorry I have to hit you. I like you."

He grinned. "Don't worry about it. I'm always happy to help. And one more thing…"

Evans reached into one of his pockets and withdrew a device about the size of a Pez dispenser. It had a silver handle and cap but the rest of it was black.

"This is the bomb you requested."

I swallowed, trying to keep the anxiety out of my voice. "Oh."

"It's pretty simple." He flicked his thumb against the cap, revealing a red button.

"Squeeze the handle and press the button. You'll have five minutes to get clear if you set it off this way. There's also a backup instant detonation switch if things get..." He paused, choosing his words. "...hectic. It's on the bottom. It detonates in ten seconds. The bomb creates a very large explosion but based on the size and dimension of the Bergleute's ship, you would have to be in the main engine room to destroy the entire vessel. Otherwise, it'll cripple the ship, but not obliterate it."

"Got it. Thank you." He handed it to me, and I carefully closed the cap and put it in my pocket.

Evans glanced at the elevator's dropping numbers, sparing me a small smile. "Good luck."

I returned it. "Thanks."

Our moment was disrupted as the elevator stopped on the wrong floor. The doors slid open and revealed the second-to-last person I wanted to see right now.

The guard I'd knocked out. Simmons.

Evans quickly hid his surprise and cleared his throat, nodding to the guard as he stepped onto the elevator. "Simmons."

He glanced between us, his brown eyes narrowing when he looked at me. "What are you two doing?"

"Taking her to see Bridgewater," Evans answered nonchalantly. I had stepped toward the rear of the elevator when he came in and started to ease the gun into my waistband at the small of my back. The heavy cotton sweatshirt could conceal the lumpy shape of the weapon, but not if we got off before he did.

"What floor?" Evans asked, his gloved finger hovering over the buttons. We hadn't chosen our level yet since we had been discussing how to fake my escape. Things could go sour very quickly if we indicated that we were going to the cargo hold where the escape pod was kept.

"Interrogation. Just got on shift." He sent me a nasty look. "That's where I work now because of you."

I kept my mouth shut, merely looking away. Simmons frowned. "What? You don't have anything to say to my face now, is that it?"

Evans tried to intervene. "C'mon, don't do that. She's just some hard-headed punk. Not worth your time."

Simmons snorted. "Not worth anyone's time. 'Cept maybe Hallstead's."

We both froze. I knew I shouldn't have said anything, but the words slipped out before I could stop them. "You wanna run that by me again?"

"Like you don't know. Why else do you get all the special treatment? The nice room, not rotting in jail for the rest of your life? Don't pretend like you're not fuckin' him."

"You son of a bitch!" I launched myself toward him, but Evans caught my arm, holding me back. I heard a brush of cloth and then a click and Simmons' gun was drawn, pointed at my chest.

Evans drew his just as quickly, his voice level. "What the hell are you doing, Simmons?"

"No, I think that's what I should be asking you, Evans," he sneered. "Why are you helping this bitch escape?"

"Escape? What are you talking about?"

He let out a bitter laugh. "I got the call five minutes ago. She and her brother are taking the alien off the ship. Rosewood figured I'd enjoy the payback, so he sent me to intercept you. Would have come for you himself, but apparently he's indisposed on account of your brother tazing him."

The elevator stopped at the interrogation level, but Simmons hit the Close button before the doors could open. He then pressed the prison cell level, keeping his rifle aimed at me and not Evans. If anything went sour, I'd be the first to die. No way around it.

"So this is what's gonna happen: you're gonna get off this elevator and walk back to your nice little cell, and you're gonna spend the rest of your life remembering that I put you there. Maybe if you're nice to me, I'll let the two of you share one."

"We're not going to do that, Simmons," Evans growled. "You know that."

Simmons smiled, but it was more like a baring of teeth. Like a lion with its jaws wrapped around an antelope's throat.

"Yep. I do."

His rifle went off, nearly deafening me. I expected an explosion of blood and agony going through my body, but then I realized *he hadn't shot me.*

Evans lay in a heap against the wall of the elevator. The acrid smell of gunpowder and blood burnt my nostrils as I knelt next to him, shouting his name. The bullet had hit him in the upper body, just below where the collarbone connected to his right arm. He moaned, clutching the wound with his good hand, his own gun forgotten on the floor.

Simmons aimed his gun at me again, catching my attention.

"What did you shoot him for, you shit?!" I screamed.

He shrugged. "Collateral damage. They'll believe me if I tell them he struggled."

"If he dies, I swear to God, I'll *kill* you," I said, my voice thick and hoarse.

"Tall talk, sweetheart. But you touch that gun on the floor and I'll shoot you too."

"I'll risk it," I snarled through my teeth, reaching for the gun. Just as I did, the lights went out in the elevator, swallowing us in darkness.

Except for sparks of light when three shots were fired.

Silence.

The elevator had stopped moving. Someone cut the power. I stood motionless, straining my ears to hear something other than Evans' labored breathing. There was at least another three feet around me that Simmons could occupy, but it was too dark to see if my bullets had hit him. Only one thing to do. I had to get the lights back on.

I carefully sidled over to the panel where the buttons were and felt for the hatch that would open the manual controls. I pried it open and closed my eyes, concentrating on the texture and length of each wire, feeling the weight and letting it tell me what I needed to know. Luckily, this thing had a temporary emergency power back up and I switched it on, filling the elevator with dim light and the lurching sound of it moving down toward the prison floor.

Simmons lay on the opposite side of the elevator with a bullet in his gut, wheezing and shaking as he stared at the wound. I walked over to him, raising the gun so that it was level with his forehead. He glowered up at me and spat in my general direction. I smiled the same cold way that he had only moments earlier.

"You should learn to respect your betters, Simmons."

"Fuck you," he strained to say. "Shoot me."

"Oh, don't tempt me. I would love to shoot you...but I think I'll let you live with the knowledge that I beat you and got away, making this your second failure. You'll probably be assigned to cleaning toilets after this. You're pretty qualified for it, being that you're full of shit."

With that, I kicked his rifle farther away and hit the floor for the cargo bay before I went back over to Evans to help him dress the gunshot wound.

"I'm so sorry," I whispered. He shook his head, looking pale but not near death. The medical personnel would probably find him soon and he'd be okay. Except for getting in trouble with Bridgewater. I tried not to think about it.

"S'okay. Just get out of here alive and this new scar won't be in vain."

"I will. I promise."

The elevator doors slid open. I kissed him on the cheek and lifted the borrowed gun as I walked out only to find my worst nightmare.

"Hello, Miss Nam."

The enormous escape pod rested in front of a hatch with huge metal doors with windows, displaying the endless blackness of space, but that wasn't what caught my attention. In front of the pod stood General Bridgewater holding a gun against my brother's head. But that still wasn't what caught my attention.

Captain Hallstead held a gun against Hatwer's temple.

I felt sick. Nauseous. Scared. Helpless. It took a couple of tries for me to speak, but I somehow managed it.

"What are you doing?"

General Bridgewater arched a gray eyebrow. "Stopping you from making the biggest mistake of your life."

I glared at him. "I'm not talking to you."

Surprise stole across his face. I looked at Hallstead, tightening my grip on the gun.

"What...are...you doing?"

He spoke only two words. "My job."

"I trusted you," I whispered. "I don't trust anyone but my brother."

"Well, Hallstead always was the perfect soldier. Not even you could change that." Bridgewater lifted his other hand. He snapped his fingers, and I heard the collective sound of several rifles being cocked. I lifted my eyes to the floor above me where there were at least ten soldiers with their guns trained on me. There were ships lined up beside the launch pad where the escape pod stood, but metal crates populated the remaining space, probably filled with food and supplies. Good cover if there hadn't been almost a dozen guns pointing at me.

"It was a nice effort, really, but you're outmatched and outwitted. Put the gun down or your brother and your little alien friend die," Bridgewater said.

I narrowed my eyes at him. "If either of you even twitch, I'm going to shoot you in the face. If they die, you die."

"I've got ten rifles that say you won't make your mark. Are you willing to risk your brother's life to save some alien?"

My gaze wandered to Duke. He had a black eye and a gunshot wound in his shoulder. The very sight made my heart shudder inside my chest. My fault. Always my fault.

I took a deep breath, trying to remain steady. "We decided to do this, come hell or high water. I'm willing to die for this and so is he. Do your worst, General."

To my horror, he actually smiled. "Then I shall. Captain Hallstead?"

"Yes, sir."

"Shoot her brother in the head."

Bridgewater lowered his gun and stepped aside, gesturing toward Duke. I aimed the gun at Hallstead just as he lifted the barrel off of Hatwer. Everything in me screamed at once for him not to do it because if he did, I was going to kill him, and I didn't want to because he was the only goddamn person I had ever met who seemed to understand me.

"Don't do it," I whispered, not sure if I were talking to him or myself. "Don't make me kill you."

Silence stretched into eternity as he stood there with the gun pointed at the only family I had left, staring at the back of my brother's head with those dark gray eyes.

"You're wrong."

I started to answer, but then he turned around and aimed his gun at General Bridgewater's head.

"I'm not the perfect soldier anymore."

All of the guns in the room shifted to point at him. General Bridgewater's face turned red. "Captain, have you lost your mind?"

Hallstead smiled. "Not even a little bit."

"You are about to sacrifice your life and your entire career on a half-cocked idea from a worthless orphan brat," Bridgewater spat.

"And I'd do it again. No offense, Scarlett."

I almost smiled. "None taken."

"So here's what gonna happen—you're gonna let them on the ship and they're gonna try to save Hatwer's people. If you move a muscle out of line, I pull this trigger. I can handle life in prison. It's better than having to work for you anymore."

"He's bluffing. Shoot him."

"Am I? I think we both know at this range you'd be dead before any of them fire."

Bridgewater stared at him, then glanced at me, then at the soldiers, and then back at Hallstead. I could see the gears turning in his head as he calculated the outcome of our current predicament, and so could Hallstead.

"Drop the gun."

Bridgewater's weapon clattered to the floor.

"Now step away from the launch pad."

He walked backward with his hands up. I kept the gun pointed at him and hurried over to my brother, helping him to his feet.

"Oh God, *Oppa*, I'm so sorry. I'm so sorry," I murmured, hugging him with one arm.

He shook his head. "It's okay. We need to get going. We don't have much time."

I looked at Hatwer, who seemed confused and anxious about what was going on.

"Are you okay?"

"Yes. I am glad you are here. We were ambushed. I am sorry that I could not defend your brother."

"It's okay. Open the ship; we have to leave right now."

Hatwer went over to the ship. It was oblong and black with strange dark blue markings on the hull. The little alien reached beneath it and dug his claws in. Then, like magic, a hatch opened on the top of the vessel, sliding backward. Hatwer climbed inside first, and I helped lift my brother in next. The interior was deceptively large, but it made sense, as the Bergleute were at least seven feet tall. Just before I went in, my eyes found Hallstead's and he gave me the barest nod. I crouched behind the massive chair and told Hatwer to get us out of here.

The console of the escape pod was unlike anything I had ever seen. Instead of buttons or controls, there was a smooth, liquid-like substance that Hatwer stuck both of his hands into. The gel conformed to his claws all the way up to his forearms. The inside of the cabin lit up, and I felt a humming beneath my feet, indicating that the propulsion system came online. I pointed to the enormous metal doors across from us that led to the vast outer space and Hatwer eased the ship toward them.

Outside, Hallstead went over to the controls and opened the doors. We floated through them and into the launch room. The doors shut behind us, sealing the room, and then the other set of doors opened. Hatwer steered us through the exit and into outer space.

The pod glided forward in an amazingly smooth path away from the *Titan*. I turned my head and looked out of the window as we flew, my jaw going slack as I realized just how enormous the vessel was. The *Titan* was shaped like a cruise ship, but the number of levels on it were nearly impossible to count. We looked like a tiny teardrop in comparison to it.

"We'd better punch it," my brother said, casting a concerned look at the *Titan*. "I don't know how long Hallstead can hold them off. They'll come after us as soon as they've captured him."

He glanced at me from over the alien's head. "He had us fooled for a while. I take it that wasn't part of the plan?"

I sighed. "Hell no. Something must have gone wrong on his end and he had to improvise. I hope he'll be alright."

Duke lifted an eyebrow. "I'm the one with the gunshot wound. Your priorities kind of suck, Lettie."

"Drama queen."

He chuckled, though it wasn't very steady. Both of us were trying desperately to hide how scared we were. Humor served as a deflection method, a distraction from the horror of the reality that we were flying toward death itself.

Among the items Hallstead had left for us, there was a first aid kit, so I opened it and went to work patching up my brother's shoulder as best as I could. I cleaned the wound—it was a through-and-through, thankfully, so no slug to remove—and tied it tightly to reduce any bleeding. He was tough. He'd be alright for now, but we'd have to get back to the *Titan* soon to make sure there wasn't any internal bleeding.

If we survived this, anyway.

As promised, Hallstead had left two spacesuits for us, so we got dressed. They were a lot like the ones in the movies—form-fitting, black, with a helmet that had a thick-reinforced glass that had a light built in near the temple. Once donned, it immediately gave me readings about my environment like temperature and kept a reminder of my remaining oxygen. It also immediately linked up with the nearest suit's communications link, meaning Duke's.

I placed my hand on Hatwer's shoulder, getting his attention. "Can you let me know when the Bergleute ship comes within range?"

"Yes. What are we going to do?"

"You're going to go into your pod form and remain completely still like you're dead so that it thinks we jettisoned your body into space. He'll either come on board or just scoop up the vessel and take it back to the mothership. We'll get on, rescue your family, and take them all to New Earth."

"You are certain they will not simply destroy this vessel instead?"

I winced. "Relatively certain. A vessel is a vessel. You said yourself that the Bergleute considered us to be a threat, so they would want to know what we did with their ship and if they can learn anything else by taking it back."

"Very well."

HALLSTEAD

The cot beneath me was absurdly uncomfortable. No matter which way I tried to sit on it, my weight felt unevenly distributed. Then again, they had been chosen for their low costs. The world's governments were always in agreement about pinching pennies.

"Why'd you do it, Hallstead?"

General Bridgewater's voice was so cold it could give a polar bear the flu. I smirked, glancing at him through the prison bars. "I thought I made that clear."

Anger darkened his weathered features. "This is not the time to be a smart ass. Treason is life in prison. Do you want that? Because I can damn sure give it to you."

"Whatever makes you happy."

"Goddamn you!" he snarled. "We had a system that worked, Hallstead. Rules. Orders. What were you thinking when you let them go with the alien?"

"I was thinking that maybe the best way to serve others was doing something besides following orders."

"You're supposed to serve your *own* people, not a bunch of aliens you've never even seen," he shot back.

I shook my head. "That's your problem, General. You're too short-sighted. Protect and serve. That's my job. No one ever said it was exclusive to human beings."

He let out an ugly growl and massaged the bridge of his nose. "What's the plan, Hallstead? Just tell me what the Nam siblings are up to and we can end this right now."

"What makes you think I know?"

"Good authority. Sergeant Rosewood's in the infirmary being treated for a nasty shock, but he was well enough to tell me that Duke Nam was looking for you. That leads me to believe you're in on everything, not just letting them go. So what's the plan? Break out the Shasar and take them to New Earth?"

"You're the great strategist, sir. You figure it out."

He narrowed his eyes. "Don't think that because you served under me for two years that I will hesitate to bring someone down here to get the answers out the hard way."

"I'd never think that, sir. Because after two years of loyal service, you still don't trust, respect, or listen to me. Think of me as ammunition. When the clip's empty, you throw it away."

I stood then, walking toward the bars and stopping when we were only inches apart. "The bullet's already hit. You just haven't noticed yet."

His blue eyes burned into mine. "Then we both know where we stand. No mercy."

"I wouldn't have it any other way, sir."

He turned and walked away, snapping his fingers as he went. The guards unlocked the door and put me in handcuffs. I didn't resist. We all had a price to pay, and now it was my turn.

CHAPTER FOURTEEN

DUKE

"It's here."

Scarlett and I bent over either side of Hatwer. He had spoken in her mind and told her that the ship was approaching. I still wasn't used to the whole telepathy thing.

On the console, a bright yellow bubble formed beneath the gel and drifted toward the blue bubble that represented us.

"How far out is it?" Scarlett asked the alien. His black eyes darted to hers and a couple seconds passed and then she looked at me. "We should be getting a visual in a couple of minutes. Let's go ahead and hide."

The entrance to the vessel was a hatch in the floor activated by touch like the controls. It would be our only advantage over the alien based on how Scarlett described them. If it came aboard, we would have to act fast. I had moral qualms about killing human beings, but I didn't think I would feel bad slitting the throat of the creature that helped make me an endangered species.

"What the hell are these things?" Scarlett asked, brushing her gloved fingertips across something hanging on the wall behind her.

I stepped over the hatch, peering at what looked like two armored gauntlets. "Dunno. Maybe they're some kind of weapons?"

She glanced at me, a bit nervous. "Think it's worth a shot? No pun intended?"

"I don't see why not." I pulled one down from the peg and found a sticky note attached to the other side that read, *"Thought you might need these. –H"*

I showed it to Scarlett, unable to keep from smirking. "Gifts from your boyfriend."

She crumbled the note in her fist, rolling her eyes. "He's not my boyfriend."

Chuckling, I gave the weapon a careful examination. The Bergleute had three fingers on each hand so I had to double up my first and middle and ring and pinky stub in order for it to fit. The gauntlet went all the way up to my elbow and conformed to my skin like it was alive. Above my knuckles lay a small round spout that I assumed was the barrel for the weapon.

After determining it was safe, Scarlett slipped the other one onto her right arm. If Hallstead had recommended them, we were probably in good hands. No pun intended.

"They're here," Scarlett murmured, motioning for me to squat behind Hatwer's chair. The alien withdrew his arms from the controls and shifted into his pod state. Silence permeated the vessel. I tried to breathe as quietly as possible, my eyes glued to the hatch. Sweat beaded on my forehead as the first minute passed by and we could hear nothing. Then, I caught sight of an eerie white light above our heads. It looked like some sort of scanner. They were scanning Hatwer's body for signs of life. I knew nothing about his anatomy, but I hoped it didn't give off any vital signs in that state.

After a couple of seconds, the light vanished and we were left in darkness once again. I felt Scarlett touch my hand and tap out a question: "Should we look yet?"

I tapped back, "No, wait until we start moving again" and we kept still, scarcely breathing, eyes locked on the hatch.

Then, I felt the ship shift forward and start gliding again, though much slower than we had been going earlier. The Bergleute was bringing us in. I let out a long breath. So did Scarlett. Part One of our suicidal plan was over. Hurray.

"Where are we headed when we get on board?" I asked her.

She closed her eyes, likely concentrating on her memories. "Hatwer told me the parents and children are kept in separate cells, but he's pretty sure they're in the same location—on a bottom deck below the engines. It's much harder to reach the escape pods from that level, so that's where the prisoners are kept. But I guess that's good news for us with this bomb and all."

She patted her pocket, which made me nervous. Trust Scarlett to be casual about carrying an explosive device. "I'm thinking I should take the lead on the way out."

I started to frown but she gave me a pointed look. "You have a hole in your shoulder, Duke. Don't be a stubborn ass."

"No, that's your job," I grumbled, but I knew she was right. As much as I wanted to protect her, I knew I had become more of a liability than anything else due to my shoulder wound. It still sent a crippling pain down my arm and across my ribs every time I breathed. The blood had finally dried, making my skin itchy and one side of my clothing dark red.

"What do you know about the Bergleute's biology?"

"A few things. Carbon-based life forms, thick skin, five senses, about seven feet tall."

"What kind of vulnerabilities should we be looking for?"

She paused. "According to Hatwer's memories, they seem to keep the ship rather dark. Plus, the Shasar runs the engine room and primary weapon. The Bergs are probably vulnerable to light. I'd aim that thing—" Scarlett pointed to the weapon on my arm. "—at their eyes. The key to this operation is moving fast and not letting them catch up with us. We don't have a lot of advantages, but the element of surprise is the biggest one. If we lose that, we're screwed."

"Agreed. I suggest we keep Hatwer between us when we go. He'll be able to lead us around. How much air to the suits have in them?" I asked, nodding to the space suits hanging on a peg near the rear of the pod.

"Hallstead said five hours. It's definitely a last resort. Hatwer's memories suggest the atmosphere inside the ship should allow us to breathe, but not well. They're oxygen-based life forms, but there are a lot of other gases that they breathe in. That's why he sent the suits."

"More good news," I said with a grimace. "I don't suppose you know what kind of trouble we'll be facing if we make it out of this mess alive?"

She flashed me a dangerous smile. "Nope. Maybe the death sentence, if we're lucky."

"Excellent. I'm glad to have you for a sister."

Scarlett chuckled. "I know. I'm just the best, aren't I?"

I touched her hand, letting my voice grow serious. "I mean that, Lettie."

The smile slid away from her lips. She held my hand. "*Oppa*...don't start."

I shook my head. "I know, I know, we're not supposed to get mushy on each other, but...if we don't make it out of here, I don't want my last words to you to be some stupid cliché or a joke. I love you."

"I love you too. Thanks for always being there to save me."

"Thanks for letting me save you." I kissed the back of her hand and she smiled again. In the darkness, I could have sworn I saw a tear at the edge of her eye, but I let it go because there was an eerie blue light filling the cabin of the pod. We were approaching the mothership. It wouldn't be long now before we docked.

The light poured in around us where we sat, and I could see faint shadows here and there that told me we had entered their airspace. I wanted to stick my head around Hatwer's seat, but it would give us away. Even with thousands of vicious aliens around me, my curiosity still ate at me like a parasite. Silly, but true.

After some time, I felt the vessel slowing down and the blue light switched to white. Scarlett and I met eyes, and I nodded. She crept toward the far end of the hatch while I stayed where I crouched, lifting my gauntlet. My heart thudded in my chest like a trapped animal against the bars of its cage. This was it.

The pod settled on the ground and its propulsion automatically shut off, swallowing us in darkness. We waited for a handful of seconds and nothing happened. I mouthed to Scarlett that we'd jump out on the count of three and she held her breath, watching my lips.

On three, I leapt out of the pod, weapon ready, steeled with determination, ready to face the threat in front of me with my sister at my back. We were Dante and Virgil at the first circle of Hell.

Out of the frying pan and into the fire.

The interior of the docking bay was dark, but there was a circle of odd blue light that reminded me of the bioluminescent lights of deep-sea fish. The ship that had towed us was parked a few feet from ours, but nothing jumped out of it, so it may have been remote-piloted. I wheeled around in every direction, my pulse hammering in my throat, expecting to see one of the towering aliens, but I didn't see any. It could be they were en route, so I gestured to Scarlett and Hatwer to move off the platform.

The docking bay was huge and reminded me of an airplane hangar. It had three levels with much larger vessels than the escape pods on the ground floor, then smaller battleships stored above the big ones.

We walked over to a raised panel in front of the landing platform to see a screen similar to the one inside the pod. It had two dots indicating the active ships that had just landed. There were also colorful buttons with symbols I obviously couldn't decipher, so I glanced at Scarlett.

"Ask him if he understands how these controls work."

Scarlett looked at Hatwer, then replied, "He says this button here—" She pointed to an oval white button toward the top of the console. "—will remove the seal between us and space. The ships automatically breach through some kind of sealant, almost, that protects the ship from what's outside of it without creating a vacuum, but it can be opened. The green one is for communicating with the deck, the red one is for the prison level, the blue one is for the engine room, and the black one is for the weapons vault."

"Okay," I said after memorizing the symbol for the engine room. "I think you and Hatwer should head for the prison level and I'll take the bomb to the engine room."

I glanced above us at the ships that seemed built for passengers. "We'll need to load the Shasar on those or on as many escape pods as possible. They need to get far away from here but keep communications open so we can tell them where to go once we've escaped. The Bergleute are definitely going to give chase and we can't lead them to New Earth, so we'll have to figure out a rendezvous point away from the *Titan*. If we succeed and we blow up this battle cruiser, we'll have to head back and face the music. If the ship isn't completely destroyed, we're gonna have to try and distract them to chase after us so they don't target the Shasar that are escaping."

Scarlett nodded tightly. "Got it. Don't forget that there might be biometric scans to enter the engine room, so you may need to pop a Berg quietly and use it to open the engine room. Things are probably going to get messy once we reach the prison cells, but I'll try to stay undetected until then."

She held out her hand. I gripped it and squeezed her fingers. "Give 'em hell, Lettie."

Scarlett grinned fiercely. "You too, *Oppa*. Good luck."

With that, we split up.

And I prayed it wouldn't be the last time I ever saw her.

SCARLETT

If nothing else, being a thief prepared me for being stealthy in enemy territory. Though I obviously never thought the enemy would be seven-foot-tall vicious aliens.

I tried to keep my footsteps light and my breathing even lighter as Hatwer and I made our way toward the nearest stairwell. I kept the gauntlet weapon at the ready to fire at any moment. I didn't know what would happen when I did, but I hoped it would be effective. The heads-up display in my peripheral along the helmet's lining told me about the environment. The Bergleute's ship had an atmosphere that was only partially oxygen; it had other elements mixed in for them to be able to breathe. I had a feeling the living quarters and the work environment of the Shasar would have completely breathable air since Hatwer seemed fine when he was aboard the *Titan*.

The hallway that went to the stairwell was lit with bright circles in the ceiling and was forty feet long and about twenty feet wide. The halls had large plaques with alien writing on them indicating where they led. I couldn't quite tell if the ship's interior was made of stone or metal. We reached the corner and I motioned for Hatwer to stop as I checked it on both sides. Clear. For now, anyway.

We turned right based on the sign and found the stairs—which looked like regular stairs since the Bergs walked upright—then descended. Once we reached the landing before the last flight, I peeked around the corner.

And there stood two Bergleute.

They wore plated armor on their chests as well as their thighs and shins. I spotted some kind of device attached to their wrists that looked as if they were made to remote control something. It could be they accessed the doors on each floor with the wrist devices, but it could also be how they spoke to each other long distances. Their mouths didn't appear to be capable of producing words. The Berg in Hatwer's nightmarish memory had communicated through telepathy, so I postulated that their language aloud would probably be a series of sounds like that of a cricket.

I turned to Hatwer, my voice low. "Talk to me about being an Empath. Can the Bergs hear my thoughts?"

"No. Telepathy only works if they are aware another being is present and they focus their energy to connect minds. If they see you, then yes, they could attempt

to communicate with you through your empathic abilities, but if they don't know you are there, they cannot."

"Got it. Can they communicate aloud?"

"Yes. I am afraid I do not know much of their language."

"That's okay. I have an idea. It's gonna happen pretty fast. I'm going to make some noise to draw one or both of them out and then I'll open fire. Hopefully, this thing doesn't have a loud discharge noise and it won't draw any attention yet. However, I don't know if an alarm will go off when we open the prison barracks, so as soon as you can, grab their weapons. Your people may be peaceful, but I'm sure we can find a couple willing to help us fight."

Hatwer touched my left wrist gently. *"Be careful."*

I smiled to cover up how afraid I felt. "I will. I promise."

I took a deep breath and eased my way onto the first step around the corner from the landing. They wouldn't be able to see me just yet with the stairwell overhang in the way. And I was counting on it.

I blew air through the side of my cheek. It created a weird creaking noise. I heard a couple of guttural clicks from the two guards below.

Then footsteps.

I crouched and aimed the gauntlet weapon.

The second the Berg's horned head appeared, I squeezed my hand into a closed fist.

A red beam shot out and blew it to meaty green chunks.

Its huge, heavy body slumped back on the floor. The other Berg made a furious clicking noise and rushed forward. I tucked my head and rolled down the rest of the stairs as it opened fire, missing me by mere inches. As soon as I hit the floor at the bottom of the steps, I rolled onto my belly and fired at the Berg's kneecaps. The armor didn't quite cover them and the beam punctured both of its knees. It screeched in pain and hit the floor on its side. I fired twice. Both shots took out the upper part of its skull, leaving greenish-brown brain matter to leak out.

Shaking, I pushed onto my feet and scooped up both of their weapons, then called out to Hatwer. "All clear."

Hatwer peeked around the corner, clearly nervous—and who wouldn't be?—but then descended the stairs. He stepped over the bodies, and I handed him one of the guns, then turned to the terminal beside the door to the prisoners' living quarters. There was another oval blue panel like the one I'd seen before on the ship. I glanced at the dead Berg on the floor. It looked around the size of its hand, so I dragged the alien over to one side and heaved its giant arm up enough to press its palm flat onto the gooey panel.

And just like that, the door opened.

"Thank God I've watched so many movies," I muttered as I unsnapped the device from its forearm and affixed it to my left arm. It had adjustable straps, thank God, so it wouldn't fall off as I moved. I stuck my head just inside the open door to see two hallways on either side of the exit. No other Bergs in the prison wing, at least for now, but I couldn't assume I knew when they switched shifts, so I motioned for Hatwer to follow me.

And I finally met the rest of the Shasar.

The two hallways appeared to be split between the adults and the younglings. The adults were housed in huge, wide cells with a glowing forcefield that I suspected would electrocute anyone who touched it based on the humming sound it made and the static that popped under my suit and made the hairs on my arm stand up. The adult Shasar were around my height rather than Hatwer's small stature. Each had different dark green patterns and markings on their shell-like exoskeletons, like how leopards had unique spots. As I looked at them, I noticed one group was slightly bigger and more muscular than the other, so I gleaned they were like us and had male and female species. The men were in one cell, the women in the cell opposite, crowded together for warmth since they had no bed, blankets, or anything that would keep them warm on this frigid ship.

Once I walked into their line of sight, all eyes were on me. I counted thirty men and twenty women. Christ. They had it even worse than we did.

When Hatwer was visible beside me, they all stood up and hurried toward the edge of the cage, clearly trying to communicate with him. "Do you see your parents?" I asked.

"Yes!" he said, sounding both heartbroken and overjoyed. *"They survived."*

"Thank God. Tell everyone to stand back; I'm gonna open the cells."

Hatwer raised his arms, as if quieting a rabble I couldn't hear, and the Shasar in both cells obeyed, stepping away from the forcefield that held them captive. I headed over to the panel on the side of the wall of the women's cage, examining it. I saw markings that matched one of the buttons on the Berg's forearm device and pressed it. The forcefield powered down immediately, and the female Shasar flooded outside of their cell. One of them raced over to Hatwer and embraced him, dark tears running down her face, her forehead pressed to his. My throat tightened as I saw them, but I pushed the feeling of envy away and went over to the men's cell and set them free as well.

One of the male Shasar fell to his knees and hugged Hatwer, wrapping his arms around his mate as well. Many of them did the same—hugging their long lost loved ones—until the hall was crowded with Shasar reuniting with one another.

I went to the other side of the hallway to the children. There were at least forty of them, either Hatwer's size or smaller, separated by gender as well. I freed them and motioned with one hand to encourage them to come along. They were too scared to move at first, but then the adults came over and plucked them up, which gave them the courage to leave their cells. The parents matched up with their children and then I asked Hatwer to address them on my behalf.

"This is my friend," Hatwer told his people. *"Her name is Scarlett. She is here to help us escape. We must listen to her so that we can get out of here. We need at least two volunteers to help keep everyone safe. It will require us to harm our enemies. I am sorry, but there is no other way. I know that we practice peace on our world, but our captors do not and we must act accordingly."*

The Shasar glanced at one another, seeming unsure. *"I know it is dangerous, but Scarlett protected me and she will protect you too."*

Hatwer looked at me. He had no facial expression, but I could somehow see the fondness in his eyes. *"I trust her with my life."*

And that was the moment that I knew I'd do anything to keep him safe.

Hatwer's parents both stepped forward. They looked to their son, then to me. *"They want to know if they have your permission to communicate with you."*

I nodded to them politely. "Yes, I accept."

Their eyes focused on me intensely for a few seconds. Just like before with the first time I spoke to Hatwer, a strange sensation seemed to flutter over my scalp. His mother spoke first, her tone in my head sounding both gentle and strong. *"Hello, Scarlett. I am Wyla."*

His father spoke to me next, his voice firm and reassuring. *"And I am Gendon. We are so grateful to you for saving our son. We hope we will be worthy of protecting you in return."*

I smiled at them. "I know you will be."

Hatwer and I handed them the guns. "Pull the trigger to fire. Make sure the barrel is never pointed at one of your people, only at theirs. My brother, Duke, will meet us in the hangar. We'll get everyone aboard the ships, and you'll need to get as far away from this ship as you can. We intend to blow it up, or at the very least, disable it so they can't pursue us. Do you understand?"

"*Yes*," they said in unison.

"I'm going to be up front. You two will guard the rear of the group so that no one comes up behind us. Keep everyone together. Don't let anyone wander off. Most importantly, if something happens to me, I want you to keep going. Don't stop, don't wait for me, don't come back for me —just go."

Hatwer's eyes widened. "*You...want us to leave you behind if you are hurt or captured?*"

I nodded. "You have to, Hatwer. I can't risk everyone's safety. Leave me behind if it comes to that."

"*But—*"

I touched his shoulder gently. "It's okay. Your people have made enough sacrifices. It's time someone made one for you." I looked up at the Shasar. "Everyone ready?"

Wyla and Gendon observed the crowd, then said, "*Yes, they are ready.*"

I straightened up and prepared to open the door. "Then let's get the hell out of here."

CHAPTER FIFTEEN

"I apologize for the abruptness of this assembly," General Bridgewater said as he stared down at the many faces of the military recruits seated in the auditorium in front of him. It had a long aisle down the center. The men sat on one side, the women on the other, their superior officers standing on the outskirts at attention. "But unfortunately, we have encountered a serious setback in our current venture toward a potential planet that we can inhabit."

He waited for the murmurs to quiet before continuing. "As you might have noticed, Captain Hallstead is absent. He is indisposed at the moment. He has been colluding with two stowaways aboard this ship. In short, we were contacted by an alien who claimed to be seeking help after having escaped the Bergleute warship. It came here and made contact with one of the stowaways. We brought her in to let her translate for the alien and it took over her mind. She shot one of our men and convinced her brother, the other stowaway, to steal the ship and lead the Bergleute back to the *Titan*."

General Bridgewater stopped pacing and faced the shocked assembly before him. "It pains me to say it, but somehow, she managed to corrupt Captain Hallstead into allowing them to escape. We now face total destruction as a result. I will be frank with you: this assignment is not going to be easy and there is high risk involved. We have done our best to continue your combat education, but the time has come for us to take up arms and prevent this threat from wiping out the rest of humanity. You will be deployed to form a perimeter around the *Titan* and you are to defend this ship with your lives. We cannot allow the return of this stowaway and the alien who corrupted her. You will shoot to kill, without hesitation, or everything is lost."

He turned on his heel and paced to the other side of the stage, his hands folded behind his back, his expression grave. "If it turns out that the Bergleute's warship is en route, we will have to leave you behind and move the *Titan* to somewhere safe. If that should happen, you will be given instructions on what to do and how to survive until we have escaped their detection and you can return to the ship safely. Be prepared in the event that the contingency plan needs to be enacted. Remember: it's for the good of the human race. The needs of the many outweigh the needs of the few."

Bridgewater faced them again. "It is an honor to serve with you. Dismissed."

"What the hell," Sam muttered, his face ashen. "Duke was a stowaway this whole time?"

"Makes sense," Han grumbled, crossing his arms. "I always knew something was off about him."

Sam licked his dry lips, frowning. "I know, but...Hallstead? Really? He's the most do-right man I've ever met. Might as well have been Captain America."

"Bridgewater said the alien corrupted the girl. Perhaps it did the same to him."

Sam shook his head. "That doesn't smell right to me, Han. Come on, you can't tell me you're just gonna let them feed you that bullshit story."

"Why would he lie?"

"I don't know, but whatever he just told us was a crock of shit. I may have only known Duke a few days, but he's no traitor. Maybe he's not supposed to be here like all the people we lost back on Earth, but I'll be damned if I believe he deserves to die."

"He's not one of us," Han said tersely. "Never was."

"So what? He could've tattled on you about the bug, but he didn't. You're telling me that doesn't count for something?"

Han's jaw clenched. He continued staring at the spot where General Bridgewater had been standing as they waited for the lines to filter out of the seats so they too could leave. He glanced at Sam. "I will admit that Hallstead would not risk his career and his life for nothing. Maybe Duke

159

betrayed us, maybe he didn't, but what do you expect us to do about it? We're foot soldiers. We have no authority. We just do what we're told."

"The kind of person who tells you to take orders without question is the wrong person to be leading us," Sam said, narrowing his eyes. "You heard him. Bridgewater would sacrifice our entire squadron without blinking an eye. If he sends us out there to die, what'll become of the people left on the *Titan*? I know we're only the infantry and the more seasoned soldiers are still aboard, but we outnumber them. If the Bergs get within the *Titan's* vicinity, they're gonna finish what they started."

Han grimaced. "What do you suggest?"

"We dig into what's really going on here. See if we can get to Hallstead and find out the truth."

"That's suicide."

Sam gestured to the infantry filing out of the auditorium. "So is this! I'd rather die informed and making my own choice than because of Bridgewater's lies. What about you?"

Han searched his eyes for a long moment. He glanced at the men and women around him. They were his age. Too many of them looked scared and unsure. If they went to war, what would be the cost?

Han sighed. "How do we get to Hallstead?"

Sam grinned. "Easy-peasy."

Then he collapsed onto the floor.

"Is this a common occurrence as far as you know?" the nurse practitioner asked as she held Sam's wrist and checked her watch. She was a short-haired brunette in her forties, fit, wearing blue scrubs and booties. Han had fireman-carried Sam to the infirmary after the initial hubbub in the auditorium. Since the other recruits had seen him faint before, they trusted Han to bring him there alone instead of waiting for someone to find a stretcher.

Han shrugged. "Not sure. It's only happened twice so far, but maybe he has some kind of undiagnosed condition. Maybe it's a side effect of being in space. Could be stress from our training program, too. It's been pretty intense lately."

"Mm. Well, his pulse is normal, and I didn't detect anything unusual during the initial intake exam. My best guess is low blood sugar or anemia." She glanced over her shoulder at the other patients. "We'll keep him under observation for another hour or two. Would you mind staying with him and finding me once he wakes up?"

"Sure, I can do that."

"Thanks. It's a big help." She tucked Sam's arm under the blanket again and then left, pulling the curtain around their bed for some extra privacy.

And once she was gone, Sam opened his eyes. "I'd like to thank the Academy."

Han arched an eyebrow. Sam sighed in disappointment. "Duke would've gotten that reference. Alright, so here's the plan: once it's clear, I'm gonna sneak out of here and try to get to the prison level."

"How are you going to do that? There will be at least one guard."

"They gave us the *Titan's* layout during orientation, so I know where the guards' armor and things are stored. I can take a spare one and tell the guard on duty to take a break and see if I can talk to Hallstead."

Han exhaled through his nose. "Even if you somehow pulled that off before the nurse gets back, what do you expect to find? If he confirms that Bridgewater was lying, what do you think you're going to do?"

"Save him," Sam said firmly. "Duke's one of us, man. We can't just let him die because Bridgewater's trying to cover his own ass."

"What does it matter? Even if you save him and his sister, you'll be thrown in jail right alongside them for treason."

"Look around you, Han. Tell me we're not already in a prison."

Han swallowed thickly. He couldn't deny that he'd already begun to feel the claustrophobia of the ship's interior. No sky, no wind, no outside world. Just a cold ship on all sides and millions of unfamiliar stars.

"You don't have to help me," Sam said as he sat up and pulled off the thin covers. "I can do it on my own, but I think deep down, you know something's off about Bridgewater's story and about Hallstead's incarceration. If I get caught, that's on me and you can play innocent and still go on with the mission. It's up to you from here."

He pulled on his boots and angled himself near the edge of the sheet, watching the general movement in the infirmary.

"I must be losing my mind," Han muttered. Then, louder, he said, "I have a better idea. Less dangerous, too."

Sam eyed him. "I'm listening."

"The general said one of the men was shot when the Nam siblings were escaping the ship with the alien. Why don't we find out if he knows anything first before you try to talk to Hallstead?"

Sam blinked. "Huh. That's pretty smart, but how will we know which guy it is?"

"I don't think anyone else aboard has gunshot wounds, so he should be pretty easy to identify based on his chart. We'll wait for the nurses to leave for their rounds and then see if we can talk to him. If not, then we can go with Plan B."

Sam smiled and slapped him on the shoulder. "Glad you're on board."

"For now," Han grunted, then headed to the other side of the curtain to watch. After several minutes, the nurses left the room. The two soldiers slipped from behind the curtain and began checking the charts on the patients. There were ten beds total in the room counting the one Sam had been occupying, each with their curtain pulled for privacy and to let them get some rest.

"This guy," Sam murmured, pointing to the paperwork attached to a clear adhesive pouch on the outside of the curtain. "GSW to the gut, but he's been out of surgery for a few hours."

Han frowned, pointing a thumb at the bed across from him. "But this man was shot as well. Why did Bridgewater only say one guard had been shot?"

Sam chewed his lip. "Maybe he's trying to cover something up? Someone had to help Scarlett get to the alien on her way out, so maybe Hallstead had an inside man."

He crept over to the side of the curtain nearest to the bed and peeked. He nodded to Han. "He's handcuffed to the bed, so I think this is our guy."

They checked again to be sure no one saw them and then walked around the curtain.

Evans lay in his hospital bed in a gown, his upper body bulky with bandages underneath it. He had an IV in his arm, and the heart monitor attached to him beeped every few seconds. His dark hair was sweaty and unkempt, his skin still slightly pale after what he'd been through.

"Hey," Sam said quietly as he nudged the guard's shoulder. "Wake up."

Evans stirred and slowly opened his eyes. Sam smiled. "Sorry to bother you, but we're here to ask you a couple questions about what went down with Scarlett and Duke Nam."

Evans glanced between the two of them, his expression hardening. "Did Bridgewater send you? Is this an interrogation? If so, you're missing a washcloth and a bucket of water."

"No, it's not like that," Sam assured him. "We're actually a couple of foot soldiers who worked with Duke."

Evans eyed them. "Name and rank."

They told him. "Ah, then you're in Rosewood's group. That checks out, at least. Why do you want to know what happened?"

"Bridgewater ordered us to defend the *Titan* and kill Duke and Scarlett if they try to board the ship."

Evans' brown eyes widened. "Shit. What about Hallstead?"

Han shook his head. "He's in prison for treason."

"Damn it. I was afraid this would happen." He shifted to sit up straighter in the bed, the handcuffs jangling noisily as he positioned himself. "If I tell you, what is it you plan to do?"

"Not shoot them out of the sky, for one," Sam said. "We want to know the truth. Bridgewater's about to sacrifice our fleet if the Bergs' warship is on its way here. We want to help our infantry too, if we can. There's got to be a better way, but we can't act unless we know all the facts."

"Before I say anything…if this goes tits up, your necks are on the line. Bridgewater will throw you in the slammer same as Hallstead."

"We know," Han said. "But what the general is doing isn't right. What makes us human beings is not being as barbaric as the Bergleute."

Evans nodded. "Alright. Well, I'll try to condense as much as I know, but here goes."

He filled them in. Sam sat on the stool beside the bed, listening intently. Han paced back and forth, also keeping an eye to make sure the nurses hadn't returned yet.

"Best case scenario is the Nam siblings succeed and either blow up or cripple the warship and then take the Shasar somewhere safe," Evans said as he finished up. "Worst-case scenario is they get captured and the Bergs come after the *Titan*."

Sam shook his head, his jaw clenched. "I knew it. I knew Bridgewater's story didn't add up. All those innocent lives and he's willing to just let them die instead of trying to help."

"It's tactical," Han said. "But cold-hearted given that the little alien risked everything to get to us."

He faced Evans. "What can we do?"

"Your best bet is to try to get to Scarlett and Duke and warn them that if they try to return to the *Titan*, the infantry has orders to shoot them on sight. After that, it's up to you. You wouldn't have the resources to survive in space on your own, but if the Shasar have knowledge of things we don't, you may luck out and be able to survive without coming back here to be imprisoned. In fact, I'd bet they'd welcome you with open arms."

"But what about Bridgewater?" Sam demanded. "He's just gonna remain in command and not pay for lying to our troops and risking their lives?"

Evans winced. "That's how the cookie crumbles, kid. He's the highest authority on the ship."

"And there isn't a system of checks and balances?"

Evans shook his head. Han paused, thinking. "Let me ask you this: aside from the guards and Rosewood, did any of the other superior officers for the infantry know the whole story?"

"Probably not, I'd imagine. It was a closed loop. Only the security guards and some of the relevant medical personnel knew the truth. If the other officers below him motioned to remove him from command for violating code of conduct by manipulating our troops into military action under unnecessary circumstances, it might hold, but it depends on how you'd get them the proof that everything I just told you is true. There'd have to be hard evidence he's lying, and I'm sure the few people in the loop have already been intimidated into silence."

"Evidence," Han muttered. Then he snapped his fingers and looked at Sam. "The bug. What if we bugged him and gave them the recording? Would that be enough?"

"It might be, but how do we get him to admit to everything?" Sam asked.

"Hallstead's still in interrogation, I'd imagine," Evans said. "Bridgewater's probably going to go check on their progress. If you can bug him before he gets there, you might have a shot."

Evans then nodded to his gear, which was folded up on the chair beside his bed. "You can wear my stuff as a disguise and use my credentials to get to that level; it shouldn't flag it until it's too late since I haven't been tried for treason yet while I'm in here recovering. You'd better get moving."

"I'll go," Sam said as he hurried over to the chair. "Han was almost in trouble with Bridgewater earlier so he might recognize him, but I'm just a small fry."

He redressed quickly. "If I get the evidence we need, who can I trust?"

"Anybody but Rosewood. I don't think they've had enough time to replace Hallstead yet, but the next one in line to take over would probably be Colonel Sierra Rochester. We didn't get everyone off the Earth the way we planned, so there are gaps in between military rankings. She's a straight shooter like Hallstead and she'll hear you out. Plus, if I remember correctly, they served together. She's a friend of his, so I'm sure she's already trying to put in a good word for him and stop the enhanced interrogation."

"Okay." Sam took a deep breath. "Here goes nothing. Thanks, Evans. I'm sorry things went down the way they did."

"Just make sure Scarlett makes it out okay," Evans said firmly. "I owe her one."

"I'll do my best." Sam glanced at Han, who nodded to him from where he stood by the curtain.

"You're clear. Good luck."

Sam crossed himself. "Amen."

And then he slipped out of the infirmary.

CHAPTER SIXTEEN

HALLSTEAD

High pain tolerance was one of my most valued talents. I was grateful for it. In the past, I'd been able to succeed where others failed because of it. My fellow soldiers sometimes joked that I was the Terminator; I just wouldn't stop until the job was done, come hell or high water.

And high pain tolerance was the only reason I was still conscious.

I couldn't even guess how long they'd been waterboarding me. Or, rather, how long *he* had been waterboarding me. I'd briefly seen the hesitation on one of the guard's faces before they put the washcloth over my face.

But there was no hesitation on Staff Sergeant Rosewood's face. He'd wanted to do this to me. After all, the Nam siblings had made a fool of him not once but twice, and I was their accomplice, so in his book, nothing he did to me was wrong. It was retribution in his eyes.

At whatever point, Rosewood stopped. My ears barely registered much, but I'd heard someone knock on the door. I took in as much air as I possibly could—and it wasn't much—to keep from passing out. While I lay there coughing wetly, I heard Rosewood, then a female voice that sounded a lot like my colleague, Colonel Rochester.

"What?" Rosewood demanded.

"This has gone on long enough," Rochester said tightly. "If he was going to crack, he would have already. I'm not going to stand here and tolerate this any longer. You get him off that table and back in his cell."

"I'm under orders, Colonel," Rosewood said smugly. "Your discomfort is noted, but I'm not about to disobey the general. He told me to get answers, and I haven't gotten them yet. I'm going to continue until he talks."

Movement, as if he were walking away, but then I heard cloth rustling. "Take your hand off me, Rochester."

Steel entered her voice as it lowered into an angry hiss. "I served with that man for five years. He is an upstanding human being and one hell of a soldier. I don't care if you're under orders. I'll take the heat myself, but you are not going back into that room to torture a good man. Not while I'm here."

"You wanna throw down, Colonel? I'll put you in the cell right next to him for treason."

"I'd like to see you try."

A caustic silence fell. "Fine. I'm gonna take my lunch break. See if you can do any better."

Vindictive anger filled his voice like a hive of bees. "But if I come back and he still hasn't talked, we're back in business."

I heard the thump of the bucket being dropped and then more footsteps. A door closed in the distance. Rochester sighed. I heard her shoes on the hard floor as she walked over to my table.

The restraints on my arms loosened, then she peeled the wet washcloth off my face. My eyes burned like hell, so I could just barely see her. She was around my age, with warm brown eyes that matched her skin, her wavy hair held back in a bun, fit and trim like any good soldier. She smiled at me, her voice a bit hoarse. "Hey, stranger."

I gave her a weak, crooked grin in return. "Sierra."

She walked over to the table on the other side of the room and came back with a towel. She dried my face and then helped me sit up. She held out a small, shallow pan, and I heaved up a good bit of the water in my stomach and lungs, exhausted by the time I was done. Everything hurt. I ached in ways I'd never known before, and I was so grateful for a second of peace that I wanted to hug her. I didn't, but I wanted to more than anything.

She draped a fresh towel around my neck to help a little with the ice-cold temperature of the room and then she stepped back with another tired sigh. "You don't deserve this, Travis."

I shrugged. "My own fault. I decided to help them. I knew there'd be consequences."

"Even so, this is...wrong. To do this to one of our own, even if you went against orders and committed treason. We're all we have left of the human race and this is how we treat each other?"

I snorted. "You've always been an idealist, Sierra. Nothing's changed but the world dying. People are still people. And they're still terrible."

She crossed her arms and shook her head. "We have to evolve if we're ever going to survive out here. Bridgewater's out of line."

"Hey," I said, narrowing my eyes at her. "Don't you start that talk. I don't want you on this table after me, alright?"

"You know I'm right," she said hotly. "What kind of leader does this to his men?"

"Someone focused on the big picture," I grunted. "His favorite phrase, 'The needs of the many outweigh the needs of the few.' Which is ironic since Mr. Spock would despise him if they ever met."

"Tell me about it." Rochester nodded toward the door. "Rosewood will kill you. And won't lose any sleep over it, either. Isn't there something you can tell him to get him to back off and just let you be?"

"Not how it works, I'm afraid. If I give them away, then everything is lost."

She studied me. "You really believe that? Enough to give your life up for it?"

"Yeah. I do."

"Damn you, Travis. I don't want you dead. You're my friend. I haven't got many of those left. We lost a lot of the good people we knew when the Bergs struck. I don't want you to join them."

"And, what, you're the good cop in this interrogation?"

"No. I just...if there is some kind of middle ground, then I want to find it. I know you want to protect the Nam siblings, but you can't do that if you're dead, Travis."

"They don't need me. They've gotten by without me this long."

"It's not just about them. *We* need you. The people on this ship need someone with a heart, not someone who quotes a Vulcan without understanding what he's even saying."

"That hurts my feelings."

Rochester jumped as she faced the open doorway to see General

Bridgewater standing there. She saluted him. "Sir. Sorry, sir. That was rude of me to say."

"You're entitled to your opinion, Colonel," the general said as he walked the rest of the way inside. "Just make sure you won't be overheard next time."

He folded his hands behind his back. "If you don't mind, I'd like a moment alone with him."

"Yes, sir." Rochester sent me one last meaningful look and then left. The hesitation in her eyes was touching. I hadn't had anyone care about me in a while, not since...

I winced. *Shit. Dangerous thinking there. Stay focused.*

Bridgewater glanced at the door after Rochester shut it behind her. "That's one thing I could never do, you know. Be relatable. Personable. Have my men trust and like me."

"Gotta have a personality first."

Bridgewater let out a dry laugh as he walked over to face me. "Point taken. I've always envied you. You know how to rally the troops. Earn their trust and respect. Me? I'm always the authority figure. The designated villain of the story. I make the decisions that hurt some people and spare the others. It's a lousy job, but somebody's gotta do it."

"Yeah, well, forgive me if I don't applaud you for it. Now what do you want?"

"Bumped into Rosewood on his way to lunch. He hasn't reported that he made any progress, so I thought I'd stop by."

I wiped away some of the water running down into my eyes, unable to help sounding bitter. "Wanna pick up where he left off? I thought you don't like getting your hands dirty."

"We've all got dirty hands, Hallstead. No one serves this country without dirtying them."

"This country?" I said with the utmost scorn. "You mean the one floating through the abyss in a million pieces? Wake up, General. It's all gone. The only person you're serving now is yourself."

He glared at me. "At least I'm in service to someone worthy. You'd throw a brilliant career and your life away on a couple of orphan brats."

I smirked. "A couple of orphan brats who outwitted you."

A sour look entered his features. I kept going. "And that's why you can't let this go. You know that what they're doing makes sense, but you can't handle it because it's not part of the plan. You want everything neat and clean, no loose ends, no accidents. Life doesn't work that way,

General. You can't just see everything in black and white. You're going to get more people killed thinking like that and we can't afford to lose anyone when this is all that's left of the species."

Something occurred to me. I sat up straighter, scrutinizing him. "That's why you're here, isn't it? You want to bargain with me."

Bridgewater crossed his arms. "I would be willing to forgo trying you for treason if you tell me the Nam siblings' plan."

I stared at him. And laughed heartily. "Wow," I said, shaking my head. "So you really don't know me after all, huh?"

"You're making a mistake—"

"And it's mine to make!" I barked. "So go get your lackey back and keep waterboarding me, 'cause I'd rather die than spend another second talking to you."

Bridgewater exhaled through his nose. "You never learn. This is the long game, Captain."

My mouth flew open to insult him again, but then I noticed something. Bridgewater always wore his full military regalia, badges, awards, and all, over the suit.

And there was a tiny little thing that could be mistaken for a button on his right shoulder.

A bug.

Someone bugged him.

Quickly, I rephrased what I'd been about to say so as not to tip him off. "Oh, yeah? What's the long game, General? Please enlighten me."

"Because of your selfishness, I now have to assume the Nam siblings are going to come back here with those filthy aliens in tow. And I have deployed the infantry to protect the *Titan* and blow them out of the sky if they try to come aboard."

I seethed. "You fuckin' coward."

"It's us or them, Captain."

"Your fear is not an excuse to murder two civilians trying to help. The Shasar could be the key to our survival out here and you want them dead just because they're the unknown factor that blows your best laid plans to kingdom come. They could unlock the universe for all we know but you'd rather kill them so you don't have to face the fact that deep down, you're nothing more than an empty suit."

Bridgewater gritted his teeth. "I am doing this for the good of everyone here, including you, so you ought to show a little respect."

"Oh, yeah? Did you tell the infantry the truth? Or did you lie to them so they'd be compliant?"

"I told them what they needed to hear and that's it. Everyone is not privy to truth on this vessel, and I am going to keep it that way." He took a step closer. "Now for the last time, Captain Hallstead, tell me what they have planned." His eyes narrowed to slits, his voice a whisper. "Or I will have you executed."

"Go right ahead. See what happens. I bet it won't even take twenty-four hours for the troops to mutiny and throw you out of an airlock. I'm the only thing between you and oblivion, General."

He stared me down for another moment and then straightened up, his voice as ice-cold as the room around me. "We'll see."

Bridgewater strode for the door, but then paused and gave me an askance glance, his smile poison. "Come to think of it, maybe I won't kill the girl, Scarlett. Better to let her see your corpse first before I jettison her into space right next to you in the casket. *Alive.*"

I lunged for him without thinking. "You son of a bitch!"

With my legs still strapped to the table, all it did was lurch and groan under my weight. Bridgewater motioned for the two guards waiting outside and then left as they wrestled me back onto the table and strapped me down again.

I had to get out of here. I had to protect them.

I had to protect *her.*

CHAPTER SEVENTEEN

DUKE

Darkness seemed to be the name of the game with the Bergleute. Beneath the suit, I was covered in cold sweat as I crept around the ship headed for the engine room. Looming shadows caused me to dart into small corners to hide and give Scarlett and Hatwer as much time as possible to free the Shasar. I knew at some point our cover would get blown and we'd have to fight our way out, but I prayed it wouldn't be soon.

My new problem was that there was a long corridor over a set of cooling towers. The area was not lit well, and if one of the aliens came upon me from either direction, I'd be screwed. It would take at least close to a minute to cross it even while hurrying, so I parked it in an alcove by some of the electrical panels and tried to think it through. What I wouldn't give for an invisibility function on this spacesuit.

I shut my eyes and tried to slow my heartbeat. "Think, Duke. Think."

I thunked my head back against the wall, opening my eyes. Then I tilted my head slightly as I noticed that above me were metal panels. Not just metal panels.

Air ducts.

Jackpot.

The wall to my left was mostly whatever version of electricity they used, so there were control panels with lights monitoring the ship's systems and some bolted to the wall. I set my booted foot on one that was waist-high and hauled myself higher, setting my knee against the corner of the wall. I shimmied my way up to the ceiling—a good nine or so feet from the floor—and then pushed up against the corner of one ceiling panel. It wasn't bolted in; it fit like a ceiling tile. I applied my strength and it came up off the hinges on one side.

However, the metal let out a loud screech when I pushed it up and I heard suspicious clicking noises, then heavy footsteps. Shit!

I wedged my foot against the side of the wall and heaved myself through the opening as fast as I could, the wound in my shoulder burning white-hot with pain, blood oozing into the bandages from the extra strain. I slithered into the air vent and then pushed the panel closed again, sliding out of sight barely a second before the alien rounded the corner into the alcove. I kept perfectly still and didn't even breathe, listening intently.

Silence now.

Then, after half a minute, the footsteps echoed away toward the corridor.

Thank God.

I flipped on the light in the visor of my helmet. Dust coated the inside of the air duct in thick patches and clumps, swaying with the mix of oxygen and other gases that the aliens needed to breathe. It was narrow, but I could wriggle forward using my elbows and forearms as long as I kept my legs straight. It took everything in me not to repeat any lines from *Die Hard*.

I belly-crawled around the corner to the section above the long corridor to find that the air duct indeed followed it parallel and there was enough space for me to fit. After I got through, I'd hang a right and make it into the engine room.

I flattened my hands to the walls on either side of me and pushed my way through the duct, wincing and slowing at times when I could hear my gear scraping against the bottom. I got about halfway there when I heard another Bergleute approaching and froze in place, breathing light, listening hard.

The cooling towers below created a whirlwind of noise, so it was hard to distinguish, but I knew from the distant thump of their boots and the unnerving bug-like noises they emitted. It was worse than I thought; I heard a second pair of footsteps and more clicks. It could be two of them that knew each other were standing there talking. I wasn't sure how loud the cooling towers were nor how good their hearing was, so I stayed put.

And that's when things got worse.

My helmet's heads up display turned red and blipped a warning at me that said *Organic Life Detected.* I frowned, wondering if it had picked up the signal of the two aliens beneath me, but there was an arrow pointing...*behind me.* Confused, I craned my neck as best as I could over one shoulder.

And there, at the end of the air duct, was a creature I could only describe as a slug the size of a labrador.

My jaw dropped.

The slug-like alien had two tendrils that oozed out of its torso and collected thick tufts of dust that it then held over the middle part of the front of its body. A mouth-like opening appeared and it placed the dust bunnies inside. They sizzled and dissolved on its flat purple tongue—or perhaps the bottom of its mouth, hard to tell in the dark—and the slug crawled forward into the duct, seeking more.

My helmet's flashlight had partially illuminated the slug. Its two stalks for eyes focused on me, beady little things that blinked slowly, and then it glanced down. I did too. My shoulder wound had reopened and some of it pooled in the chest area of my suit, so my blood had smudged against the inside of the duct. The slug alien touched the blood and sampled it on that flat, disgusting tongue. Ew.

Then it looked at me even more intently than before. It glanced at the dust, then me, then the dust again.

And it dropped the dust bunny.

Shit.

The slug's body increased in mass without warning. It expanded to the point that I could no longer see behind it, its fatty tissues bulging until it filled the space of the duct where it was on all sides.

And then it slithered toward me.

I cursed under my breath and then propelled myself forward as fast as I could. I couldn't do anything else—there was no room to roll over or turn around, so I just crawled toward the other end of the air duct.

Below me, the Bergleute's footsteps echoed in my direction. Shit. They'd heard me. I'd have to come out of the duct blasting if I wanted to survive.

I made to the end and shuffled around the corner.

And there, above the entrance to the engine room, was a huge fan.

I stared at it. "Of *fucking* course."

A tendril wrapped around my left ankle.

I choked down a scream as the slug alien tried to yank me back into the air duct with it. I kicked at the tendril first. I left a big fat boot print in the middle of its fleshy torso, but it just filled in a moment later, leaving no mark at all. It was like the black and white Blob horror movie from so long ago. It would probably try to swallow me whole and dissolve my body inside it. I was not about to die like this, not after all the shit I'd been through.

The slug alien entangled both my legs and tried to wedge my feet into its mouth. I struggled until I made it onto my side and then pulled my legs up toward my torso, which brought it closer to me. I grabbed the alien by both of its eyestalks and then heaved with all my might, dragging it up across my body.

And directly into the spinning metal blades of the fan.

The slug didn't stand a chance. The blades chopped off its eyestalks and half of its upper body, splashing inky yellow blood and gore all over my helmet and upper body. However, the rest of its body was so dense that it stopped the blades from spinning.

I wiped the ichor off me so I could see and wedged my hands into the corners of the fan, shoving with all my might. The fan finally popped out of the end of the air duct and hit the ground below. I scooted back a few feet and then listened.

The two Bergleute who heard the commotion had opened the door to the engine room and had gone inside. I heard them communicating and waited, then peeked out slightly. Neither of them looked up at me, pointing to the remains of the slug alien. They must have thought the slug was what they'd heard in the vent. I thanked my lucky stars.

One of them dragged the broken fan and slug corpse out of the engine room, and the second Berg followed it, shutting the door behind them as they went. I waited another minute just to be safe and then jumped down from the air duct.

My landing wasn't great or stable, but I didn't break both legs or ankles, so it would just have to do. I stayed on my knees for a second to see if the noise had brought more Bergs. Nothing yet. I lurched onto my feet and surveyed my surroundings to get a bead on where I was headed next.

The engine room consisted of a huge chamber with what appeared to be five main engines and then fuel lines feeding into them that ran underneath the metal grates of the floor. It appeared to be powered by some-thing bluish-white. Each engine had a large panel on the side with statistics in bar graphs that had the Bergs' native language symbols to indicate the working order of the engine. There were enormous panels where I assumed one could open them to fix any damaged parts and replace the mechanisms inside it. I walked alongside the one closest to me, inspecting it, and then on the other side, I found that the readings all fed into a central command center.

The command center was like the ones you'd see in *Star Trek*—about waist-high with dozens of buttons and five screens that had a diagram of each engine. They showed a status with a symbol in the center that looked to mean that all but one was in perfect condition. The far-right engine had a few symbols blinking on it, indicating problems. I'd need to plant the bomb somewhere that a routine check wouldn't make it easy to discover, so I kept going past the central diagnostic console and checked around the other four engines. Once I was done, I hailed my sister.

"Scarlett," I whispered as I palmed the control near my ear. "Do you read me?"

Static. Then a garbled reply. "I read you, *Oppa*. You okay?"

I grimaced as I glanced down at the sticky guts all over my suit. "Somewhat. Did you get them out?"

"Yeah, we're in the stairwell headed for the hangar. Did you make it to the engine room?"

"I did. I'm about to plant the bomb and meet you there. Things are gonna get hairy really fast—there's only one way out of here, and I think I'm gonna run into the enemy on my way out—"

I heard the whoosh of the engine room doors opening again.

I immediately crouched and then hurried over to the side of the engine facing the entrance. One Berg stood there holding a metal circular panel. It stared around the engine room, so I ducked back behind the engine and waited before checking again. The Berg walked over to just below the air vent and tossed the metal panel down after pressing a button. It floated a couple feet off of the ground, emitting a white light on top, and the alien placed both its giant feet on it. The panel lifted it up until it was just below the air duct. The Berg examined the alien slug's smeared blood on the walls and then peered farther inside. Uh-oh. It might have been piecing things together.

And then I realized.

I was covered in the slug's guts and would have left a trail when I climbed out of the vent.

"Duke? Duke, you still there?"

The Berg's head tilted down toward the right of the air duct.

The jig was up.

"Scarlett, go now," I hissed. "Take the Shasar and go, I'm blown."

The Berg let out a growling noise and jumped down from the floating platform, stomping around the first engine to follow my trail. I'd seen something on the central controls that looked along the lines of a security alarm, so I hurried toward the opposite end of the fifth engine and readied the gauntlet weapon.

The Berg bounded around the corner and I opened fire.

A beam shot out of the gauntlet that hit it in the upper shoulder, injuring it, but the wound was superficial. Its head whipped around as it spotted me, and then it fired in return, forcing me to take cover beside the fourth engine. Sparks popped in the metal grate where its shots hit near me. It was laying down cover fire so it could get to the alarm.

I dove from behind the engine and rolled, coming up on one knee. I fired several times, aiming for its gauntlet. It raced toward the console, but my fourth shot hit it in the middle of the gauntlet. It seared a hole straight through the creature's forearm. The gauntlet lit up with red energy and electrocuted the alien in mid-stride. It screeched and fell to its knees, dripping green blood all over the floor. Its six spidery eyes fixed on me, and I felt the naked hatred in the glare as it lunged for the console.

I raced over and grabbed its thick wrist, applying all of my weight to hold its working hand from hitting the alarm. It snarled and bit my right thigh. Pain lanced up my leg. Finally, I let go with my right arm and fired the gauntlet at it one last time. The shot took the creature right through the throat. Its arm felt limp in my grasp, and it made a gurgling noise for a couple of seconds.

The hatred in the Berg's eyes dimmed to nothing. It slumped back to the floor, dead. I stood there, shaking and panting, staring at its corpse to be sure it didn't so much as twitch. It didn't.

I took the bomb over to the third engine and crouched, feeling for the fuel lines underneath that fed out to other parts of the ship. I took a deep breath, set it, and then placed it out of sight.

Five minutes.

I had five minutes to escape an alien-infested warship, or it would kill me, my sister, and the Shasar along with the Bergleute.

KYOKO M.

Tempus fugit.

CHAPTER EIGHTEEN

General Bridgewater valued punctuality, so it concerned him that the infantry had not launched according to plan at the time they had been instructed to report in. He had hailed the docking bay more than once, but there hadn't been a response, so he left the bridge instead and took the elevator down there himself.

When he arrived, his soldiers were all standing in formation. Puzzled, he walked to the edge of the banister and addressed Colonel Rochester. "What's the hold up, Colonel? We don't have much time left."

She glanced up at him. "I'm sorry, sir, but we have a problem."

Bridgewater heaved an angry sigh and then marched down the stairs to the bottom level to address her face-to-face. "And that is?"

Her brown eyes bored into him like twin drills. "You."

"Excuse me, Colonel?"

A thin smile touched her lips. "You ordered a military strike under false pretenses and threatened to murder a member of your ranks."

"Preposterous," General Bridgewater spat. "What in the hell is the matter with you? Those aliens are on their way here right now to kill us and you want to accuse me of treason?"

"I'm sorry, sir, but this takes precedence."

He folded his arms. "You have no proof that what you're saying is true."

Rochester's smile widened. "Oh?"

She tilted her head to one side, glancing behind her. "If you would, Sam."

One of the recruits in formation marched forward and handed her a small recorder. She held it out and pressed play.

Captain Hallstead's voice cut in on the recording. *"Oh, yeah? What's the long game, General? Please enlighten me."*

General Bridgewater blanched.

"Because of your selfishness, I now have to assume the Nam siblings are going to come back here with those filthy aliens in tow. And I have deployed the infantry to protect the Titan *and blow them out of the sky if they try to come aboard."*

"You fuckin' coward."

"It's us or them, Captain."

Rochester skipped ahead a few seconds and played another bit from the recording. *"Oh, yeah? Did you tell the infantry the truth? Or did you lie to them so they'd be compliant and wouldn't question you?"*

"I told them what they needed to hear and that's it. Everyone is not privy to the truth on this vessel and I am going to keep it that way. Now for the last time, Captain Hallstead, tell me what they have planned. Or I will have you executed."

"General Bridgewater," Colonel Rochester said calmly. "You are hereby under arrest for ordering the unlawful slaughter of two civilians and a military officer. You are relieved of command, effective immediately."

"This is—you can't—that is sensitive information that is vital to the survival of every person on this vessel—" He didn't get any further as the other officers came forward and took both his arms to hold him back as he tried to rush Colonel Rochester. She slipped the recorder into her pocket and then stepped forward, unholstering his firearm from his waist.

"Let go of me!" he snarled. "You don't have the authority to remove me from command!"

"And you don't have the authority to remain in command after showing us what you really are," Rochester said as she removed the magazine from the gun and shucked the bullet out of the barrel without even blinking.

"They'll kill us all!" Bridgewater shouted, struggling in vain against the two officers as they put him in handcuffs. "Do you hear me? We'll all be dead, same as the Earth!"

"Thank you for your input, sir," Rochester said mildly. "We'll take it under advisement."

Rochester turned around to face the infantry. "Now then, it would seem we're down a leadership position by one. Anyone have any suggestions?"

"I've got one," a smoky voice called out from the level above them.

General Bridgewater's head whipped around to see Captain Hallstead casually strolling down the staircase toward them. He walked over to where they stood and smirked at the gob-smacked look on his former commander's face, sliding his hands into his pockets. "Any chance I can be of service, Colonel?"

Rochester smiled at him. "You read my mind, Captain. I motion to temporarily grant you command of the infantry until such a time as the imminent threat has been neutralized. All in favor, say aye."

Every single infantry and officer standing behind them chorused, "Aye."

"All opposed?"

Not a single soul spoke.

"The motion carries." Rochester leaned in slightly toward Bridgewater. "You're dismissed, sir. Take him to the brig."

Hallstead winked at him. "Told you so."

The officers hauled Bridgewater away and out of the docking bay.

Rochester turned to her friend. "The floor is yours. For now, that is."

"Much obliged, Colonel."

Hallstead walked forward. "I am sorry for the poor leadership you've all experienced and I will do my best to make sure I don't make the same mistakes as my predecessor. I know Rochester has told you the truth about Scarlett and Duke Nam. Knowing what you know now, I believe it is your right to decide. We already have one volunteer—" He clapped a hand on Sam's shoulder lightly. "And I will be joining him. Any and all others are welcome as long as you understand that the stakes are high and we cannot afford to let ignorance be the name of the game. We're all we have left of the human race. Everyone's life matters, so everyone gets a choice from here on out."

Hallstead stepped away from the platform, headed for the containment room where the spacesuits were held. "So choose."

SCARLETT

The Shasar and I made it through the stairwell before all hell broke loose.

I knew something was wrong when the arm device I'd stolen off a Berg began to beep repeatedly. It had an alert with a symbol that looked a lot like the one on the control panel of the prison cell where the Shasar had been held. My best guess? It had sent an alert that the cage doors were open for too long, so the automated system alerted the guards.

Which meant shit hit the fan.

"Get ready," I told Wyla and Gendon as I reached the top of the landing and pressed myself to the wall adjacent to the open doorway. "I think they're coming for us. I'll clear a path for everyone; just follow my lead. When I say go, run."

The two Shasar nodded, then telepathically communicated my instructions to the others. I peeked around the corner. We had to clear at least three hallways to return to the docking bay where Duke would meet us now that he'd set the bomb. The hallways were wide enough to fit probably three people shoulder to shoulder, but there was no cover. The only advantages were being smaller and faster than the Bergs and the element of surprise.

Shadows gathered at the end of the hall. It was now or never.

"Go!"

I bolted into the hallway and sprinted, my boots pounding against the floor. Three Bergs had just turned the corner at the other end. I fired wildly to draw their attention to me, aiming high. I hit the one in the middle right through the forehead, but the other shots bounced off the armored chest plates of the Bergs on either side. They drew their weapons from their waists and barreled toward me, firing back. I ducked low and the shots missed me.

At a dead sprint, I reached them in only a couple of seconds, so the one on the right went for the gun and swung an enormous arm at me. I dodged it by getting in between its arm and its body, blasting at the weak point in its armor between the chest plate and the holster for the laser gun. It died instantly, slumping over, which partially blocked me from the view of the third. It tried to fire at me, but I hid under the dead Berg for cover and fired back until I hit it in the right arm. The Berg stumbled, clutching the wound, and passed the gun over to its left arm, taking aim again.

This time, two shots rang out from Wyla and Gendon.

And they had great aim.

The Berg didn't see it coming: one shot to the head, the other in the throat. Its twitching corpse thudded to the ground beside the other two. I heaved the corpse aside and nodded to the two brave Shasar before motioning for them and the others to follow me. I'd programmed a timer to make sure we boarded before our five minutes were up and we'd used another precious thirty seconds with that encounter. I crouched long enough to grab a large knife that one of the Bergs had been carrying and then turned the corner into the second hallway.

We made it halfway through the next hallway when two more Bergs caught up from behind, firing at the helpless Shasar in the rear. I yelled for Wyla and Gendon to take command up front and flattened myself to the wall, laying down cover fire as the Shasar fled past me. I knelt and concentrated my shots at the Bergs' exposed kneecaps. I managed to cripple one of them, but then the other grabbed an oval object from his belt and hit a button. A bright blue shield formed and my shots bounced off it.

Fuck. What little luck I'd had ran out.

The shielded Berg lurched toward me. I backpedaled and stayed as low as possible so its shots would go over my head, but it had better aim than the others. A shot grazed my left shin, and I screamed in agony as it burned like a red-hot poker. I shifted as much weight as possible to the right side of my body and limped for the end of the hall. I made it just barely as the shots kept coming and pressed myself into the wall directly beside the hallway opening.

The Berg's shadow loomed on the opposite wall.

I took the knife in my left hand and plunged the blade into the gap in his leg armor at the back of the knee.

The Berg's entire leg crumpled, bringing it down. I yanked the blade out and stabbed it in the throat two, three times, not stopping until my arm was drenched in its blood. The alien hit the floor face-first. I snatched the glowing shield out of its limp grip and hefted it, quickly noting that it had a button on the outside of the handle that turned it on and off. I tapped it with the bloody blade and it held strong, so I took it with me as I hurried to catch up with the escaping Shasar.

Three minutes left.

Tears leaked out of my eyes from the strain of running on my injured leg. I'd never felt anything like it; my body screamed at me to sit or lie down or just plain die to make the agonizing streaks of pain shooting up my left side stop. Wyla and Gendon had gunned down another Berg along the way, but there were three Shasar bodies. I rounded the next corner and yelled for them, brandishing the shield. Gendon saw me and moved through the crowd of the Shasar, hurrying to my side.

"Take this," I told him. "It should be good cover. I'm gonna try and find another one for Wyla."

"*Thank you,*" he said as he accepted it. He then offered his hand. "*You are hurt. Let me help.*"

I shook my head. "I'm gonna slow you down. I need to take a rear position and try to bottleneck the Bergs coming up from behind once we reach the docking bay."

"*That is suicide,*" Gendon said sternly. "*I will not allow that.*"

I gave him a tired, crooked grin. "Who put you in charge, Daddy-O?"

"*You did,*" he said in a clipped tone, then grabbed my forearm and pulled my arm across his shoulder to take the weight off my left leg. He held the shield in his other hand in front of us, his four eyes gleaming with determination. "*I shield, you shoot.*"

I shook my head. "No wonder your son's so stubborn."

"*I consider that a compliment.*" Gendon helped me through the rest of the corridor—his eyes ahead of us, mine behind us.

We made it to the docking bay exit, which was a large opening roughly fifteen feet across with sliding metal doors. By now, the ship's alarm system had been activated, so we knew reinforcements would get here soon.

And my heart clenched as I noticed Duke hadn't made it here yet.

"The console," I told Gendon, pointing to the upright panel beside the docking bay doors. He helped me over to it, and I found the symbol matching the one on the prison cell door. I figured it was their word for open or close. "Go help the others find space-worthy ships and evacuate. Get as far away from here as possible. We only have two and a half minutes before the bomb goes off."

"*What about you?*" Gendon asked.

"I can't close the doors until Duke makes it."

Gendon hesitated. "*And if he doesn't?*"

I just stared at him. Gendon touched my shoulder. Then he handed me the shield. "*Good luck, my friend.*"

"Thank you, Gendon. Get clear. Keep everyone safe."

He gave me one last lingering look and then headed off to help the Shasar board the escape pods.

I propped myself up against one side of the control panel, facing the open doorway, the shield held in my left hand, the gauntlet weapon in the right. "Duke, can you hear me?"

Nothing. Just my panicked heart rate in the suit's heads-up display. "Duke, do you read me?"

No response. I gritted my teeth as I stared at the end of the hallway where I knew a hoard of Bergs would approach any second. We had so little time left before detonation, yet all I cared about was my brother, my protector, my *oppa*. If I died without seeing him one last time…

"Goddamn you, Duke!" I cried. "Answer me!"

A slanted shadow stretched across the other end of the hall. I got ready to open fire.

My brother staggered into the hallway, splattered in yellow and green alien blood, an oversized laser pistol in his hands. "Jesus Christ, Lettie, gimme a second to catch my breath."

"You stupid jerk!" I stifled a sob as he hobbled to my side and hugged me to him. I slammed the docking bay doors shut and aimed the gauntlet at the panel. I blew it to pieces just as the doors began to rock back and forth from the Bergs catching up.

"That's not gonna hold for long," Duke said as we turned toward the hangar. About half of the Shasar were left now boarding the pods and leaving through the sealed barrier of the ship out into space. "There has got to be another way to stall them or they're just gonna chase us."

"One of the smaller pods might do it," I said, pointing to the ones on the far end. There were four or five vessels that were meant for only two passengers in an emergency, so they were about the size of a speedboat. "We can fly it over and block the door with it."

Sparks flew out from the edges of the doors; the Bergs were blasting through the metal.

"Worth a try," Duke said tightly. Together, we limped over to the escape pod. I climbed inside, noting the same set up as the one we'd used to sneak aboard. "I've got this. Prep the other one so we can get the fuck out of here."

Duke accessed the other pod while I pulled down the top and fired up the engine. Lights winked to life on the console and I grabbed the piloting globe, pulling backward. The escape pod hummed with energy as I guided it away from the edge of the ship and turned it around. It scraped loudly against the metal floor, but it still managed to fly toward the creaking doors to the docking bay. I landed it between the broken remains of the console and the doors not a moment too soon. The top half of the door bent outward from the giant aliens bashing against it. The ruined section of the door made a crunching sound and then something on the controls beeped in warning. I realized why a second later.

They'd pinned me in.

I couldn't get out of the pod.

"Lettie!" Duke said, his escape pod hovering above the exit. "We've got to go, come on!"

"It's stuck," I whispered. "The pod door won't open. If I move the pod, they'll get out and shoot you down."

I took a deep, trembling breath. "You have to leave me behind, *Oppa*."

Duke fell silent at first. "No. No way, Lettie. No fucking way. I am not leaving you here to die."

I smiled through my tears. "It's okay, *Oppa*. I owe you one anyway, remember?"

"No!" my brother shouted. "Lettie, you have to get out of there!"

I pressed my gloved hand to the windshield and looked at him. I knew he could see me. The pod rocked harder, back and forth, as the Bergleute tried to free themselves. "It's okay, Duke. I love you. Always. Take care of them. They need you."

"Lettie," Duke said hoarsely, his voice choked with tears. "Don't do this to me."

"You have to go, *Oppa*," I said gently. "For me. Please."

"I love you," my brother whispered. "I love you so much, Lettie."

"I know."

Duke took one last long look at me, tears coursing down his face, and he piloted the ship outside into the vast reaches of space.

He would be safe.

And that was all that mattered.

HALLSTEAD

"First things first," I said to the six brave souls flanking me in identical battle-ready ships from the *Titan*. "Do not fire unless they fire first. The plan was for the Shasar to use the Bergleute's escape pods, so they will be in the enemy ships. We want to avoid friendly fire at all costs. They may not be able to communicate with us unless Scarlett is with them, so wait for my mark before firing. The last report from our satellite indicates we had incoming hostiles before the Nam siblings made it aboard. I counted eight of them, so we're outnumbered, but it doesn't mean we're down and out. Copy me?"

"Copy," the soldiers said in unison. To make it easier, we'd taken designations of T1 through T7, starting with me as T1. We had three women and three men in our squadron.

It still didn't quite hit me—even as I saw the sparkle of distance stars—that I was mere minutes away from fighting an alien race of murdering miners to save a girl I'd met less than a week ago. Life's funny that way. Oddly enough, though, flying a spaceship was reminiscent of my days as a pilot earlier in my career. The same eerie calm filled me and narrowed my focus. No place for emotions in the cockpit. Kill or be killed. That's all there was to it.

And yet anxiety gnawed at the pit of my stomach.

I knew there were too many variables with the Nam siblings' plan. Plenty could have gone wrong by now. Hell, they could both be dead along with the Shasar, but I knew I had to see it through to the end. I'd given up everything on a leap of faith, something I'd never done before in my entire life.

But I had to know if they'd made it.

If she'd made it.

"Sentimental jackass," I muttered under my breath, flexing my hands on the pilot stick as we sailed toward the last known sighting of the Bergleute battleships. I'd had enough time to study the fighter ship's controls and interior in the tense months leading up to the Bergs' arrival into our solar system. The recruits had gotten the schematics not too long afterward, but it wasn't supposed to be this way. The plan had been to give them months' worth of training and they'd practice in virtual until they could do it for real, but it had all gone to hell the moment the world's military couldn't stop the warship. Only those who had made it through the screening process made it onto the *Titan*, so I'd have to put my trust in their skills.

"Hallstead," Rochester said over the comms. "We're showing eight bogeys up ahead. We're steering the *Titan* heading away from the danger. Coordinates have been sent to your onboard computer. Eliminate the threat and rendezvous with us there. We're still awaiting satellite imaging to confirm if the warship is still where it was when we last saw it or if the Nam siblings were successful."

"Roger that, Colonel. Good luck. Travel safe."

"Kick ass, Captain."

I smirked. "I plan to."

I had just enough time to see over my shoulder that the *Titan* had begun to gradually change direction, which was no mean feat given her size. All the more reason we had to eliminate the threat. As far as we'd come along with our technology, we didn't have warp speed or light-speed like in the movies. The *Titan's* propulsion could only do so much, and much smaller vessels could catch up with her. Other infantry had been deployed to create a perimeter, and I hoped they wouldn't see battle.

The console beeped to alert me that we were now within range to target. In the inky depths of space, shuttles rarely showed up to the naked eye; sometimes only the propulsion or if the ship had a shiny metal exterior. I had to trust my instruments since I couldn't see a damn thing.

"Standby," I told the other soldiers. "I'm going to attempt to make contact."

"Copy that," they chorused.

I slowed the ship to a stop and my men did the same so that we formed a blockade of sorts. Our scientists had rigged the wings of the ship to flash Morse code and several different attempts at non-verbal communication. I made sure the channels were all open and took a deep breath. "This is Captain Travis Hallstead of the *Titan* vessel. We are attempting to make contact with you. Please respond if you're receiving this message."

Silence.

Lots of it.

The ships didn't budge, either. I calculated them to be a half kilometer away, just stationary, their oversized oblong vessels motionless, same as ours. My eyes narrowed.

"We cannot allow you to proceed further unless we receive some form of response," I tried again. I listened intently.

Then the ship in the center veered toward me.

It didn't move quickly or aggressively, so I matched its speed as it approached. I still couldn't see anything through its windshield. I decided to pull up side by side in case it was one of the Shasar trying to get visual confirmation.

Once we were parallel to one another, I used sign language to indicate everything that I'd just said over the channel.

More silence.

"Sir," one of the soldiers—Sam, I believe, designated as T3—said uneasily.

All at once, the pair of ships on either end of the blockade turned inward and fired at me.

"Shit!" I yanked on the piloting stick upward and just barely avoided getting hit. "Squadron, you are clear to engage! Open fire, open fire!"

I spun around and fired at the vessel next to me, but it veered off to one side and took evasive action as I pursued. "Rochester, hostiles engaged; I repeat, hostiles engaged! Deploy the defenders!"

"Roger that, Hallstead."

"Squadron, you are not to allow a single ship to approach the *Titan*, do you read me?"

"Yes, sir!"

"Let's go to work, people. Divide and conquer. Separate a bogey and take it out of the equation. If two try to gang up on one of us, call it out and we'll converge. Do not let any of them get within firing range of the *Titan*."

"Speaking of which," Sam said. "Got two on my tail now. Han, do you copy?"

"Copy," the soldier replied. "I'm closing in now."

My own bogey had immediately taken evasive action toward the *Titan* looming in the distance. I poured on the juice and concentrated every iota of my focus to get it in range for a direct hit. It was deceptively fast for a craft nearly twice the size of mine. It might have had to do with whatever power source it had, but I wasn't about to let it get off a single shot at the *Titan*.

I fired to the right of the craft. Predictably, it banked to the left to avoid it, and I aimed slightly ahead of it and then fired again. Our ships shot from two barrels up front, so one missed, but the other grazed the right rear side of the pod. It punched a hole that caused the fuel line to leak in weightless blobs behind the craft as it flew. My in-flight console calculated that its speed was rapidly dropping. It tried to throw off my aim by going into a barrel roll, but I hit it a second time on one of the rear fins. The ship's trajectory skewed hard to the right, and it tried to correct, but one of the other enemy ships fleeing in that direction clipped it hard enough to tear it right in half. I spotted the eviscerated corpse of the Bergleute piloting it in the wreckage, a sense of vindictive satisfaction welling up in my chest. One down, seven to go.

I veered off and targeted another pod that was trying to escape our notice to head for the *Titan*. As I closed in to lock on, T4 spoke. "Captain, you've got one on your six and closing in."

My onboard computer showed an image of the enemy ship approaching from the rear. It didn't have a lock yet, but it would if I didn't break off into evasive action, but then I got an idea. Not a good one, but an idea nonetheless. "Copy that, soldier, do not engage. I've got this."

I locked onto the ship up ahead and as I did, the onboard sensor detected that the enemy ship had locked onto me as well. I waited just a second more and then shot straight up.

The enemy ship had fired the same time I moved. It blew the ship in front of me apart. I circled to be behind the other one and shot it four times until it shattered into wreckage. Five left now.

"Good catch, T4," I told him. "Follow me."

We flanked another one and forced it to constantly zig-zag to avoid a hit. It clipped one of the other fleeing ships, which caused an engine shut-down, and then we took it out. Four left.

My right wing jerked hard and the console flashed red. "Shit, I'm hit. It's at our three o'clock."

"On it, sir, hang in there." T4 angled the ship straight up and fired on the pod, spinning to avoid the shots that kept coming. I dodged an oncoming ship, just barely missing it, and the status screen showed me a diagram of the damage. Turning wouldn't be much fun, but I could still manage it. The bigger problem was losing air. My suit had air, but a limited amount. If I had to jettison, there was a chance I'd go floating out past my men and be lost in the vast reaches of space.

Good times all around.

My punctured wing drew the attention of another enemy, but T2 and T3 caught on. "Sir, can you make it to our position?"

"I'll damn sure try." Spoke too soon. The Berg behind me fired repeat-edly and tore a chunk out of my tail as well. My cockpit exploded with red lights all over the place. I swerved as best as I could to close in on T2 and T3 before the Berg could get a lock on me.

"Now!" T2 said. He and the other pilot dropped sharply from above and fired on the vessel until it crumpled in on itself. Three left.

"T6 to squadron, I'm hit! I need backup now!"

I caught sight of two Bergs chasing after T6. He had a fuel leak and his wings were damaged, causing him to slow enough for them to catch up. "Hang on, T6! Squadron to T6, give him some support."

Too late, the other ships converged and laid down cover fire, but the pod on the right got in a shot that tore apart the pilot's windshield, his ship shattering. I shut my eyes and grimaced. It was a horrible sight I'd never forget.

I blasted off after the pair. They split up once they saw me, so I took the one on the right. It tried to throw me off by flying upside down to end up behind me, but I followed it doggedly, firing wildly as I tried to get it within my sights. "Come on, you son of a bitch."

"Captain, you don't have enough maneuverability to catch up," T2 warned me. "You're gonna cause a system shutdown."

I clenched my jaw. I knew he was right, but it didn't help; it just pissed me off more. I couldn't get it with brute force. I needed a strategy.

A piece of broken pod bounced off my left wing. I saw the wreckage from another ship up to the right. I did some quick math, then darted off from behind the Berg's pod and flew straight toward it.

"Captain, what the hell are you—"

The side of my craft scraped the broken ship and it bounced off my hull like a basketball. The shattered ship spiraled downward…directly into the fleeing pod.

The impact cracked the hull and part of the pod's windshield. "T2 and T5 on me."

"We've got it," T5 confirmed as she blasted off toward the spinning enemy ship. "T4's in trouble, can you reach her?"

"T3, with me," I ordered as I strained to turn the ship so I could see. The ship's controls had gotten sluggish. The alerts had gone berserk with warnings. They'd have to wait.

T7 hovered in front of T4, who had zero working propulsion, which left him a sitting duck out here with two Bergs still in play. She was just barely keeping the circling ship at bay with cover fire, and we were several kilometers away.

And if things weren't bad enough, my radar beeped, indicating a fleet of ships approaching from the direction the Bergs had come from.

I clenched my jaw. It looked like the other infantry would be engaging in battle after all. "T2, with me. T3, help the others. T5, get the last straggler."

"Yes, sir."

I studied the radar. Christ, I counted three dozen ships, and they weren't all the same size, either. Some were larger, some were escape pods, and others were ships I'd never even seen before. We had enough infantry, but it would be a goddamn bloodbath with this many combatants.

"We're gonna have to stall," I told T2. "Not much else we can do while Rochester gets the *Titan's* defenses in place."

"Understood," he said tightly.

I let out a long breath. "On my mark, soldier. Good luck."

"Same to you, sir. At least I'll die following the orders of an honorable man and not a coward."

I smirked. "Same here. And in three…two…one—"

"Wait!" he said.

I froze with my finger on the trigger. "What?"

"I…I think I'm getting a transmission, sir," he said, shocked. "Hold on. Yes, check Channel 564."

I punched it into the console. Static. Then, a male voice. "Halt, do not fire, repeat, do not fire, this is Duke Nam transmitting from the vessel at your starboard."

The knot in my stomach unfurled. "Holy shit. You made it."

I patched myself through to Rochester. "Sienna, have your men stand down. It's the Nam siblings. They made it out of the Berg warship."

"That's some goddamn great news," she said, and I could hear the fierce grin in her voice. "And just when we needed it the most. I'm preparing the docking bay now. Send the Nam siblings through the blockade."

"With pleasure."

"Do the Shasar know they can just stay in our air space for now?"

"Yeah, I think that's the plan, but the little one that came to us might come aboard."

"Got it."

I hailed Duke again. "Welcome back, soldier. Follow us."

I did my best to guide my ship back to the *Titan*. It was on its last legs, and it just barely made the trip. I climbed out as Duke's ship entered and pulled off my helmet after the bay doors closed behind it. I ran a hand through my helmet hair, though I knew it wouldn't do much to make it presentable. And I pretended I wasn't doing that so I'd look less of a mess when I saw Scarlett again.

Once the pod had extended its landing gear and the engines cut off, the windshield slid back.

I stopped dead.

Duke stepped out of the pod.

Alone.

I licked my lips as I walked over to him, glancing expectantly out the window at the other ships that had congregated near the *Titan* to wait for instruction. "Hey. I'm guessing Hatwer's with his people out there. Is Scarlett with him?"

Duke removed his smudged, slightly cracked helmet. I saw his face. I saw the tears still wet on his cheeks. I saw the emptiness in his eyes.

"Duke," I said slowly, hoarsely. "Say something. Where is she? Where's Scarlett?"

His lips just barely moved. "She's gone."

I dropped my helmet. "What?"

Duke swallowed hard. "She was...blocking the door to the docking bay so the Shasar and I could escape. The door pinned her pod door closed so she couldn't get out so she...she told me to go."

"The ship, did it—"

Duke nodded a little. "Bomb went off. Vaporized the warship. The Bergs are dead, but..."

He trembled and buried his face in one gloved hand, a sob rattling in his next words. "She told me to go. I shouldn't have left her there. I should've..."

Duke collapsed onto his knees and cried.

Slowly, I knelt in front of him and gently placed my hand on his shoulder, pulling him toward me. I embraced him. No point in saying anything. After all, what could be said? She'd died saving us and the Shasar as well as the person who meant everything to her. She'd died brave and selfless.

She'd died a hero.

And really, that was the best any of us could ask for without a world of our own.

It didn't take too long to get a memorial organized. After all, it wasn't like many of the people on board knew her. All they would know was that one woman sacrificed everything to keep her brother safe and to make sure the Bergs paid for what they'd done to us and the Shasar. We would be honoring the other soldier we lost—Jon Laughlin was his name —for his sacrifice protecting the *Titan*. After that, we'd need to bring Hatwer on board to see if anyone else on the ship possibly had the

Empath trait needed to communicate. I had my doubts, but it was protocol.

I returned to my quarters and got dressed, but when I reached for my usual black suit jacket, I was met with an empty hanger. I'd given it to Scarlett. I'd almost forgotten.

Something about that made me lose it. Maybe it was just the crack in the levee. After all, I'd damn near lost everything when the Bergs destroyed the Earth and maybe Scarlett was that last little piece of humanity that I'd held in my hands. I sagged onto my bed with my head in my hands and cried. It didn't matter that I'd only just met her. I didn't know what the hell lay ahead for me or anyone else, but I knew she'd deserved a future. And she'd never see it. She'd never see the world we'd make again once we colonized New Earth. It wasn't right. It just wasn't fucking right.

Some time later, I got a handle on myself. I took a different black suit jacket with me and headed down to the auditorium. The other parts of the ship tuned in via video feed since it was impossible for all of them to fit in here. Dr. Warwick had already tried to talk to me, but I didn't want to start the avalanche right now, so I'd rebuffed her.

When I entered the auditorium, I spotted Duke standing on the far end, staring out of the window. I had a minute or two before I had to be on stage, so I went over to him.

I touched his shoulder. "Hey."

"Hey," he said, his voice hollow, brown eyes fixed on the stars.

"We'll keep it short," I promised. "No one's gonna force you to do anything, so take all the time you need."

"Thank you, Captain." A faint smile touched his lips as he glanced at me. "You're alright, you know. I get why she liked you."

I smiled back. "So, in addition to all her other faults, she had lousy taste in men."

Duke let out a small laugh. "Yeah, she did. But she believed in you even when I didn't. I'm glad she was right about you."

I swallowed past the lump in my throat. "Hopefully I'll make her proud someday." I squeezed his shoulder. "Come on."

He and I walked up the steps onto the stage and the attendees quieted. I cleared my throat again. "Today, we're here to honor the lives of two of the bravest people we'll ever know: Scarlett Nam and Jon Laughlin. Some of you might know them, some of you might not, but it's important that we remember the selflessness these two displayed when they gave their lives to keep the people on this ship and the Shasar safe. We'll have a few words first from Scarlett's brother, Duke, and Jon's sister, Misty. I hope that everyone here can appreciate just how precious life is and how important it is to appreciate what you have before it's gone."

I stepped aside. Duke walked up to the podium, dressed in black as well, holding a single red rose that he spun between his fingers.

"My sister was…well, the best way to put it was wild," Duke said. "She was volatile and untamable and passionate. She saw the world as she wanted it to be, not as it was, but I think that was always her strength. When Hatwer first came to us for help, they wanted to kill him after he stopped being 'useful,' yet my sister went to bat for him. She was determined. She knew that there was more to him than met the eye. She saw an incorruptible goodness in him and in his people that was worth fighting for. We're so different from the Shasar, yet Scarlett was able to see through those differences. She believed in them. She gave up everything to protect them."

He took a deep breath to steady himself. "I've spent my entire life protecting her. She always felt like she owed me a debt, even though I'm her brother, her blood. And today, she repaid that debt a thousand times over. She protected me. She protected us. I charge everyone here with this thought in closing: we may find a new planet to call our home, but never forget that home isn't a place, it's in the people who love us. Find those people who give your life meaning and protect them. Nothing lasts forever."

Duke held out the rose. Its beautiful color shone in the darkness. "To Scarlett."

"To Scarlett," everyone said solemnly.

He left the rose on the podium and took his place beside me.

Just as Misty went to take his spot, Rochester, who had been seated up front, touched her ear. She had a link so there wouldn't be any announcements that would interrupt the ceremony. Not that it mattered—she shot to her feet and hurried onto the stage toward me.

"The bridge just got something on radar," she whispered. "Another escape pod."

"Shit," I hissed, and beckoned Duke to come with me.

We rode the elevator up to the bridge, and the analyst who found the signal brought it up on the holographic projector. "Any communications yet?"

She shook her head. "They're not within range yet."

"Think it could be a straggler?" Rochester asked.

"I don't see why," I said. "That would be a suicide mission. They know damn well they can't take an entire blockade, not with their armada gone. There's no one to back them up."

"Maybe they're trying to negotiate?" the analyst asked.

"I met these things," Duke said, narrowing his eyes at the lone ship. "They don't negotiate."

"Did any of the Shasar get separated during the escape?"

"Everyone they know of is accounted for."

I exhaled and tried to think. "Keep trying to get through to them. We'll send a squadron out to intercept. Duke, bring Hatwer to the docking bay in case he can help translate."

Duke nodded and headed back toward the elevator. I checked the magazine in my gun and put it back in the holster. And I hoped to God I wouldn't need it.

Rochester chewed her thumbnail as we both watched the ship get closer and closer. The squadron came to a stop a few kilometers away and one of the pilots opened a channel. "This is Han Blankenship of the *Titan* vessel. You are trespassing. Identify yourself immediately."

Static. I paced around the hologram.

"I say again: you are trespassing in the *Titan's* airspace. Identify yourself."

The pod didn't move, but a moment later, lights began to flicker along the bottom.

"The hell?" Rochester said. "They've never done that before."

"No, they haven't," I muttered. I gestured to the analyst. "Can you get me a pen and paper please?"

She handed them to me. I watched the lights. They were definitely in a pattern, and they were definitely repeating. I wrote down the sequence and frowned at it. Why did it seem familiar?

And then it hit me.

Morse fucking code.

"We are prepared to use lethal force if you do not cooperate—"

"Han, no!" I shouted. "Don't fire. Escort the ship into the docking bay, now."

"Sir?"

"Do it."

Rochester stared at me, confused. "Travis, what the hell."

I grinned as I held up the paper I'd just written on and showed her the code. Her jaw dropped.

HUMAN. DO NOT SHOOT.

I didn't waste another second—I bolted for the docking bay as fast as I could.

By the time I got there, the damaged Bergleute pod had docked. Duke and Hatwer were standing by the staircase. The windshield of the pod was badly damaged, so I ran over to it and shoved with all my might.

The pod opened.

Scarlett Nam pulled off her suit's helmet and grinned at us. "What up, fuckers?"

CHAPTER NINETEEN

SCARLETT

Y ou...infuriating...impossible...little *shit.*"

Duke rushed forward, dragged me out of the escape pod, and squeezed me in the biggest, warmest hug he'd ever given me. Despite my cavalier one-liner, I hugged him just as tightly, fighting tears. I was so relieved he and the Shasar had made it out alive. I'd been terrified, flying with what was left of my reserve power to the *Titan's* previous coordinates. I'd had no idea if they'd cleared the warship's explosion and I'd just prayed they had.

My brother kissed my forehead, pulling away enough to look me over for injuries. "Are you okay, Lettie?"

"I'm okay, *Oppa*," I whispered as I wiped the tears from his cheek. "Really."

Hatwer came forward as Duke let me go finally, his voice overjoyed. *"I am so grateful to see you are alive, Scarlett. I do not understand many human customs, but I believe I am to embrace you to show my happiness?"*

I laughed and stooped enough to hold out my arms. "Yes, you're learning, Hatwer. We call this a hug."

The little alien wrapped his arms around me. *"It is strange, but I could get used to it."*

"I hope you will. I'm so glad you're safe, Hatwer."

198

He let go of me as well. I sent a sly look at Hallstead. "Well, are you just going to stand there, Cap'n?"

Hallstead smirked, saying nothing.

Then he grabbed the front of my spacesuit and pulled me close, kissing me. My eyes shut automatically. The kiss chased away the lingering cold from being out in space without much life support. Bliss flowed down my body. It didn't last long, but it was enough to make me sigh when he pulled away.

"Oh, what the *fuck* is this?" Duke demanded, pointing between the two of us when Hallstead stepped back.

"What?" I asked innocently.

"No," Duke said, glaring at us. "No, absolutely not. Fuck no. None of that shit better happen again while I'm still breathing."

Hallstead laughed, nodding. "Yeah, about what I thought. Once a watchdog, always a watchdog." He nodded to me. "What happened? How'd you get out of there?"

"The Bergs managed to get through the doors and it knocked me loose. I had less than thirty seconds, but I made tracks far enough away to escape the blast radius. However, the force knocked me off course and damaged the ship. I was at half capacity for fuel and propulsion, but I had enough of the guidance system left to get myself back to the *Titan*."

I gestured to Hallstead. "And I figured since our smart guy here knew Morse code, I wouldn't get blown to smithereens even with my comms down."

Duke squeezed my hand. "I'm so proud of you, Lettie."

"I didn't do it alone," I reminded him. "You placed the bomb in just the right place. It took out the entire warship, not just the engine room. You saved everyone just as much as I did."

I glanced at Hallstead. "So, what now?"

"A lot of things, but first off, you'd better get checked out in the infirmary and get some rest. The Shasar are doing okay so far; they're just following us to New Earth. We'll need you to help communicate the colonization plan. We've also got to find out what they know about the Bergleute. We can't assume their entire race was on that warship. If their home planet finds out we took away their greatest weapon, they'll likely want to retaliate. We need to get to solid ground before they have a chance to find us."

I nodded. "Got it. See you in a while."

Duke took me up to the infirmary. They checked me out and sent my bloodwork off to the lab to make sure I wasn't carrying any alien diseases, but since I'd been in my spacesuit the entire time, it was unlikely. My leg required a shitload of disinfectant and stitches. They gave me a pair of crutches and instructed me to stay off my feet for as long as possible. It had been a graze, but it was still damned painful. At least it hadn't broken my shinbone; I didn't want to be clunking around the *Titan* in a cast.

Duke caught me up on what happened after they escaped the warship. I was vindictively glad to hear that Bridgewater and Rosewood were locked up. They weren't fit to lead anyone, that was for damn sure, but what he also mentioned was that Hallstead was rethinking my brother's position in the infantry. After all, he'd shown enough leadership skills to be more valuable than a grunt, as did I, so they'd brief us later on what they wanted us to do from here on out.

Duke checked his watch. "I'll meet you on the bridge once they call for us. Get some rest."

I saluted him as I settled down into the bed. They'd been kind enough to lend me some clothes from another passenger that was my size: a black tank top and pajama bottoms. When it was time to go, I had a pair of plain black slacks, a button-up shirt, and flats. Not anything I'd ever wear myself, but it'd do for now. After all, I was a stowaway.

Duke went to the door, then narrowed his eyes at me again. "And stay away from Hallstead. The guy may be a hero, but he's not the kind of man you need in your life."

I rolled my eyes. "Beat it before I kick your ass, *Oppa*."

He snorted, but left all the same. I tried different positions on the bed so that my injured leg wasn't taking any weight and closed my eyes.

About ten minutes later, there was a knock at my door.

I frowned. Hadn't been expecting anyone this soon. I stood and limped to the door, pressing my palm to the scanner so that it would open. It wasn't Duke.

"Scarlett."

"Hallstead."

He stepped inside and the door slid shut automatically. For a long moment, neither of us said anything. He stared at me. I stared back. Finally, I had to say something.

"Do you want to talk?"

"No."

"Good."

What followed probably looked a lot like a UFC match. Bodies slamming against each other. Muttered curses. Full body pins. Elbows and knees jammed into places they didn't belong. Torn clothing. It was the single most violent experience of my life.

It was also the single most satisfying experience of my life.

But it wasn't all sex and violence. I felt the first genuine swell of emotion when he kissed the birthmark on my stomach—a little smudge of dark skin to the left of my navel that had looked scarlet to my mom when I was born; and a second when he kissed the blue butterfly tattoo on the inside of my left thigh. Everything about Hallstead in the real world was hard and unforgiving, but here he was selfless. Without words, he told me he knew how much of a screw up I was and didn't care. He still found me interesting, valuable, desirable, irreplaceable. Idiot.

I hadn't had sex in a long time, but not for reasons that Dr. Warwick would write down in her notepad. The places that Duke and I had lived over the years weren't nice: mostly studio apartments with cheap rent in bad neighborhoods. I'd had little to no privacy and even less of a social life. We'd keep to places with month-to-month rent, cash only preferred, so we could boogie if someone caught on to us. No time for friends, no time for relationships. Just me and my brother against the world.

And as a result, I'd really, *really* missed the touch of a lover.

Maybe that was why I couldn't help myself with Hallstead. Somewhere in there, I probably did want to make love to him, but I didn't care right now. I'd almost died. I'd given up everything and I'd expected to crossover to wherever life led after death, but I'd been given a second chance. I wanted to feel alive.

And that's how Hallstead made me feel.

I couldn't take my eyes off the sight of him above me as he drew my panties down my legs and settled one big hand on my lower stomach. The intensity of his stare could've matched the sun; it warmed my bare skin all over. I could tell he was reading me, making sure I truly wanted to go there with him, that we weren't both just letting lust and hormones call the shots.

I made it clear for him by parting my legs.

Hallstead didn't hesitate. The first moment of his lips and tongue on my sex was mind-blowing. I hadn't felt pleasure in… God, I couldn't remember the last time. He propped my legs up on his shoulders and worshiped me like a goddess. I had no idea how thin the walls were in the civilian quarters, so I flipped the pillow over my face to muffle my moans. And unlike any lovers I'd ever known, he didn't stop too soon or fumble around, not knowing what to do. He knew *exactly* what he was doing. The orgasm rushed up through me in a scalding wave of sensation, wiping out any aches and pains from my mission.

When it was over, he pulled the pillow off my face. I made a little startled noise after he tossed it onto the floor. "But—they'll hear if I don't—"

"I want to hear you," he murmured, his dark lashes low over his eyes. I shivered. Holy shit. That was a good line. Perfectly timed, no less. I was in danger of swooning at this rate.

Hallstead lowered his long, heavy frame onto me after he'd quickly applied a condom from his wallet. I wrapped myself around him as much as possible, wanting the closeness, wanting the intimacy, wanting the recklessness of it all to overwhelm me. And it did. God, did it ever. I didn't care about the initial discomfort—after all, it had been a damn *while* —not when the sultry groan that left him as he pushed inside me sounded so good I wanted to record it on vinyl. I pushed his hair out of his eyes and kissed him as he moved inside me for the first time and what I prayed wouldn't be the last.

He didn't rush it. He stayed with me, slow and steady, until I relaxed into it, until I was gasping for air around every kiss, my fingers and toes tingling, the pleasure welling up from within and spreading through my veins like only good sex could. I looped my legs around his narrow hips and held on for dear life as the heat at my center just stoked into an inferno.

He didn't hold back. There was no need. I dug my nails into his shoulder blades as my climax overtook me in a dazzling explosion of sparks underneath my skin and deep in my belly. He slowed above me, and the fact that he didn't join me just made me all the more determined. I flipped him onto his back in a rather acrobatic move I'd learned in self-defense. He did hesitate then, glancing down at my heavily wrapped calf. "Scarlett, your leg—"

I flipped my hair out of my face and smirked down at him. "I'll live."

I lowered myself onto his cock, slowly, purposefully. Hallstead hissed, his eyes closing, his head rolling back for a second, gripping my hips hard. He licked his lips and glared at me, but with a playful edge to it. "So goddamn stubborn."

He gripped the side of my face and tugged me down enough to kiss him, his other hand steadying me as I rocked myself onto him again and again. The pleasure kept building and building until we were both panting and cursing into each other's mouths. His grip on my hip wouldn't relent, keeping me centered over him as he fucked up into me faster, harder, until the edges of the world got blurry and I teetered on the edge of my orgasm. I swiveled my hips and that was that—he groaned my name in that rough, smoky voice and we both pitched off the cliff together into the blissful abyss.

I collapsed onto Hallstead's chest and let out a tired, happy sigh, my eyes drifting closed as the warm blanket of the afterglow flowed over me.

"Best mistake ever."

Hallstead chuckled and kissed the top of my head. "Damn right."

"Snowstorms."

"Lightning."

"Allergies."

"Cigarette smoke."

"Independent bookstores."

"Lunar eclipses."

"Sunburn."

"Ocean waves."

"Sand."

"Seaweed."

"Campfires."

"The Internet."

"Empire State Building."

"The Pyramids of Egypt."

"The Great Coral Reef."

"The Mona Lisa."

"Northern lights."

"Sunrise."

"Sunset."

"Railroad tracks."

"Rain."

"The Super Bowl."

"Cars."

"Traffic."

Finally, I sighed. "This is the most depressing pillow talk ever."

Hallstead chuckled, and I could feel the vibrations as they flowed down my back. I lay on my side, one hand tucked beneath the pillow, the other rather sentimentally clasped with one of his, and he lay behind me with his hot chest against the curve of my spine. We weren't exactly spooning because that was way too domestic for us, but it was remarkably similar. Sometime after the sex, he had asked me what I missed the most about the Earth and our list grew longer and more solemn with every passing moment.

"Sorry. What else should we talk about?"

I found it a little hard to concentrate. His other hand swept up and down my stomach in lingering strokes and it felt ridiculously soothing. I had almost drifted off a couple of times in the last few minutes.

"Who is she?"

He paused. I didn't need to see his face to know he was probably frowning. "She?"

"The girl I remind you of. You don't have to tell me her name, but I know there is one."

"What makes you say that?"

"The way you connected with me when we met. I could feel it. I didn't put it together until the first time I kissed you. You reacted like you were already taken, but I know you aren't. So who is she?"

For a long moment, he didn't answer. I waited. At last, he let out a quiet, resigned exhale.

"She...was an old friend. We went to college together. I was an army brat and college was the first time I didn't have to travel and leave all my friends behind. I never said anything to her about how I felt because I was too scared to cross that line."

"Mm. I think that's the first real thing you've ever told me about yourself."

"Then, in the interest of fairness," he said, sliding upward so he could look into my face. "Why a butterfly?"

"I just like butterflies."

"Liar."

Damn him. I closed my eyes. Silence built and then crumbled. "When I was a kid, they used to tell me that the butterfly represents change. That something can become greater with time. I don't know, I guess I wanted to be like that."

I opened my eyes when he touched my chin, making me look at him. "Well, guess what? You are. When you came on this ship, you were an angry selfish little girl and now you're responsible for saving an entire race. Two, if you count us in that equation. Not bad for a butterfly."

I smiled, mostly because I was trying to hide the fact that his stupid sentimental words made me want to cry. "That's pretty corny."

He grinned. "I'll take that as a compliment."

He kissed me. I savored the moment because I knew things would never be this way again. This was our time. When he left this room, he would be Hallstead again and I would be Scarlett. We weren't in love. We were just two people who needed each other and had shared something special. Nothing more, nothing less.

"How much time do we have left?" I mumbled into his mouth. He pushed up on his hands again, glancing at the nightstand, and then frowned.

"Where's my watch?"

I bit my lower lip, trying not to smile. "I think it's on the floor. You lost it somewhere during the, ah, initial assault."

He leaned over one side of the bed and I enjoyed the view of his long, muscular upper torso stretched above me. He retrieved the watch and read the time with a somewhat sobered expression.

"We have to be on the main deck soon. They're gonna give us the report of the initial analysis for New Earth."

I tried to hide the disappointment I felt with a mischievous smile, wrapping my arms around his neck.

"One for the road?"

He smirked. "If you think you can handle it."

"Shut up and kiss me, Captain."

Half an hour later, my undergarments and borrowed clothing had returned to their proper places on my body. It was just as well. The frigid air in this room was bad for my skin.

Hallstead stood by the foot of the bed, lacing his tie in the mirror perched on the wall. I watched the careful movements of his hands, noting how practiced they were. I didn't know much about him, but I could tell he probably always wore suits. He didn't seem like the jeans-and-t-shirt type. Not that I blamed him. The man could seriously rock a two-piece.

Once he was done, he turned and met my eyes, hesitating. I sat on the edge of the bed, absently drawing circles on the sheets. The customary awkward after-sex silence. I'd only heard rumors of it. Nice to know they were true.

"So."

I cleared my throat, gesturing to the chair behind me. "I still have your jacket, if you want it back."

He smiled. "Keep it. I've got more than one."

I relaxed a bit. "Is that your way of trying to get me to pine for you? It's not gonna happen."

Hallstead chuckled. "Of course not. The great Scarlett Nam doesn't need a boyfriend. She is a fiercely independent woman of the 21st century."

I scowled at him as he walked toward me. "Be more condescending."

"I can try, if you want," he teased, holding out one hand. I found it to be a curious gesture, but gave him my left hand and he tugged me off the bed until we were only inches apart. I almost shuddered as I felt the line of heat from the front of his body.

"I don't know what this is or what you want to call it, but if you need me, I'll be around," he murmured, linking my fingers with his. "I mean that. Even if it's just to talk."

I felt a rush of affection at his words. He knew exactly what I needed, somehow. That seemed to be a miracle in itself. "I'll keep that in mind."

"But just to be safe, if this is the last time I get to see you like this..." He let go of my hand and picked me up, wrapping my legs around his waist. He darted in for a kiss before I could even react, and I melted into it like a stupid little girl with a crush. I didn't even care that I should have been offended by the manhandling. It was by far the best kiss I'd ever had, and it made me realize I didn't want it to be the last.

After a long moment, he pulled away, and I opened my eyes, giving him a look. "You're such a douche."

He laughed. "Well, I had to make sure you had something to remember me by."

He pressed one final sweet kiss against my lips and then lowered me to the floor. "I'll see you on the bridge, Scarlett."

"Definitely."

I watched him go and knew that somehow, we would be alright. Maybe not forever, but for now, it was enough.

DUKE

When I reached the bridge, I was glad to see a couple more familiar faces: Han and Sam were among the people standing around chatting as we waited for Scarlett and Hallstead to arrive to start the meeting.

"Well, well, well," I said. "Who invited the riff-raff?"

"Didn't you hear?" Sam said with a grin. "We're being promoted."

"No shit. Congratulations. What's the new assignment?"

"The initial thought is they're going to need a squadron to go down to the planet's surface," Han said, as stoic as usual, but I could see pride in his eyes. He wasn't the kind of guy who'd be happy with being a grunt his whole life, so I got the feeling this was a big deal to him. "We'd escort the craft and then set up a perimeter while the scientists have a look around. They're assembling the team as we speak."

Sam nodded to me. "And I take it they want you to recount what you encountered on the Berg warship?"

"That's my best guess, yeah. It was…something else." I fought down a shudder. "I'll just say it's a good thing we blew them to hell and leave it at that."

"I believe you. Fingers crossed their whole species was on that warship." Sam then snorted. "And I don't even believe myself, to be honest. I think we've got a helluva fight on our hands if the rest of them find us."

"An eye for an eye," Han rumbled. "They shot first. We merely retaliated."

"I would make a 'Han shot first' joke here, but we both know you won't get it," Sam mused.

Han just rolled his eyes, then glanced at me. "I owe you an apology."

My eyebrows rose. "For what?"

"For being suspicious of you. I thought you'd turn me in, but you didn't. You kept your mouth shut and you saved us. You have my respect from here on out." He offered his hand. I almost gaped at him.

I shook his hand once. "Thank you, but you don't need to apologize. I was sketchy to begin with and you were right to be suspicious."

"Even so, we owe you." His eyes wandered to behind me and his stature straightened. I turned to see Hallstead enter the bridge, which resulted in the military personnel saluting him. It took a lot of effort not to glare at him as he appeared; I still didn't appreciate whatever the hell was going on between him and my sister. I'd made that boyfriend joke insincerely. I didn't think for a second she liked him or vice versa, and I was going make damn sure nothing came of it aside from some sort of flirtation.

"At ease, gentlemen," he said as he stepped up to the platform with the holodeck in the center. "We're just waiting on our Miss Nam and we'll get started."

His gray eyes flicked over to me and something of a smirk almost hovered over his mouth. I must not have fixed my face fast enough. "Mr. Nam."

"Captain," I said stiffly, crossing my arms. "Or is it general yet?"

"That's still up for debate," he answered, tucking his hands into his pockets. "Acting general, I guess, but we'll see."

Rochester elbowed him lightly, grinning. "Admit it, Boy Scout. You kinda like being in charge, don't you?"

"For now, anyway."

The elevator dinged and Scarlett hobbled out, dressed in her borrowed business casual outfit, which looked odd on her. I'd mostly only seen my sister in jeans, cargo pants, and sweatpants. There weren't any real occasions for her to wear business casual in our old line of work. I could tell she hated the crutches; she'd always been quick on her feet. Poor thing.

Thank God she was still alive.

"Sorry I'm late," she said with a haggard sigh. "But as you can see, I'm not terribly mobile right now. What'd I miss?"

"Nothing yet," Hallstead said. "What we have here is a little think tank, basically. The way I see it, we have three groups that need to catch each other up to speed before moving forward."

Hallstead gestured to Han, Sam, and me. "These three gentlemen agreed to escort the first ship down to the planet's surface. Once there, they will set up a perimeter and escort the exploration team around until they find somewhere to make camp."

He then gestured to the group standing to his right: four men and three women. "Our exploration team consists of the top minds in relevant fields who survived Earth's destruction. We've got a biologist, a botanist, a geologist, a civil and mechanical engineer, a wildlife zoologist, and our two astronauts. Everything they gather will be sent to an even bigger team of experts who will then create an action plan, and then we'll assign who will go to observe if the landscape is safe enough and has enough resources for colonization."

Last, Hallstead gestured to Scarlett. "The team will then be advised by the Shasar, whose technological advancements and knowledge of the known universe might be helpful to us. In exchange, we're prepared to share what resources we have and help them build a new settlement for themselves. At this time, we're not aware of anyone else on board who happens to be an Empath like Miss Nam, so we'll need her to communicate with them until we've developed an alternate form of language with their species."

He hit a couple of buttons on the console and brought up security footage from what looked like a common recreation area of the ship on one of the mid-level floors. The Shasar were congregated there. The furniture had been covered in plastic, as were the floors, and I could see evidence of quarantine and hazmat materials. "We've gotten them all on board and comfortable for now since their vessels wouldn't survive the trip on the amount of oxygen available. Shortly, Miss Nam will figure out if they require food and water like us, and we can ration out what we have available from surplus."

"And how long is it going to take to reach the planet?" I asked.

"168 hours. Right now, we sent the probes ahead of us to capture as much data as possible so that we know what we're anticipating. The first set of photos and video ought to be to our onboard satellites within the next 48 hours."

"How long can the people onboard the *Titan* survive on what we have now?" Scarlett asked.

"The last numbers I saw indicated between two and three years, but with our added guests, that is going to affect the original projection. That's why we need to move immediately on exploring the planet and moving the Shasar planet-side first, if possible. If it's not safe, they'll remain with us until we get a handle on protecting them and our exploration team. The *Titan* runs on a revolutionary self-perpetuating energy source, so we're not worried about losing power or oxygen running out— just food and water, and the initial reports from our satellites indicate the planet should have drinkable water and edible vegetation similar to Earth."

Hallstead's expression hardened. "And that brings us to our last concern. If the Bergleute's entire race was not aboard the warship when it was destroyed, we have to put a contingency plan in place in case they try to pursue us. The *Titan* is our lifeline. We have to protect it at all costs. It's going to be important to get as much information from the Shasar as possible so that we're ready for them, but that's also why Duke and Scarlett are a part of our think tank."

He glanced between my sister and me gravely. "We need to know everything you know about the Bergs."

Scarlett smiled fiercely and held up a tiny rectangular device. "Lucky for you, my heads-up display recorded everything and survived the trip."

She handed it to him, and he inserted it into the console. We watched the grisly footage. The scientists took notes on their tablets and notepads. Sam looked a bit pale while Han's eyes stayed narrowed, his jaw clenched, the entire time. Scarlett had as bad a time as I did aboard that ship, and it was gut-wrenching to watch her goodbye to me again. I could tell a few of the observers were moved by it as well, especially Hallstead, who swallowed hard.

"Thank you, Scarlett," the captain said, clearing his throat and turning off the footage once it had reached the point where she'd come aboard the *Titan*. "Duke, what else can you tell us about them?"

"Whatever they are, it seems to me like the ones we encountered were the brutes," I said, carefully thinking over my own horrific experience. "Given how sophisticated their type of fuel was and how the ship was designed, it could be that this is only a fraction of their whole race. I can't see big monsters like those ones working on electrical grids where the slightest miscalculation could get you killed. We also saw a lot of different ships, so it's possible that the Shasar are just their latest victims. Maybe they've enslaved other alien races to build for them or there are Bergs back on their home planet who interpret things they learn from other aliens. The other reason I theorize that is at one point, I had to go through the vents to avoid detection and I ran into—I shit you not—a carnivorous alien slug."

The people gathered around me gave a start. "A what?" Scarlett demanded.

"You heard me," I said with a snort. "Which indicates that maybe there were other aliens on board their ship or they'd accidentally carried something from their home world onto the ship. It seemed very much like a parasitic creature that just snuck onto the ship and since it lived in the vents, they had no idea it was even there since they can't fit into the air ducts."

Hallstead ran a hand through his hair, then sighed. "This just keeps getting weirder, doesn't it?"

"Oh yeah. Weird as hell."

"I'll put in a word with the *Titan's* engineering team. Maybe the best way to avoid another conflict is if the *Titan* lands on the planet and the Bergs can't find it. In the meantime, let's get Miss Nam over to the Shasar and we'll reconvene once the first images from the planet's surface come through. Dismissed."

"Captain," I said, catching up to him before he got too far.

"Yes?"

"I have an odd request, but I think it might help."

"Sure, what is it?"

"Could I meet with Evelyn Rosewood?"

Hallstead frowned. "You can, but what for?"

"I don't know, I just…have this hunch about something she said when we first met. It won't take long, I promise."

Hallstead went to one of the communications officers on board and had them call down to her room. After a bit, he wrote down the meeting room number and handed it to me, then gave me a stern look. "Keep it short. She's still recovering from the launch."

"Yes, sir."

"The hell are you up to, *Oppa?*" Scarlett asked.

I squeezed her hand. "Can't explain it, really. Just a gut instinct. I'll see you in a bit."

Hallstead and Scarlett got into another elevator going down, but I stopped before getting into one going up when I noticed his hand on her upper back to steady her as she balanced on the crutches. "Hey. Hands where I can see 'em, pretty boy."

Scarlett rolled her eyes. "Go bark at the moon, watch dog."

I let out a growl, which made her laugh in spite of herself, then I got on the elevator and rode to the upper deck meeting room floor. There were open access meeting rooms that civilians could book, but these were the private rooms for the authority figures aboard. I opened the door to find a couple of wooden tables and chairs with cushions. What a relief. I'd hated those metal tables and chairs in the interrogation levels.

Evelyn Rosewood didn't look as spaced out as the first time I'd seen her. She sat up straight in her chair, and she wore a navy dress with an ivory shawl over it. Her brown eyes seemed much more focused than before. Her white dreadlocks were neatly tucked into a bun at the base of her neck.

"Mr. Nam," she said with a slight nod.

"Mrs. Rosewood," I said in return, nodding to her as well after I closed the door. "I'm sorry if this is abrupt. I hate to disturb you, but I need to ask you something."

"Is it about my son?"

"No, ma'am."

She let out a little snort. "Good. He's an asshole. You know it better than most, I bet."

Wow. Not the response I was expecting. "You're...not angry with me about what happened?"

Evelyn shook her head. "He chose his own path, and he's proud and bullheaded. I always knew it'd lead him into trouble. After all, do you think it's just a coincidence he's divorced?"

"I didn't know that, ma'am."

"Well, now you do. Trouble's always been coming for him. I warned him, like any mother does, but he wouldn't listen."

"To be honest, that's what I've come to talk to you about," I said. "That night the ships launched and left Earth, you said something to me about us being chosen. About someone waiting in the darkness."

Evelyn winced. "Ah. To tell you the truth, that was a night where I hadn't taken my proper medication. I'm old. You know how old folks get. I'm not always myself."

"Well, that's just it. I thought you were talking about the Bergleute at first, but what if you were talking about the Shasar instead? Did you have any prior knowledge about the mission and its details?"

Evelyn frowned. "I...no. I know my son told me that he was a part of a secret international organization, but he wasn't allowed to tell us any details. He just said there may come a time when we'd have to abandon our friends and family, but nothing else."

"Right, so how did you know about the aliens?"

"I..." She frowned harder. "I don't know."

"This is gonna sound nuts, but I think maybe you have some latent Empath abilities and the Shasar reached you from the Bergs' warship that night. Did you have a dream about strange creatures? Creatures that look like this?" I took out the scrap of paper Hallstead gave me and drew a very basic but functional picture of Hatwer.

Evelyn stared at it. "I...yes, I dreamt of him that night."

"The Shasar are a telepathic species. We don't yet know the extent of their abilities, but it's possible that as the warship approached Earth, Hatwer was calling out for help and you heard him. You and Scarlett might be the only Empaths right now, but if we can figure out just how you were able to hear him, then we can open up communications between them and us."

"I..." She looked back at the paper, stunned. "But I'm an old woman. I can't possibly be able to use telepathy."

"I think you might, ma'am. Would you be willing to give it a try? Just once?"

She nibbled her lower lip. "I...they're not dangerous, are they?"

I shook my head. "Not that I know of. They were a peaceful race until the Bergleute kidnapped them and enslaved them. The one you may have seen in your dream is just a child. His name is Hatwer. He's friends with my sister, in fact."

"And you're sure that door doesn't swing both ways?" she asked. "That they can't take control of me?"

"I have yet to see evidence of that, but I do promise I'll protect you." I smiled at her. "After all, I have to make amends for putting your son in jail."

She met my eyes for a long moment. "And you really believe in them? In me?"

"I do, ma'am."

Evelyn took a deep breath and stared at the drawing. "Okay. It can't hurt to try, can it?"

I winked at her. "No, it can't, ma'am."

CHAPTER TWENTY

SCARLETT

The next couple of hours were productive, but grueling, as I dictated the Shasar's knowledge for the *Titan* scientists and Hallstead. It was a lot for an ex-thief with a GED. I suspected Hallstead knew I was getting worn out, so he concluded the first session after the second hour. It hadn't been long since our escape from the ship and without daytime and nighttime, it was hard to adjust to knowing when to get some rest. Most of the information I collected had to do with the Shasar's biology, eating and sleeping habits, and if they had a written version of their native language that the linguists on board could study.

After the session let out, Hallstead met me in the hallway, still cool as a cucumber, keeping his voice low. "You okay?"

I nodded. "Thanks. I think I'll be able to go for longer once I get this sleep schedule licked. I probably need a few more hours to clear my head."

"Yeah, you do look tired."

I sent him a sly look. "That's partially your fault, you know."

Hallstead grinned. "Yeah, I guess it is. Your brother's really got it out for me, though. I might turn up in the trash chute if I'm not careful."

I chuckled. "He can't help himself. He was already overprotective long before the suicide mission. And I have a bad track record with men."

Hallstead winced. "Yeah, Dr. Warwick mentioned it. I'm sorry."

"It's ancient history, Captain."

"Well, I have something that might cheer you up."

I snorted as I watched him pull out his phone. "Something tells me you're not the kind of guy who gives a gal flowers."

He handed me the phone. "Here. Take a look at the designation."

I scrolled a little, seeing a roster of the *Titan's* occupants organized by last name. I saw mine and next to it, my new profession. "Translator."

"Mm-hmm. Scroll up."

I did and saw my brother's name. "Fieldwork Liaison."

I glanced up to see him smiling. "You're all official, Miss Nam. No longer prisoners. You're *Titan* residents from here on out."

"Travis…" I couldn't help a dopey smile as I handed him the phone. "You didn't have to do that."

He shrugged a shoulder. "I'm the boss now. Perks of the job."

Hallstead nodded toward the other end of the hall where the scientists were waiting for the elevator. "I've got to get back and discuss what's next with the eggheads. Get some sleep. We'll brief you in another eight to ten hours and then set up the next session."

"Mmkay. I'll see you then."

Hallstead flashed me that trademark smirk. "Behave yourself in the meantime, Miss Nam."

"I make no promises," I sniffed as I headed for the elevators on the opposite side of the hall. I returned to my living quarters and crawled into bed. The *Titan* was oddly silent, like a fancy hotel. I thought the quiet would help me sleep.

It didn't.

And of all the things keeping me awake, the most prominent one was Captain Hallstead.

Look, I know how it sounds, alright? Like a dumb headstrong girl with a crush. But every time I tried to push him out of my mind, he crawled right back in like a persistent cat that wanted to be inside a too-small cardboard box.

More than that, it was the first time I'd ever hidden anything from my brother.

And that was…scary.

Duke knew about Percy. Duke knew about me losing my virginity to a guy who lived in our building. He knew practically everything about me and yet…I hadn't told him about me and Hallstead.

Why?

No idea.

So I did something else stupid.

"Well, Scarlett, I have to say I was surprised to get your call," Dr. Warwick said as she settled into the cushion of her office chair. I didn't sit; I paced back and forth by the other chair, too filled with nervous energy to sit.

"You and me both, Doc." I smoothed my hands through my hair. "So, in TV and movies, there's some kind of Hippocratic oath I've seen before. You know, patient-doctor confidentiality. Is that still a thing?"

"It is for me," she confirmed.

I narrowed my eyes at her. "Even after Hallstead came to you for dirt on me?"

"That was different. In certain circumstances, if the patient is in danger of hurting themselves or someone else, some of the information can be released. And Hallstead seemed genuinely concerned about the safety of you, your brother, and the other passengers, so I cooperated. It was only for your protection."

I rolled my eyes. "Uh-huh. Well, we need to re-affirm that you're not going to repeat this to anyone else."

She adjusted her glasses, her face and voice calm. "I will not repeat it to anyone else."

"Good. I slept with Hallstead."

Dr. Warwick sputtered for a second, her eyes wide. "Come again?"

"Ha. No pun intended."

"I…" She seemed to take a second and compose herself, grabbing her pen and pad and scribbling madly. "When was this?"

"Not too long ago, after I got back to my room."

"Goodness me. That's…a lot to unpack. No wonder you can't sleep."

I quit pacing enough to rest my hands on the back of the seat. "So you know why?"

"I can probably guess. Have you had any attachment to anyone aside from your brother since you two left the foster care system?"

"No."

"And did you tell Duke you slept with Hallstead?"

I swallowed hard and just shook my head. Dr. Warwick gave me a sympathetic look. "First of all, stop beating yourself up about it. It's all over your face. You didn't do anything wrong."

I flung myself in the chair, groaning and covering my face with both hands. "But I don't know why!"

"Scarlett, he's your older brother. You care what he thinks about you. If you told him about it and he didn't approve, it would put you at odds with him. From what I can tell, he's always been on your side and any arguments you've had have been minor. A suitor he doesn't approve of could be a big roadblock in your relationship."

"Hallstead's not even a suitor," I insisted. "He's...I don't know what he is."

"Try to think of what he is to you in your own words."

"This may shock you, Doc, but I don't exactly have a frame of reference when it comes to men."

"Alright, well, let's go another route. Would you like to see him again?"

I chewed my bottom lip. "I mean...yeah? Not to be too graphic, but it was some dynamite sex."

Her lips twitched at one edge. "Oh?"

"Again, I know I have a low bar, but the captain can lay the pipe, I'll be honest."

She seemed to suppress a chuckle. "Right. Well, despite what certain parts of society taught us, sex—when it happens between two responsible, consenting adults—can be great for the body, mind, and soul, and you've been without for a long time. If you feel overwhelmed, that's normal. It was a big step, especially after you narrowly escaped being killed. Cheating death demands celebration and you seem to like and trust him. These are uncharted waters for you."

"But why can I stare down the barrel of a laser pistol and not flinch, but thinking about Hallstead makes my insides turn into jello?" I demanded. "That's ridiculous."

"It's human," she reminded me patiently. "And again, you've never had someone you liked as much as him before, so you're feeling defensive. It's not a problem that you have to solve, Scarlett. Let yourself feel something new. It might be scary at first, but you can weather the storm if you just stay aware of your own feelings."

"So...you think I should tell Duke the truth?"

"It doesn't matter what I think. It just matters what you think."

I sighed. "If I tell him, he's gonna go berserk."

"Then don't."

"But then I'll keep feeling guilty."

"Is it going to hurt Duke if you have a relationship with Hallstead? Aside from just not telling him about it?"

I thought about it. "I guess not? I mean, I'm no longer in consideration for the military branch of the *Titan* personnel. I'm officially a translator, so it's not fraternization."

"Has Hallstead made any mention of wanting to hide the relationship?"

"No, not yet. We're not even sure if it's a relationship, to be honest. Maybe it was just a one-night stand. An itch that needed scratching."

"It doesn't sound that way to me. Was it just sex? Did you talk afterward?"

I fidgeted. "There was some pillow talk afterward."

"Did it keep your interest?"

I shrugged. "I guess so."

"I think it's very possible you like Hallstead for more than sex and it's worth exploring, if only because you've been devoid of any meaningful relationships aside from your brother. There are a lot of things you've never gotten to experience when you were on your own for so long. Maybe Duke will react poorly and maybe if you explain it to him, he'll eventually accept it. At the end of the day, it's not your responsibility to keep Duke happy. He has to do that himself. If you find fulfillment with Hallstead, then keep seeing him. First, though, you need to have a talk with him about the nature of your relationship."

I groaned again. "Yes, because we know conflict resolution is my forté."

"You'll figure it out sooner or later." She gave me a thoughtful look. "Is that his jacket?"

I fiddled with the too-long sleeve on my left wrist. "It's comfortable. Sue me."

Dr. Warwick smiled. "Like I said, Scarlett. Defensive."

I rolled my eyes. "Thanks, that's a big help."

I ran my hands through my hair again and softened my tone a bit. "But I do mean that. Thank you. I guess I have a lot to think about and saying it out loud to another person helps. I don't have a best friend. Or any friends, for that matter. Not yet. I should work on that."

"Yes, you should. And the good news is now you have the time to do so. You're in an environment where that's possible."

"I'm sure everyone is clamoring to be friends with a socially inept ex-criminal, so good to know." I stood up and nodded to her. "Thanks, Doc. Really. Much obliged."

"My pleasure, Scarlett. Get some sleep."

"I'll try. Later, Doc."

I headed back to my room and then flopped into bed.

And to my absolute surprise, I slept fine.

What do you know? Maybe there is something to this therapy stuff.

Now that I was just a normal passenger, I was given what amounted to a welcome packet and access to everything that a normal occupant would have. In short, the *Titan* was a mix between a military vessel and a cruise ship—not that everything was about luxury, just that it had the basic needs of a person at sea. There were communal bathrooms and showers, somewhere to exercise and run track, a cafeteria, those sorts of things. Obviously, money was meaningless when the world and its economy were gone, so anything you needed didn't cost anything. Clothing was obtained through a sort of Goodwill-style booth in the common areas.

What was also weird was my new celebrity on the ship. After saving the Shasar and killing the Bergleute, my brother and I were regarded fondly by anyone who bumped into us. It was far cry from how we'd spent most of our lives running from the authorities and trying to be as incognito as possible. I had no idea how to feel about the spotlight on me. After all, I never considered myself a hero. I'd just tried to do right by someone who needed me.

After the second session of translating, or dictating, I suppose, information between the Shasar and our team, I pulled Hallstead aside to talk.

"I'm sure you know by now I'm not great at communications or...feelings...but I wanted to see where we were. I'm not sure. I've never..." I hesitated, trying to figure out how to phrase it. "...liked anyone before. As weird as it sounds. So I don't know what to do."

Hallstead's eyebrows lifted. "You like me? Wow, I had no idea."

I glared. "Smartass."

"You're very cute when you're defensive, you know," he said, leaning a shoulder against the wall beside us. I had a very real urge to kiss him, but I resisted it. "I had a feeling you've never done this dance before. That's why I gave you some space to figure things out."

"Oh." I nibbled my lower lip, feeling oddly self-conscious. "Well, I mean...do you want to keep seeing me?"

"Yes." He answered without a sign of reluctance. My heart leapt. Stupid heart. "But I also know that your brother isn't going to like it."

"So you want to keep it on the down-low, to use the vernacular?"

"For now. Is that gonna bother you?"

I thought about it. "I mean, I won't feel awesome about lying to Duke, but to be honest, it's none of his damn business. I could have a whole conga line of guys outside of my bedroom and it shouldn't matter. I think he needs time to mellow out. He's gonna be on serious watchdog alert for a while with what just happened and we'd have to ease him into it." I paused. "Whatever 'it' is."

"We'll figure it out," he said softly. "There's no rush, Scarlett. Like you said, you've never done this before. Nobody's pressuring anybody. We like spending time with each other. It's that simple. Everything else, we'll take it as it comes."

My stomach fluttered. God, I really did have a crush on the man. For shame! "When can I see you again?"

He glanced down at my left leg. "You know, I really should let you heal first."

"Yeah, that's not gonna work for me. I don't need my shin to bang you, so pony up, boyfriend."

He laughed. "I've got a lot going on, but after the images get back from the probes, I think I have a few free hours."

"Hours?" I said with heavy skepticism. "Don't oversell yourself, Hallstead."

His dark lashes lowered over those gray eyes, something sly and seductive creeping into his voice as he deepened it a bit for my benefit. "The first time was just the abridged version, you know."

"Is that right?" I said, adding something sultry to my own voice.

"Mm-hmm. You sure you're up for it, Miss Nam?"

"I'm more than sure I can keep up."

"We'll see about that." He was about to say something else when the overhead PA system came on. *"Hallstead to the bridge. Repeat, Hallstead to the bridge."*

"They're playing my song," he said with a sigh. "I'll call your room when I'm heading over."

"Looking forward to it, hotshot."

He flashed me a quick grin before heading to the elevator. I checked on the Shasar to make sure everyone was alright before I left to return to my room.

Curiously, when I arrived, the room phone was already ringing. I limped over to the bed and then sat down, grabbing it. "Yes?"

"Scarlett, it's me," Hallstead said, his voice tense as piano wire. "We've got a problem. Simmons and Rosewood broke out of prison."

CHAPTER TWENTY-ONE

DUKE

"How did they get out?" were the first words out of my mouth as soon as I reached the bridge with Scarlett on my heels, hustling as fast as she could on her crutches.

"The guard on duty was giving Simmons his meal, and he reached through the bars and yanked him into them," Hallstead answered from where he stood beside one of the observation consoles. "The electrified field shorted out and Simmons took his security card to let himself and then Rosewood out. By the time someone found the unconscious guard, it was too late. They're somewhere on the service levels where there are only stationary cameras. There are blind spots the two of them would know about."

"This is insane," Scarlett spat. "They know this ship is crawling with people all trained enough to take them out. What's their endgame?"

"That's what we're trying to figure out," Rochester said as she studied the footage beside Hallstead. "It could be they try to take hostages and demand to be given a vessel with provisions so they can fly down to New Earth and go into hiding. Or they want to escape and try their luck elsewhere."

"Or," I said pointedly, "they want to string me and Scarlett up for screwing them both out of a job and getting them thrown in the slam."

Hallstead frowned at me. "You think they'd go that far for revenge?"

"I wouldn't rule it out, is all I'm saying. Simmons was about to shoot Scarlett dead in that elevator and Rosewood's had it out for me since we broke into his place."

Hallstead grimaced. "Noted. You two need to stay close for now. I'm putting the entire ship on lockdown and we're deploying teams to sweep this place top to bottom until we find them. We've already shut off the access codes of the guard whose badge Simmons stole, so any log in credentials is going to get combed through until we find an anomaly."

"How big are the service areas of the ship?" Scarlett asked.

"Too big. It'll take hours to search them all. The *Titan's* got an incredibly enormous system for its propulsion and sustainability due to the number of passengers. There are dozens of backups to make sure nothing fails, and if it does, it's one section, not the entire thing at once."

"That tracks," I said. "One of the tactics Scarlett and I used when we stole was misdirection. Cause a small distraction in the store that routes the attention of the associates and then we steal in the commotion and vanish."

Hallstead and Rochester shared a look. "You're thinking sabotage?" Rochester asked.

"It's the only way to divert man-power off the search," Scarlett said. "Damage the ship and you'll have to concentrate on that instead of the other areas."

"Shit," Hallstead muttered. "Alright, so let's assume Plan A is to damage the ship and then get what you need in the meantime while we're distracted. That means food, water, clothing, spacesuits, weapons, and then a ship. With the ship on lockdown, their access should be cut off, but that doesn't rule out the living quarters. They could get to an unoccupied room and hole up in there and take what they find."

"And one more thing," I added. "Why didn't they spring Bridgewater? He has enough of a grudge against you, Scarlett, and me to want to join up with their little prison break."

"Bridgewater has to know this won't end well for them," Rochester said. "Surviving on a whole new planet with just the three of them? It's laughable at best."

"It is," Scarlett said, her voice hushed, her expression worried. "Unless you've got someone from the Shasar to guide you and be your ticket out of here."

She looked at the colonel. "Rochester, can you check the log for entry into the Shasar's living quarters?"

"Yeah." The colonel typed a few things into the interface. "My God. I'm showing a log for less than ten minutes ago. Nothing was scheduled for them for another hour at least."

Scarlett hobbledfor the elevator. Hallstead unholstered the gun on his hip and handed it to me. "Duke, go with her. I'm sending some officers down there to help. Find out what happened and report back to me."

"Got it." I sprinted for the elevator and got in with my sister, double checking the magazine on the gun. Scarlett hammered the button, muttering feverishly under her breath, her shoulders tense, worry etched deeply in her features. I prayed her instincts were wrong, but somehow the sinking feeling in my gut didn't believe it.

We arrived on the floor and hurried over to the sealed doors, which could only be entered by someone with clearance, mostly the military and scientists. Each door had a small window to see inside and Scarlett knocked frantically to get their attention. Immediately, two of them went up to the glass.

"Did two men come here?" Scarlett asked. "Did one of them take Hatwer with them?"

The two Shasar shared a look and then stared intensely at my sister. An echo of a sob left Scarlett, her eyes filling with tears as she turned to me. "Oh God, they took him. They took Hatwer."

"Lettie, look at me."

I gripped her hand hard. "We're gonna get him back. Alive. I swear it."

"I'll kill them," she snarled through her tears. "I'll kill them both with my bare fucking hands."

"I'll help you. But first, we've got to update the bridge and figure out where they went." I went to the panel beside the door and searched for the communication screen. I hailed one of the officers and she patched me through. "They took Hatwer."

"Goddammit!" Hallstead barked. "So they're either going to use him for ransom or as a hostage so we don't blow them to hell if they escape in one of the ships. We've got to get him back. Scarlett, is there any way for Hatwer to contact you from wherever they've taken him?"

"I don't know. I've never tried to mind-meld with him at a long distance."

"Hallstead, when I spoke to Evelyn Rosewood, what she told me indicates that it's possible. I think she's an Empath too, or at least partially, because she remembers having a dream about Hatwer before the ships launched during the Contingency."

"But it only happened when she was asleep, right?" Scarlett asked.

"I think so. Ask the Shasar if long distance telepathy is possible. Maybe then we can find where they're hiding and get to him."

"It's worth a shot," Hallstead said. "Go for it."

Scarlett went back over to the door where Hatwer's parents were waiting. "Is there any way to use telepathy long distance?"

She listened for a bit and then looked at me. "They said yes. Dreams put them into a sort of meditative state. Hatwer was in that state the first time he connected with me. If he's afraid, he might be in that state now. Get me to the infirmary and have them sedate me. It might work."

"You copy that, Hallstead?" I asked.

"Yeah, go, I'll have someone meet you there."

Scarlett turned to the glass again. "I'll get him back to you. I swear."

She pressed her palm to the window. They did the same. Then she turned and left with me to head for the infirmary.

SCARLETT

I still didn't like infirmaries, but they couldn't move fast enough to sedate me. I damn near wanted to grab the knockout gas myself, but they still had to do a basic check of my vital signs before they'd do it.

"This is laughing gas," the lead anesthesiologist told me. "We're going to put you under for about five minutes and then bring you back to see if you got through. You'll feel sluggish when you come out of it, but it'll wear off. Your brother will probably have to help you move around—"

"Fine, just hurry up, Orin Scrivello!" I snapped.

He made no pithy remark; he just lowered the mask onto my face. Once it was correctly affixed, he checked the levels on the gas and told me to count backward from 100.

And I was out before I got to 95.

Darkness.

Noise.

I was scared, as scared as I'd been the first time the Bergleute showed up and obliterated my people. As scared as I was when the humans hurt me during their interrogation. These men meant me harm. I wished for my parents.

For Scarlett.

"Hatwer?"

Something disconnected. Our thoughts disengaged and the darkness parted to reveal a small spotlight with Hatwer in the middle. I was back in my own body and my own head. I could see him clearly standing there, his clawed hands clutching his arms, shivering from fear. Then he blinked and noticed me there. "S-Scarlett?"

I knelt and opened my arms to him. "It's me, Hatwer."

He rushed forward and hugged me. "It's okay, I came to help you. Do you know where you are?"

Hatwer wiped his tears as he pulled back. "I am not certain."

I held his hands. "You can do it. Concentrate. What do you remember after they took you from your parents?"

"I..." He closed his eyes and slowed his breathing. "Before I went into this state, we were in one of the engine rooms. One of them said that there is a trash chute that goes all the way up to the hangar, so they could drop down there and steal a ship. I tried to escape, but one of them caught me and hit me. I fell and hit my head. That's all I remember."

I tried my best to quell my anger at one of those bastards striking an innocent child. "If you're unconscious, it means they'd have to carry you, which might slow them down. What about provisions? Do you remember them saying anything about food and water?"

"I think one of them said that each escape pod is equipped with it, enough for a week at most."

"Okay, so then they'll probably try to get aboard and then contact the bridge to tell them if they blow up the ship, they'll kill you too. They know we want you back safe. They won't kill you, I promise."

"I'm scared, Scarlett," he whispered mournfully.

My eyes grew wet. I touched my forehead to his the way I'd seen his parents do. "I know. I'm scared too. But I will do everything in my power to save you, okay? I promise. We're coming to get you, Hatwer. Hang on."

My voice came out faded as the connection began to unravel. "Just hang on."

I crashed back into consciousness screaming, "Trash!"

"Whoa!" The anesthesiologist hopped back a bit. He tried to press me flat to the bed, but I resisted, trying to see through the haze of the after-effects.

"Duke, where's Duke, trash, it's the trash!"

A blurry figure came to my right side and gripped my hand. "It's me, Lettie. I'm here. What are you trying to say?"

I gulped in a few more breaths and stared at him, croaking. "The trash chute. They're gonna go down the trash chute to the hangar and steal a ship."

"You are *brilliant*, Lettie." He kissed my forehead. "I'll tell them, hang on."

He rushed to the nearest landline on the wall. The doctor had been right—sluggish didn't even start to cover it. My limbs felt heavy and everything seemed to be buffering, as if my reaction time had taken a huge hit. Definitely not as disorienting as being drunk, but it was no fun. It was hard just to grasp a single thought as it floated by in my head. The clearest thought was that I had to get up and get ready to save Hatwer.

"Hang on now," the anesthesiologist said with strained patience as I struggled to stand. "You still need to recover. You can't just—"

"Watch me, Doc," I said as I limped over to my crutches where they leaned against a nearby chair. I didn't tip over on just one leg, but it was a close call. My vision cleared enough to see the consternation on the doctor's face as he watched me lurch toward my brother.

Duke hung up the phone, frowning at me. "Should you be—"

"Save it, *Oppa*," I said briskly. "What did Hallstead say?"

"They're going to plant men at strategic points and try to snipe them before they board an escape pod. It has to be quick and quiet so neither of them tries to hurt Hatwer."

I ran that scenario through my head and then shook it. "They're both military men. They'll be expecting it. Remember what you said about distractions?"

Duke eyed me. "Yeah?"

"We could pretend we got to them first and try to apprehend them. Draw their attention away from Hallstead's men closing in on them."

"Lettie, that sounds incredibly dangerous. And these are seasoned veterans. How do you know they won't see right through using you or me as bait?"

I bared my teeth in a grin. "You're forgetting one important factor."

"Which is?"

"How goddamn irritating I can be."

Duke gave me a measured look. "I don't want to lose you again, Scarlett."

I gripped his hand with my own. "You're backing me up. We can't lose."

He looked down at our joined hands. Then he looked into my eyes. Same mind, same heart. He squeezed my fingers. "Goddamn right. Let's go make a mess."

CHAPTER TWENTY-TWO

SCARLETT

I had to give it to Rosewood and Simmons—they were smart for asshole traitors. I took the stairwell down to the hangar to find they'd barricaded the door to stall Hallstead's men. They were both large men, which made it easier for them to climb down the trash chute without falling into the incinerator. I couldn't exactly do the same being a skinny twenty-something girl with a bad leg, so I'd opted for the approach that my brother took inside the warship: air ducts. My leg hated the strain of wriggling through it, but being slender worked to my advantage—I got to the far end of the hangar in nothing flat. I took a borrowed screwdriver and carefully undid top two screws of the vent and then peeked through the slats. No sign of them. Good.

I pushed the vent outward as carefully as possible so it wouldn't squeak. I was about eight feet off the ground it looked like, so I needed to be careful or I'd hurt my legs. I spotted a nearby shuttle and set my booted feet on the wing before easing myself onto it and then pushing the vent closed.

I didn't spot them on the upper levels of the hangar just yet as I slid down the wing and onto the floor, staying low and palming the borrowed firearm. I'd changed into one of the maintenance crew's jumpers along with sturdy boots, my hair back in a ponytail. What I wouldn't give for a bulletproof vest. None of those on board. After all, there weren't actually supposed to be any firearms discharged; the ones the guards carried were just in case the Bergs caught up with us. The ship's outer walls were doubly enforced, so a bullet couldn't penetrate the hull and compromise the entire ship unless someone concentrated fire on one spot with an automatic weapon. That being said, I really didn't think it was a good idea to open fire with only one wall separating me from outer space.

I swept my side of the hangar, didn't see anything, and then moved stealthily toward the center where the staircase and the launchpad were. I knelt and flattened myself against the wall, then peeked around the corner.

There were two *Titan* personnel lying on the floor, unconscious, with their arms and legs duct-taped together. Simmons stood by the launchpad with a hand clenched around one of Hatwer's thin arms. I was relieved to see him conscious again. He stayed completely still since Simmons had his gun pointed in the alien's general vicinity.

I concentrated as much as possible on the little alien. *"Don't move and don't say anything, but it's me, Scarlett. Can you hear me?"*

"Yes," Hatwer said, relief in his voice.

"I'm around the corner to your right. Duke is on his way now. We're going to try and distract them so that Hallstead's men can take them out. I promise you won't be hurt, okay?"

"I understand."

"Do you know where Rosewood went?"

"Yes. He is prepping the escape pod for launch. One level up to my left."

I tilted my head, listening in. Faintly, I could hear the propulsion system humming to life. Shit. I had to move fast.

I took a deep breath and prayed the plan wasn't a mistake.

I whirled from around the corner and shouted, "Drop it, asshole!"

Simmons didn't waste a single second; he opened fire immediately. I dropped to one knee and rolled behind the nearest ship. He cursed and then hollered, "Of course you came to the alien's rescue, you miserable little bitch."

"That's Miss Miserable Little Bitch to you, you shrimp-dicked fuck-knuckle," I shouted back, pushing up from my hiding spot and aiming the gun at his head. He aimed at mine, his other arm around Hatwer's throat to keep him close enough to be a partial shield. "Let him go, Simmons. You know you're not gonna get away with this shit."

He let out a nasty chuckle. "That's where you're wrong. I've got leverage and you ain't got shit. You're gonna let us go and maybe if you're nice, we'll send your little friend back to you one piece at a time."

"Running and hiding like the cowards you are," I said with a sharp smirk. "I'm glad you've finally showed your true colors. Tell me whose ass you kissed to be invited onto this ship. We clearly know you're no credit to the human race."

Simmons' face reddened as he sneered at me. "I served my country. That's how I got here. I didn't sneak in and then sleep my way to the top."

I laughed. "I'd tell you to go fuck yourself, but you're so repulsive the attraction wouldn't be reciprocated."

"Better than being a no-account slut."

"Yeah, well, this no-account slut just saved everyone on this ship, including your sorry ass, so maybe you should thank me."

He narrowed his eyes at me. "This is your last chance, bitch. Get out of my way or I will kill you."

"Like you did in that elevator? I was two feet away and you couldn't even hit me. Face it, Simmons. You're a failure. A gutless worm. A flunky. You wanna know why I piss you off so much? It's because you're nothing more than a mediocre white man who realized that even with the rest of humanity dead, you'll never amount to anything because there is nothing special about you."

"Fuck you!" Simmons gauntleted his right hand with his left and shot at me.

I dove to one side and yelled, "Hatwer, now! Go!"

The little alien leapt off the launchpad onto the floor below, rolled, and then took off to find a hiding spot.

"No!" Simmons snarled, turning as if to run after him, but I returned fire and forced him in the opposite direction.

Bullets punched divots into the metal floor near my feet, so I strafed as I laid down cover fire, careful to keep count of how many bullets I had left. He took cover over by the staircase and yelled, "Rosewood, we're blown! Get that damn thing in the air now!"

"It's fueling!" Rosewood yelled back. "I can't make it go any faster."

I needed to draw Simmons away from the stairwell; that was where Hallstead's snipers were going to come through, so I crept around the left side of the hangar past the launchpad until I was across from Simmons, though still obscured by one of the ships.

I checked my magazine. Ten bullets left. Shit. I'd have to be careful.

"This isn't gonna work," I called out to Simmons. "You lost Hatwer. You're just a liability now. He's gonna leave without you."

"Shut up!" I ducked down as a couple more bullets punched metal dents into the wing of the ship near me.

"You really think he's gonna risk his freedom for you? After you've shown just how incompetent you are? You should have just stayed in your cell."

I spotted Simmons climbing up another flight of stairs, hoping the higher vantage point would give him a better shot at me. Perfect. While he moved, I limped over to the bottom floor staircase entrance as fast as I could. There was a broken pipe someone had shoved into the door handle to keep it shut. I wrenched it free. As I did, I heard Simmons swear when he noticed that I was gone.

"Where are you, you little bitch?" he shouted in frustration. "You call me gutless and then run and hide? You're not better than me and I'm gonna prove it when I kill you."

"Forget her!" Rosewood ordered from the upper level. "Get the alien back now, dammit!"

Heavy footsteps on the staircase again. He was coming down to search for Hatwer. Damn it. If he found him, we'd be back to square one.

I closed my eyes and concentrated. *Hatwer, where are you?*

There is a door that leads into a room with spare parts for your spacecrafts. I am hiding there under a piece of scrap metal.

I stuck my head out enough to look around the hangar, and I spotted the door to the far right of the hangar. Simmons was searching nearby, but he was bound to try there in a minute or two. If he holed up in there, the snipers wouldn't have a good shot and he'd have his hostage back. I didn't have any good ideas. Just a bad one.

I climbed onto the launchpad as stealthily as possible, given my bad leg, and then got on my knees. I aimed the handgun as carefully as I could as Simmons approached the door to the supply room. Then I prayed and pulled the trigger.

I missed center mass, but the bullet grazed his right shoulder. He cried out and then whirled around. I hit the floor on my belly and scooted past the edge, just barely making it before the bullets whizzed over my head.

"It's over, little girl," Simmons gloated as he closed in on me. I tried to crawl to the opposite end of the launchpad to drop down, but he was too quick. "Freeze."

I did. He'd reached the top of the small set of stairs onto the launchpad and I was on all fours with the gun in my hand, my back to him. No way I could draw it before he shot me. I'd gambled and lost.

"Slide the gun off the platform."

I clenched my jaw for a second. "I'd rather die armed."

He let out another filthy chuckle. "At least you know you're dead meat. That's good enough for me. Turn around. I want to see your face when you die."

My heart hammered in my chest, but my voice didn't waver as I spoke. "Fuck you."

Simmons grabbed the back of my hair and kicked the gun out of my grasp. He dragged me up to my knees and put the barrel of the gun to my forehead. He yanked on my head nearly hard enough to break my neck, forcing me to look at him. "I win."

I grinned fiercely up at him. *"Annyeonghi gaseyo,* asshole."

He frowned at me. "What?"

Unbeknownst to him, a red dot had appeared on his forehead.

The sniper's bullet struck his head dead center.

He died confused.

Simmons' body toppled backward onto the platform, a chunk of skull and brain matter missing from the back of his head.

I stood on my shaky legs and kicked the gun away from his still-twitching fingers. I should have felt horror at the scene of death before me, but all I could think were two words.

Good riddance.

I looked away from the corpse to see the smoking barrel of the rifle that had shot him and who was holding it. But I didn't have to look. I already knew.

"Thank you," I said breathlessly.

Hallstead shouldered the rifle and nodded to me in respect. "You're welcome, Scarlett."

Then he gestured for the two men at his side to head toward the next landing to catch up with Rosewood.

DUKE

"Why did I let her talk me into this shit?"

I had several more feet to go before I'd reached the hatch to the trash chute, but the stench and the strain of putting my back to the wall and slowly lowering myself down was enough to make me want to scream. I wasn't claustrophobic, but this sucked. And I had to stay as quiet as I could; I didn't know if anything was audible on the other side of the wall.

What also didn't help were the slimy walls where food had smeared on its way down into the incinerator, so I'd had to bite my tongue to keep from reflexively shouting the couple of times I almost fell. The combat boots helped immensely, but it was a delicate operation, to say the least.

I finally reached the hatch. Very little food would come from the hangar—maybe just meals from the people on shift down here. The main items deposited in here would be broken parts from the ships that weren't recyclable. The reason I'd taken this shit suggestion, though, was that the fleet of escape pods were on the side of the hangar near the trash chute, which gave me a prime opportunity to sneak up on Rosewood. He was a certified pilot in addition to his other duties, so Hallstead knew he'd be the one to fly it and Simmons would be the one to keep control of their hostage.

I reached forward with both hands and gripped the rim of the chute, straining to hold my body up as I set my knees on the slide and cautiously looked through the clear plastic cover to see outside of it. No sign of Rosewood. There were three ships parked near me. He'd probably be fueling it up; most of them had only half a tank to keep from wasting fuel if they weren't needed. The jet fuel dispenser would be against the other wall.

I hauled myself out of the chute and then pressed myself to the nearest wall. I took a few seconds to catch my breath and then double checked the handgun to be sure it was locked and loaded. Time to go.

God, I hoped this wasn't a mistake.

There were four vessels on this side, so I stayed as low as possible and crept toward the tower in the middle of the level where the fuel was stored. It could be accessed on any of the floors of the hangar, and I finally caught sight of Rosewood with the sleeves of his prison jumpsuit rolled up, pumping the fuel into the escape pod. It was about forty feet to the edge of the ledge where the launchpad would be, so I couldn't see it from here, but I'd heard shouting and gunshots just a moment ago in the chute. I wanted badly to check on Scarlett, but that would give me away. I had to trust my sister.

Rosewood pulled the fuel pump out of the jet and then sealed it shut, his back to me as he did so. I was a couple yards away, but I was no marksman; I'd never held a gun until all of this shit with the Starlight Contingency started. I didn't want a kill shot—just a distraction.

Well, it turned out I worried for nothing.

Rosewood's posture straightened, and he spoke without turning around. "Mr. Nam. I should have known. You're too much of a do-gooder to let this slide."

I almost demanded how he knew it was me, but then I noticed my reflection in the escape pod's metal paneling and cursed myself. Rookie move, Duke.

"It's over, Rosewood," I said as I planted my feet and kept the gun aimed at him with both hands. "You know you won't get far. Do you really prefer death to imprisonment?"

"Death of the soul is the death of the body, son. Being locked in a cage for twenty to thirty years is the same as being dead in my book. I'll take my chances out there, thanks."

Rosewood turned his head to give me his side profile. "And besides, we both know you ain't got the guts to pull that trigger."

I smiled. "On the contrary."

I shot the spot right beside him. Fuel immediately began to leak out onto the floor.

Rosewood cursed as it splashed onto his slip-on shoes and he whirled around. He had a snub-nosed pistol instead of a handgun, probably taken off the guard they'd knocked out. Time slowed as he aimed at me, ready to fire.

Before he could, another shot rang out from down near the launch-pad. Rosewood's head snapped to one side on instinct. He darted to the other side of the fuel tower, out of sight, and I suspected he wanted to know what had become of Simmons.

I backed up a few steps and checked over the edge as well, trying not to panic as I thought about my sister.

There, on the launchpad at my sister's feet, lay Simmons.

With a bullet in his brain.

I spotted Hallstead and two of his men on the staircase, who had been let inside the hangar by Scarlett as planned. He must have had no choice; I knew he didn't want to give them away before both suspects had time to change their gameplan.

Before I could move, Rosewood sprinted and leapt into the escape pod.

"Dammit!" I ran toward it as I heard the propulsion system roar to life. I fired at the cockpit, but the bullets just pinged off harmlessly. No way Hallstead's rifle would make a dent in it, either.

"Rosewood, this is your last chance," I said as I stood in his path.

I saw his lip curl as he glared at me, his voice coming out through the pod's speakers. "You just don't know when to quit, do you, boy?"

I glared right back. "Neither do you."

Rosewood flew the pod straight at me.

I stepped to one side and then shot at the floor.

The bullet caused a spark. That spark ignited the jet fuel on the floor under the vessel, then followed the trail up to the leaking tank.

Rosewood's pod had just become airborne when it exploded.

I took cover behind the fuel tower. The pod crashed onto the landing pad, nothing more than a hunk of burning metal. I'd seen Scarlett clear the pad shortly after Simmons had been shot, so I knew she and the others were safe.

And I'd just taken a human life.

Jikineun-gae.

The watch dog. Just like my mother said.

I took a deep breath and let it out slow. I'd given him a choice, and he'd chosen wrong. It was as simple as that.

Or that was what I'd tell myself from now on.

I holstered the gun and took the staircase down. My sister met me halfway and literally tackled me in a hug. I smacked the far wall and wheezed as she nearly crushed my ribs. "Geez, Lettie, it's okay, I'm okay."

"You idiot!" she said when she let me go. "You almost got yourself killed standing in front of that pod. What's the matter with you?"

"Ah, so now you know what it feels like," I mused. "Fancy that."

She rolled her eyes. "Fancy that."

I watched as the other *Titan* guards put the fire out with extinguishers and then tended to the two tied-up men. Hallstead came over once he was sure they were alright and had called for medical assistance. Scarlett returned from the supply room with Hatwer in tow and the little alien clung to her arm, but otherwise seemed like he might be okay.

"Well, this certainly was...messy." Hallstead offered his hand to me. "Thank you."

I shook it. "Had to be done."

He sighed. "Yeah. A shame, but they made their beds. I'll take care of the bodies. You guys get Hatwer back to his people and then I'll brief you on what we found on New Earth."

He moved as if to leave, but Hatwer touched his arm. Hallstead stopped. Scarlett smiled. "Hatwer says thank you."

The captain reached out and lightly patted Hatwer's shoulder, his features softening. "Anytime, kiddo."

He went over to his men to help clean up the remains of the pod. Scarlett and I left, taking the staircase to the next level up that had elevator access. She'd strained herself quite a bit during this fight, so I helped take some of the weight off her hurt leg. She nudged my shoulder once we were inside the elevator with Hatwer. "You gonna be okay?"

I tried not to wince. She could read me like a book. "Eventually."

She held my hand. Said nothing else. Didn't need to, really. I tried not to remember the moment she'd walked into that kitchen with my mother lying on the floor, her blood decorating the floor and the counter and the table. I'd run to her, trying to keep her from seeing. She was so small, so young, so innocent, and my father had taken away any semblance of a life from her when he murdered our mother. He'd left behind a broken home and two broken children. I'd never known what had become of him, but with the Earth gone, did it still even matter?

It did, somehow. Maybe I should have hunted him down and made him pay. Maybe I'd have done that had I not needed to take care of Scarlett. She asked me once if I wanted to find him, but I told her no. Because revenge was a path I refused to take and I'd never let her take it either. *"He who seeks revenge should dig two graves."* I wouldn't bury my sister, not after all we'd been through, and had Rosewood lived, there was no guarantee she'd be safe.

I closed my eyes. I could still see his face right before he flew that ship at me. An empty, angry man.

Just like my father.

And I swore to myself that I'd never become him.

Ding!

The elevator doors parted. I walked out with Scarlett and Hatwer. She returned him to his family and they embraced us both, told us they were grateful for everything we'd done. I felt so terrible for them only having one person—or possibly two if Mrs. Rosewood was indeed part Empath—to communicate with after the abduction of their son. The Shasar had placed an enormous amount of faith in us and we'd already let them down once. I hoped we wouldn't again any time soon. When we left, it was time to go to the bridge for the briefing.

"The initial images look promising," Hallstead said, scrolling through them on the holographic projector. It showed a dry, rocky terrain with a large lake and waterfall nearby.

"We've confirmed the presence of an atmosphere. The planet's temperature seems to be bearable and it's oxygen-rich. The gravity will take some getting used to—we predict it's 10% greater than that of Earth. Our satellites are continuously recording information so we have an idea of the axis, seasons, and the effect the local star will have on it long term. We've confirmed with the land rover's imaging that there is vegetation like moss around this vicinity. We don't want to land too close to the water in case it draws some of the planet's fauna, so we'll have the exploration team land about a mile away and begin the land survey. We'll air drop supplies once a week until the team has gathered everything needed to make a good judgment about its sustainability as a new home for us. Two of the Shasar's engineers agreed to accompany the team to do the same for them. If everything on the planet suggests it's habitable, we could have a colony built within six months and then begin moving people over from the *Titan* in about a year."

Hallstead put his hands on his hips and exhaled. "And that's it, folks. Now we just need to get there in one piece."

"And what if it's not habitable?" Scarlett asked. "What's Plan B?"

Hallstead changed the holodeck image to show a list of designated planets. "We've managed to locate five other worlds with potential, but this was our astronomers' number one choice because of the presence of water. Even if it's not drinkable, it's possible to test it for desalination. The initial scans of these other planets don't suggest they have surface water, though some may have it underground or at the poles like people used to think about Mars. The problem is distance, time, and fuel. The ship could make the trip. It's us I'm worried about. Hopefully, the Shasar have better ideas for long-distance space travel to help us out if we need to keep looking."

"Any sign of the Bergs?" I asked.

"Nothing yet, but we've got sentinels strategically placed around this solar system to tip us off if something approaches."

"And what if there are hostiles planet-side?"

Hallstead smirked. "Hopefully, between you, Sam, and Han, you can take care of any threats, but we can send reinforcements should the survey come under heavy attack. If it's too much to handle, you'd return here for safety and be kept under quarantine until the medical team clears you. Once this region has been surveyed, we'll be organizing expeditions to continue exploring the surrounding areas. It'll take a long time to explore this world—we're talking decades."

"I pray none of that colonialism bullshit tags along," Scarlett said, crossing her arms. "We don't need a repeat of Earth's 'discovery' period in history."

"The policy we have in place is not to occupy any land with sentient life on it. If we have neighbors, we're staying out of their hair unless they express any interest in us."

"What if they consider it their planet and don't want to share?"

Hallstead winced. "We'll cross that bridge when we get to it. We want to avoid any military engagements. If we can find middle ground, we will."

"And if you don't?" she demanded. "What, we're going to kill them and take the planet for ourselves?"

"Lettie," I said, touching her arm. She relaxed a bit.

"There aren't enough of us left to try for a hostile takeover," Hallstead said. "At best, we could defend the colony, but if it came to that, we'd evacuate and try somewhere else."

"Good. Because we just got a pretty good reminder of how awful human beings can be thanks to Simmons and Rosewood and we don't need to bring any of that bullshit to this planet."

"People are people," Rochester reminded her. "They do stupid stuff when they're cornered. We'll be doing our best to mitigate it, but be aware that mistakes and accidents are going to happen and we'll have to learn how to deal with them. We have no world power left for support or guidance. Just us."

Scarlett snorted. "Well, if we do build a new country, I vote we don't go with capitalism this time. It was kinda fucked back on Earth."

That got the group chuckling. Scarlett was always good for one-liners, after all.

"In the meantime…" Hallstead pointed to the conference table a few feet away where there were heavy portfolios stacked. "Everything we have is detailed in those files. Review them and we'll meet again once the satellites, rover, and probes send us back new data."

The meeting adjourned. I grabbed a folder, about to offer it to Scarlett, but she wasn't beside me. I glanced up to see her walk toward the edge of the bridge near the massive windows. We were in deep space, so no planets nearby. Their gravitational pull would endanger the ship, after all. Just a thick black blanket with stars glittering every so often like diamonds; the kind we stole back on Earth.

I rested my forearms on the railing as I stood beside her. She didn't look at me, too captivated by the view. "I keep thinking I'm gonna wake up on the floor of that mansion and this will all have been some crazy dream."

I snorted. "Better not be. What a rip-off."

She laughed. "I know, right?"

We watched for a while longer before she spoke. "Do you think Evelyn was right? That we were chosen to survive out here when everyone else was lost?"

"I don't know," I said softly. "Not sure I believe in fate."

"Me neither, but..." Scarlett shook her head. "We were all alone. No friends, no family, no loved ones. Predisposed to violence and having to think on our feet. Survivors. What are the odds that we're the ones who ended up here with the rest of them?"

"If there is some divine plan, why did it have to involve me getting shot? 'Cause let me tell you, that shit sucked."

Scarlett brandished her heavily bandaged leg. "No shit, Sherlock."

"I don't know if there is some kind of ineffable plan, but I do know one thing."

"What's that?"

I smiled at her. "That I'm proud of you, Lettie. You did the impossible backward and in high heels, as the saying goes. You fought and you bled and you rallied the troops and you won."

I took her hand, lowering my voice. "And I know you still blame yourself for what happened with Percy and those thugs, but I want you to let that go. That's not who you are anymore. You are Scarlett Nam. You're not just a survivor—you are *the* survivor. You've gotten yourself in and out of trouble better than anyone I've ever known."

She glanced away, her eyes wet. "Duke—"

I bumped my forehead against hers. "I mean it. You're strong and smart and you're the best person I've ever known. We're gonna go out there into this new world, together, and we're gonna kick some ass."

Scarlett looked up at me then, grinning. "We're gonna kick some space ass."

"Hell yeah, we will."

FIN

DUKE AND SCARLETT NAM WILL RETURN IN
THE EDEN PROTOCOL
BOOK TWO

ACKNOWLEDGMENTS

To my parents, my mother and father, who stuffed down their fears and encouraged me to pursue the tempestuous field of writing and publishing. You inspire me every day to work my ass off and become someone great. I hope someday I make you proud.

To my brother, who remained brutally honest while reading my work. Thank you for verbally abusing my characters and forcing me to write better.

To Sharon, who pushed me to do the best I could with this story and remained a voracious reader throughout the trials and tribulations of the Nam siblings. You believed in this story long before I ever did. It definitely wouldn't have made it without you.

To Erica, who patiently thumbed through these pages and told me what needed to stay and what needed to go. I am eternally grateful.

To John Hartness and the awesome team at Falstaff Books, thank you for being my support and backbone while I went off the rails with this insane story.

Thank you all. I am forever in your debt.

ABOUT THE AUTHOR

Kyoko M is a USA Today bestselling author and a fangirl. She is the author of The Black Parade urban fantasy series and the Of Cinder and Bone science-fiction series. The Black Parade has been reviewed by Publishers Weekly and New York Times bestselling author Ilona Andrews. Of Cinder and Bone placed in the Top 30 Books in Hugh Howey's 2021 Self Published Science Fiction Contest.

Kyoko M has appeared as a guest and panelist at such conventions as Geek Girl Con, DragonCon, Blacktasticon, Momocon, JordanCon, ConCarolinas, and MultiverseCon. She is also a contributor to Marvel Comics' Black Panther: Tales of Wakanda (2021) anthology as well as the Captain America: The Shield of Sam Wilson (2025) anthology.

She has a Bachelor of Arts in English Lit degree from the University of Georgia.

ALSO BY KYOKO M.

FRIENDS OF FALSTAFF

Thank You to All our Falstaff Books Patrons, who get extra digital content each month! To be featured here and see what other great rewards we offer, go to www.patreon.com/falstaffbooks.

PATRONS

Dino Hicks
John Hooks
John Kilgallon
Larissa Lichty
Travis & Casey Schilling
Staci-Leigh Santore
Sheryl R. Hayes
Scott Norris
Samuel Montgomery-Blinn
Junkle

www.ingramcontent.com/pod-product-compliance
Lightning Source LLC
Chambersburg PA
CBHW020617110726
47899CB00002B/548